Julie Williams-Nash was born in Dundee, Scotland, in 1964. She grew up in Northern Ireland (but stays in touch with her inner child). Julie studied English and Psychology at Queen's University and also has an MA in Media Studies from Ulster University. Her career has covered magazine journalism, copywriting, press and public relations, research, policy and public affairs. She is divorced and has two grown-up children and two cats. She loves to run, travel and do yoga.

For

R & R & B

with all my love…

and to all the "Little Odds" all over the world—we are family!

Julie Williams-Nash

The Little Odds

Austin Macauley Publishers™
London • Cambridge • New York • Sharjah

A CIP catalogue record for this title is available from the British Library.

ISBN 9781035843657 (Paperback)
ISBN 9781035843671 (ePub e-book)
ISBN 9781035843664 (Audiobook)

www.austinmacauley.com

First Published 2024
Austin Macauley Publishers Ltd®
1 Canada Square
Canary Wharf
London
E14 5AA

Thanks to Austin Macauley for giving *The Little Odds* the chance to see the light of day! Written in 2011, I was too shy to do anything about this *Little Odd* trilogy, until Austin Macauley took a chance on me. Thank you to Ali P for the initial cover designs back in 2012 and to the editors and production team at Austin Macauley.

To my family, my friends, my teachers—anyone and everyone who has ever taught me a lesson in life, one way or another.

Most of all, to my children, Rory and Rowena—I am so proud of you both—and to Beryl, also my daughter effectively—my beloved trinity, you three hold my heart and soul.

Finally, in loving memory of the best mummy and daddy, I was very lucky I got you two to parent me, even if I was a little odd.

Table of Contents

A note to readers of all ages: *The Little Odds* is an allegory, but it's also an incredible adventure that invites readers of all ages to unlease your imagination and let it run riot. It's intended to be just good fun—but older readers may notice various references to poetry and music—for example, the poems of TS Eliot, or WB Yeats or even Shakespeare. Other readers may pick up on references to well known and loved songs, and if you do, just enjoy the ride. *The Little Odds* is intended to be fun, but there are some themes throughout about the planet, and our place in it—or on it. If you are a grown up reading it for children, probably a few chapters at a time is enough to keep their attention. If you are reading it as a grown up, then just enjoy the adventures for what they are—a chance to keep in touch with your own inner child, and remember how it feels to indulge your imagination.

Part One

Chapter One
The Little Odd

One day, something funny happened to the Little Odd.

LO and Behold, it slipped through its cloud and landed without ceremony in a BUA (that's a Built Up Area).

The Little Odd was frightened. It had never left its cloud before. It was called a comfort zone. The Little Odd felt safe and loved and happy there, but now this strange thing had happened.

The Little Odd just stood there, trembling. Alone; and very, very worried.

The Built Up Area, which the Little Odd knew was also called the Big City, looked very different now. The Little Odd had only ever watched the city from its cloud. The Little Odd had to lie flat and hold on tight and look over the edge to watch it from afar.

The Little Odd had a special gadget called a cirrusoscope that allowed it to see things up close when that was necessary.

From the safety of its cloud, the Little Odd would watch all the comings and goings, like:

- the little dots which scurried here and there;
- the little tin boxes on wheels that hurtled higgledy-piggledy this way and that. Sometimes they stood still, and when that happened, the Little Odd could hear the strange noises they made—

BEEP-BEEP-BEEPETY-BEEP.

It wasn't music; it was just noise;
And so the Little Odd would cover its Odd ears and La-La-La to itself.
The Music in the clouds was so much prettier.

It was called melody.

***

The Little Odd stood there all alone, looking around at everything it could see. Everything was very interesting to look at, but the Big City was oddly very quiet today. The Little Odd realised it was not quite dawn yet. It could see a little bit of early light shining through.

'Ah,' the Little Odd says out loud. 'So the Big City just hasn't woken up yet! Well, that explains everything!'

You see, the Little Odd had fallen asleep on its watch.

Ooops! Ooooops! Ooopsy-daisy!

It had rolled over and fallen out of its special cloud.

'Ooooh no! What's to become of me? How will I ever get back again!'

The Little Odd flumped down and cried,

Big Sad Sobs…

Poor Little Odd—all alone in the world without a friend to its name.

☹

'Go away,' says a voice. 'You're disturbing my beauty sleep.'

The Little Odd couldn't see where the voice was coming from.

All it could see was a bundle of old rags skew-whiffy in a shop doorway.

'I'm sorry,' says the Little Odd to no one it could see.

'I'll go in a minute. I just need to sit and wait until the tears pass by.'

'Grrrr, blagh, grump—well hurry up and leave me in peace!'

'Oh, are you in peace? That's nice, I'd like some of that right now,' the Little Odd says to the bundle, for the voice seemed to come out of there.

'I am frightened and all alone in the world right now. I just need to sort myself out and then I'll be out of your hair. Do you have hair, dear bundle of rags?'

'Excuse me?' says the voice.

It was a nice voice actually, from a female of the species.

The bundle of rags started to move this way and that, and soon a little head appeared.

'Yes, I have hair. Everyone has hair, don't they?'

The Little Odd was now sitting upright, crouched against the doorway. The voice from the rags sat the exact same way, still wrapped in rags, in the other corner.

The Little Odd could see that clearly, she had hair.

Lots and lots of it—the most beautiful colour ever seen, ever!

(Now, you don't see that every day, thought the Little Odd quietly, but its eyes lit up).

'Oh, hullo!' says the Little Odd.

The girl voice watched this odd creature suspiciously.

She had big green eyes like space-saucers that seemed to dazzle the Little Odd until it got a bit confused.

'Who are you and why are you here?' says the girl voice. She looked at him trying hard to look tough and mean, but the Little Odd could see right through her, and knew she was just as frightened and worried and alone and lost in all the world.

'I'm… I'm… uh… I'm a Little Odd, pleased to meet you.'

And it held out its hand-paw-thing and put on its happiest shiniest smile.

The Little Odd saw the faintest flicker of a smile,

'I'm a Runaway.'

'Well then, hullo Runaway.'

The Little Odd went quiet, but they continued to look at each other.

The Runaway looked at the Little Odd curiously.

The Little Odd kept its shiniest happiest smile on its face.

It didn't want to scare her.

The Runaway had been expecting lots of questions next, and because the Little Odd didn't ask, she thought it could stay for a few moments more.

At least it had stopped crying now. And had a nice smile; so she smiled back now and says, 'You really are a Little Odd, aren't you?'

And then they burst out laughing.

Even though nothing was funny. Nothing was funny at all.

☺

'Why are you here?' she asked.

'Dunno.'

'Where are you from?'

The Little Odd pointed to the sky, but the Runaway just rolled her eyes to heaven and says, 'Don't be silly.'

Then she pointed at the Little Odd and says, 'Do you know anyone in the Big City?'

'No.'

'Have you any friends?'

'No, not here.'

'Do you like ice cream?'

'Dunno. I like candy floss,' says the Little Odd, 'especially when it comes in pink. That's my favourite colour!'

'That's a funny favourite colour for a boy. Are you a boy Little Odd?' asks the Runaway, for she'd never seen anything that looked quite like the Little Odd before.

'Dunno,' says the Little Odd. It felt its cheeks go pink. So it just looked at those Little Odd misshapen feet-things, because it was so shy.

***

The Runaway felt awkward now too and says laughing, 'Now I'm the one asking all the questions, silly me! Let us go then you and I. I want to introduce you to ice cream.'

They stood up, dusted themselves down, and she took the Little Odd's paw-hand thing in her hand, and skipped down the street singing…

'I scream, you scream, we all scream for ice cream…'

They sang it over and over again until they were out of breath from too much skipping and laughing.

They were both very happy now.

The Runaway says, 'My mummy used to sing that.' And the Little Odd saw her face grow sad for a moment. Then she says, 'Come on, before all the ice cream melts away!'

☺

They found a Little Café. She put the money on the high counter and says to the man with a round face like a full moon, 'Two of your finest ice creams, please.'

What colour?

'Pink, of course!'

So the Little Odd and the Runaway found a warm seat beside a window of the Little Cafe and watched the world go by.

Then the Runaway says, 'Do you Trust me?'

And the Little Odd says, 'What does Trust mean?'

The Runaway says, 'Do you believe I won't hurt you or be mean to you?'

The Little Odd thought for a while and then says, 'But why would you do that? I think you are my friend, perhaps.'

They both go quiet for a while.

The Runaway watches the Little Odd eat the ice cream.

She watched its face change from cautious curiosity to joy and happiness.

The Little Odd got ice cream all over its face, so the Runaway gave it some napkins; then she smiled her shiniest happiest smile. She nibbled on her ice scream—tiny, tiny bits, one at a time, with a tiny spoon. She kept her eyes downcast; for when she looked into the eyes of the Little Odd, she felt funny inside.

The Little Odd's shiniest happiest smile was there all the time now.

The Little Odd says, 'Yum-yummy-yum-yum,' over and over again.

When the Little Odd had finished the ice cream, they went outside. The Little Odd says, 'I feel so much better now, because today I have made a new friend, and I have tasted ice cream… what will we do now?'

'I suppose we will have to get you home Little Odd. Where do you live?'

'I'm not sure where exactly, but I've heard it said I live in hope!' it says with that Big Smile still on its face. 'It's somewhere up there.'

The Little Odd pointed at the fluffy clouds passing by. 'But I don't see my cloud just now.'

They both stood there for ages, in the middle of the Big City, looking at the clouds.

The Runaway says, 'I might know your cloud when I see it. My mummy used to say that I always have my head stuck up in the clouds.'

'So I say, Mummy, it is always nicer to have your head stuck in the clouds, than stuck in the sand.'

The Runaway looked sad again, just for a moment. Then she looked thoughtful.

'If we had some balloons, we could float up there and have a look around.'

The Little Odd thought this was a great idea. It had once caught a balloon that was just floating by, lonely as a little cloud. The Little Odd had held tight to the balloon in its paw-hand thing until one day, the balloon slipped away, when the Little Odd was sleeping.

'However, Little Odd, you are innocent in the ways of the world, and the Big City can be a very dangerous place for the likes of you. Therefore… you will have to live with me until we can find a way to get you home.'

'That would be nice, thank you,' says the Little Odd, bashful again. 'Do you live in that doorway back there?'

'Oh no,' says the Runaway, 'I live in the Dump.'

☺

So the Little Odd just followed the Runaway in whatever way she went. She knew the way to the Dump like the back of her hand, she says, 'Please don't worry Little Odd. Every little thing will be okay, for at least we have Faith.'

'What's that?' asks the Little Odd.

'Faith,' says the Runaway, 'is a good friend of mine. She lives in the Dump and is a very kind old lady—like a favourite grandmother. She has a sister called Joy, like a favourite aunt. Let's go find them. They'll know what I should do with you.'

The sun is shining in the sky, and the Runaway takes the Little Odd's paw-hand thing and says, laughing; 'Let's run, like the hammers…'

So the Little Odd put his paw-hand thing in her hand, and they ran laughing, all the way to the Dump. The Little Odd asked the Runaway, 'What are the hammers?' But she didn't know;

'It's just a thing people say in my Small Town, for everyone has a hammer there and everyone likes to bang it on things; or bang on about things, depending…'

'Oh,' says the Little Odd.

And when they got near the Dump, the Runaway says, 'I need to confirm, that you really are my friend?'

The Little Odd jumped up and down and says, 'This is all I ever wanted, to be a friend, to have a friend, and I'm so happy that my friend is you.'

The Runaway says, 'Do you promise to always be my friend?'

'I promise.'

'Do you promise to stick with me through thick and thin, bad times and good?

'Uh-huh.'

'Do you promise to not laugh at me behind my back, or say mean things?'

'Yup.'

'Will you never, pretend to be my friend when you really don't like me anymore?'

'I promise,' says the Little Odd, with a very serious face, 'but I'll always like you!'

'And even when I have nothing nice to share with you—no ice cream or candy floss, will you still be my friend?'

'Yes, sir!'

'And when we've found a way to get you home, will you never forget me and always think nice things about me? Will you watch over me from afar?'

So then the Runaway promised to be and do all those things back to the Little Odd, and they jumped up and down with Joy, who had watched everything from afar.

The Little Odd felt very strange but happy. Joy says there was a place in the Dump where they could stay. Joy says they should make it feel like home for now and fill it with love, for love is all you need (Joy was a happy hippy).

She says, 'Let's go find Faith, for she always has cake.'

The Runaway gave the Little Odd a big hug. The Little Odd didn't have to ask what love is.

The Runaway cast her eyes to the clouds and says, 'Little Odd, you turn up unannounced in my doorway and now look what you've done!' the Runaway says, through her shiniest, happiest smile,

'My dear Little Odd, we have so many adventures ahead of us.'

'So let us go then, you and I, into the Dump,'

'Who knows what we may find there—what treasures…?'

Chapter Two
What a Dump!

The Little Odd Makes Itself at Home

The Little Odd is very excited. It has never seen a dump up this close before.

The Little Odd looks all around in wonder, and says out loud,

'The Dump is the most beautiful place in the whole world.'

The Runaway says, 'Hey Friend, Don't get carried away.'

'Would I get carried away? What would carry me away?' says the Little Odd, its wee face worried now.

The Runaway rolled her eyes then pulled a face and says, 'I don't mean you'll actually get carried away. It's just a turn of phrase.'

'What's a turn of phrase?' asks the Little Odd.

'Grrr,' says the Runaway, 'am I going to have to explain everything to you?'

Then she put her hands on her hips and looked bossy, so the Little Odd went a shade of pink and put on its shy face and says, 'No, not EVERYTHING!' The Little Odd says this back to her, the same way she says EVERYTHING to it, just so that she knew it could talk bossy too!

Then they smiled, their shiniest happiest smiles.

'Come on then,' says the Runaway, 'let me show you around this Dump.'

Here's what the Dump looked like to the Little Odd.

It was giant—the size of a small country! (Of course, it was actually just the size of an average dump, whatever that might be).

There were so many interesting things to see ...

Mountains made out of tin cans;

Valleys made out of broken things.
Forests full of planks of wood and smashed-up furniture.
Rows of little house tents made of sheets and old clothes tied together;
Mounds made up of metal, nuts and bolts, hinges, joints and brass rings.

'There are so many wonderful and interesting things to see,' says the Little Odd, 'I have never, ever seen a landscape quite like this so close up.'

(The Little Odd says, *'Landscape,' to sound grown up. The Little Odd didn't want the Runaway to think it hadn't seen other places and planets before).*

The Runaway looked at the Little Odd with a funny screwed-up face.
'The Dump is full of rubbish!' she says.
'Well then, I have never seen such beautiful rubbish before,' says the Little Odd, knowingly.
The Runaway folded her arms. The Little Odd tried to copy her, but its paw-hand things wouldn't work that way, so it changed its mind.

☺

'I'll take you around and show the places that are safe for you and me to go, and I'll show you the places where it is dangerous. Do you understand?'
'Oh yes,' says the Little Odd, but it didn't really know what dangerous meant.
However, the Little Odd thought inside its own head,

'*I will have to find out for myself what dangerous means, without having to ask another silly question. It is a good and useful thing, to find out things for yourself.'*

The Little Odd followed the Runaway wherever she went, and decided that was how it should be, for now. She would lead and it would follow.
The Runaway knew her way around the Dump. She knew so many important things. She says she would look out for the Little Odd, to make sure it came to no harm.

The Runaway explained the lay of the land.

'Tin Can Alley is over there. It leads all the way to the magical and mysterious Aluminium Mountain. It should always be treated with reverence.'

'Oh,' says the Little Odd, who hadn't a clue what reverence meant either, but if it was a treat thing, it must be good, like cake or candy floss.

'Next,' says the Runaway, 'I'll take you along the Rocky Road. But I'm worried about your Little Odd feet things. They will be sore.'

So she thought for a moment, then noticed some old rags hanging from an old bush over there. She got the rags and very carefully, wrapped them around and around the Little Odd's misshapen feet things.

'There,' she says, 'How's that feel?'

'Very nice indeed,' smiled the Little Odd. 'Let us go then, you and I…'

And they walked, close beside each other, along the Rocky Road.

From time to time, one or other would stumble, for there were so many rocks of so many different shapes and sizes. When that happened, they would hold each other up, and the Little Odd learned new things to say like "*Steady on there*" and "*woops-a-daisy*" even though there were no daisies about.

They passed twisted prams, bicycles and wheelbarrows. The Runaway would explain to the Little Odd what these things are so that it didn't have to ask.

The Runaway now realised that the Little Odd was a bit worried about asking way too many silly questions.

There were old toys, tractors and other machinery scattered around. They saw a big blue machine that made a munching sound as if it had big sharp teeth inside.

The Little Odd was a bit worried.

There was a man with a dirty face, and he just stood there, feeding the Big Blue Machine cardboard boxes. One after the other after the other, all day long, that was all he had to do!

'The Big Blue Machine must be very hungry indeed,' thought the Little Odd inside its own head; and as they passed by, it let out a big loud "burp"!

The Runaway explained, that the Big Blue Machine crunched cardboard boxes all day long, but sometimes, it got jammed.

'Oh,' thought the Little Odd inside its own head, 'so the Big Blue Machine gets jam from time to time. That must be nice!'

☺

The Runaway says, 'Hullo Bert.'

And Bert says, 'Hullo my Little Runaway. Who's this then?'

'This is my new friend, Bert, but don't worry, it's just a Little Odd.'

Bert tipped his woolly hat—'Nice to meet you.' He smiled,

The Little Odd smiled its shiniest happiest smile and walked on.

'I think everyone and everything is very nice here. I think I will be very happy until I can find my way home. I think I have landed on my misshapen feet things!'

'How are your feet things Little Odd?' asks the Runaway, 'Do they hurt?'

'No, not at all, my feet are very cosy and comfy. Thank you for asking.'

The Little Odd felt happy inside because the Runaway cared enough to ask.

☺

Now, they arrived at a place where four roads met each other. The Runaway called this the Crossroads. The Little Odd hoped the roads weren't very cross, because up until now everything and everyone it had met—Joy, Faith, and Bert—had been very pleasant.

'Okay,' says the Runaway. 'The Crossroads is in the exact centre of the Dump. Try to remember that. The way ahead is North… it's called the Road to Nowhere because it is a dead end.'

'Is that where all the dead things live?' asks the Little Odd, with its scaredy-cat face on.

'Yayyyyeeeeessssss,' says the Runway in a spooky voice just to tease the Little Odd.

'Funny enough that is where the dead go to get buried.'

'You see, it's very important that we keep the Dump as clean as possible. GDH is very important here, or else everyone and everything will get claried in germs and get sick, or worse, get dead.'

'Excuse me, but I really don't know what GDH is?'

'Ah yes, sensible question at least—Good Dump Hygiene,' she says knowingly.

'Ah… I see,' it says, nodding sagely with its serious face on.

'So we won't go up the Road to Nowhere today. I won't be able to show you everything today, just enough so you know your way around. I will need to take you home soon and show you where we live now that you are my full-time friend.'

'Before we get tired and hungry, let me finish up the guided tour. Tomorrow, if you like, we can go exploring some more.'

'Oh yes, that sounds very exciting—like a real adventure!'

'Indeed, but just don't go getting yourself into trouble mind you.'

'Okay,' says the Little Odd, but it wasn't very sure what trouble was, or how to find it, or even get into it!

The Runaway says, it should keep an eye out for trouble, so the Little Odd thought inside its own head, that it would make sure to do that, tomorrow.

The Little Odd is starting to get very, very tired and hungry—and soon it will be time for bed. The Little Odd rubs its eyes with its paw-hand things. The Little Odd can see the sun getting steadily lower and lower in the sky.

So the Runaway says, 'I'll just show you the road to the east while we're here. It doesn't actually have a real name—just the letter E and lots of numbers. It goes from E1—just over there, to En-finity—which is a magnetic field I think, far, far away.'

'Some people say you have to walk forever down that road to find it. No one has ever actually made it to the end, and if they did, they never came back to tell anyone what it was like. I'm sure it's very nice.'

'Oh,' says the Little Odd, who was finding it hard to concentrate because it was so tired and hungry.

☺

'And finally,' says the Runaway. 'We live at the end of this road, my dear. This is called Roguery Road, and it takes us into the west, to our des-res.'

'What's a …'

'It's a place called home.'

☺

So the Runaway and the Little Odd walked into the west. They could watch the sunset along the way until the Runaway says, 'Look over there!'

The Little Odd looked over there and saw, a wigwam made out of old blankets and sheets and colourful things. The Little Odd thought it a very des-res.

On either side of the door stood Joy and Faith for they are the good neighbours.

(They have looked out for the Runaway since she arrived, and no one knows how long ago that was any more, maybe weeks or months or even years).

And although Faith and Joy are like her kind old aunts, they are very happy that the Runaway has found a friend around the same age and size, even if it is a Little Odd.

☺

Faith and Joy have made a cake of chocolate fudge and honeycomb. They get a whole quarter each and sit on the ground smiling, and everyone says, 'Yum-yummy-yum-yum,' over and over again, until the Little Odd yawns, and falls fast asleep in a ball.

(*It was a burst ball no one wanted anymore, so from this day forward, it would be set aside for the Little Odd's bed—a place to rest its weary head).*

☺

The Runaway watched the Little Odd sleeping and thought:

What a queer day indeed. This morning, I woke up in a doorway, all alone in a bundle of rags, for I went a-wandering way too far and got too tired. It got too late to make it back to the Dump and when I awoke I met the Little Odd all lost and lonely in the world! And now I have a BFF and so has the Little Odd in me! Oh, Happy Day!

Then the Runaway gets inside her Sleeping Bag and says out loud, to no one in particular, *'Who knows what tomorrow will bring?'*

'Good night sleep tight, Little Odd,' she says out loud but the only sound that came in return was…

ZZZZZzzzzzz…

Chapter Three
The Little Odd Gets into Trouble

The Little Odd wakes up and doesn't know where it is! Usually, every morning, when the sun floods the heavens, the Little Odd wakes on a bed of fluff-cloud. It is very comfortable and warm.

This morning poor Little Odd is cold and damp. The Little Odd looks around, and then it remembers how it got curled in a ball, inside a wigwam. For a moment, the Little Odd feels very sad, lonely and far from home. Then the Little Odd bounces up and thinks inside its own head,

'I am very far from home, but I am just having an adventure for a little while, and I have made a best friend already.'

The Little Odd looks at the Runaway. She is fast asleep and still. The Little Odd doesn't want to wake her just because it is an early riser.

The Little Odd is always excited about each new day and all the possibilities, but up on its cloud, that usually means just watching everything from afar, sometimes with the cirrusoscope, up on cloud Ninety-Nine-a-Hundred (for that was the Little Odd's address).

Suddenly, the Little Odd is excited about this new day, and all the possibilities.

'I will pretend I am on my holidays,' it says; and so the Little Odd stepped outside into the morning light and looked up at the clouds to see if it could see its very own cloud, Ninety-Nine-A-Hundred, but there was no sign today.

The Little Odd saw a few clouds it recognised though and so it waved at them, just in case they were watching from afar. They would be able to tell everyone up in the clouds that the Little Odd was clearly having a nice time on its holidays.

'Ah this is the life!' thought the Little Odd.

‘Wouldn’t it be nice if I could go find yummy things to eat? I could look for ice cream and candy floss and cake to bring back for the Runaway. That would make her happy, and she would wear her shiniest happiest smile.’

So the Little Odd wandered off, for it had no sense; no sense at all; an innocent in a dangerous dump.

You see when you live in the Dump, you have to look out for yourself. You have to be very, very careful for it’s dog eat dog out there. The Little Odd didn’t know that yet. The Little Odd had never even met a dog! The Little Odd had so much to learn. The Little Odd had never, ever heard, of the Law of the Jungle or even the Law of the Land, but it would live and learn, for that’s what life is all about.

So the Little Odd went in search of nice things to eat.

The Dump was just starting to come alive. The Little Odd only understood time from the sun, so it knew it was still very early in the morning. The Little Odd could see the sun just rising above the horizon, way over there in the Far East and it thought, that would be a good place to start.

‘Go east, Little Odd.’ And so it did, for then it would be easy to find the way back…

‘Then just turn around and walk west, Little Odd,’ it says inside its own head.

The Little Odd knew if it went in a straight line, it couldn’t go far wrong, for the Dump was the size of a small country, and it would be so easy to get lost and never see the Runaway again. That would make it very sad, very sad indeed.

The Little Odd could see real people rising from the ashes, from the mounds of rags, wigwams and tents. The Little Odd watched as they stretched and greeted the new day. The Little Odd wondered what they did with themselves all day.

Look for food too, it guessed. Or maybe they all had work to do, places to go, people to see—like the folk in the Big City.

There are some children, in ragged clothes, starting to roam around in the morning sun. Some have shoes, some don’t.

Some play tag. Some don’t.

Some laugh and shriek and play. Some don't.

The Little Odd walks on by. It has forgotten to tie the rags around its misshapen feet things. It will have to be careful not to end up on the Rocky Road. The Little Odd goes a-wandering taking in all the sights and sounds it sees around the Dump.

The Little Odd is too busy looking this way and that, so it doesn't see what's right in front of it. The Big Digger!

But it doesn't even know what a Big Digger is, poor thing!

The Little Odd hears this screeching piercing sound.

'Look out, look out, look out,' cries a voice from nowhere. But it's too late!

The Little Odd is lying on the ground. The Little Odd doesn't know what's hit it.

The Little Odd looks up at the sky and thinks it is floating way up to its cloud.

Then everything goes blank. Black.

☹

When the Little Odd comes around, it sees lots of people's faces peering down at it.

One says, 'It's one of those Mutations man. We told you that if you didn't clean up the Dump this would happen. The germs would mutate and turn into monsters, who would invade this place of peace and tranquillity. Look, now there's one of them right before our eyes. It's a Mutation, I tell you. A Mutation!'

The angry man says to all the people gathered there, 'Go spread the word around the Dump—we have been invaded by Mutations. We need to take this one prisoner and ask it lots of questions, so we will know more about the Mutations; who they are, where they come from and what damage they might do. There might even be Mutations amongst us who look just like us—who knows how long it takes for a Mutation to mutate!

'We will need to lock up this Mutation and throw away the key before it can do any more damage. We must search among ourselves for the possibility of Mutations hiding amongst us!'

(The Little Odd wonders what damage it has done. Has the damage not been done to it?)

The people nod their heads and say, indeed, it seems there is an invasion of Mutations in the Dump. The people say, 'We warned that this would happen, but would they listen!'

The Little Odd sat up dazed and when it spoke, the people dropped their jaws and stood and stared.

'I am NOT a Mutation. Well, at least, I don't think I am.

'I am not sure what a Mutation is. All that is known is that I am a Little Odd. And I am lost and far from home but yesterday I made a friend, and she brought me to this place, for she says I'd be safe and happy here. For I was lost and lonely in all the world without a friend to talk to.'

The people stopped and stared again.

'What's a Little Odd?' they asked.

'I am.'

Oh, they say, for they did not know how to answer that and some scratched their heads in disbelief and others chin-wagged this way and that.

The angry man who'd been doing all the ranting and raving up to now said, People, listen up! We will have to ask the Council about this. We warned them about the Mutations but did they listen? Now we have proof that Mutations exist.

'Take this creature into captivity, until we can figure out what's to be done with it.'

A rough person ties a rope around the Little Odd's paw-hand things. Someone else wraps a chain around its little leg things, then lifts the Little Odd over his shoulder and carries it off, to who knows where…

The Little Odd is thrown without ceremony into a dark Lock-Up Bunker.

The Little Odd hurts all over but no one seemed to care about that.

The Little Odd can't move its paw-hand things or its little leg things.

The Lock-Up Bunker is pitch black. The Little Odd can see nothing, nothing at all.

The Little Odd is too terrified to cry. So it curls up in a ball—a pretend one—and shivers and shakes.

The Little Odd does not know how long it stays like this, but something disturbs it, so the Little Odd sits up and realises it can see a little bit in the dark.

Then something makes the Little Odd almost jump out of its skin stuff!

A shuffling noise—

Shuffle shuffle

Scuffle scuffle

Whatever can it be?

The Little Odd rubs its eyes and looks around the Lock-Up Bunker.

Over there—in the corner—is this strange-looking creature—quite small, with little beady eyes and a long nose; tiny ears and a very, very long tail.

It is made up of furry brown stuff.

'Oh, hullo,' says the Little Odd blinking. 'I thought I was all alone in here.'

The small creature doesn't answer—it appears to be chewing something;

Chew-chew

Chew-chew

Over and over again.

So the Little Odd tries again. It puts on its shiniest happiest smile, even if it doesn't really feel like it and says, 'Hullo I'm a Little Odd, pleased to meet you' (because the Little Odd was brought up with nice manners).

The small creature looks startled and confused. No one has ever spoken politely to it before. So it doesn't answer…

The Little Odd tries again…

'I think I might be in Trouble! The Runaway warned me not to get into Trouble. I didn't mean to—it just turned out that way, and the morning started off so sunny and full of possibilities.'

'Now I am afraid I will never see the light of day again or my best friend the Runaway. She will be very worried about me because she says I am not fit to be let out alone.'

The Little Odd was feeling a bit nervous now. The Little Odd knew it was that because it always talks too much when it gets nervous, in case the small creature thinks it an idiot, when in fact, it is just a Little Odd.

The small creature sits up tall and rubs its little paw-things together for a while as if considering what to say to the Little Odd. The small creature looks at the Little Odd for a few moments more, still chew-chew-chewing and says, 'I'm Vermin; you really don't want to talk to me. Now let's just share this small dark space and get on with being alone and unwanted and misunderstood. For there's no point in talking… no one really listens.

'And there's no point in trying to be my friend, for they will turn you against me and then you won't want to know me anymore, and you will say, *yuk-yuckety-yuk-yuk. Oh, yes, Vermin—I used to know him! Horrible, horrible he was,* for that's what they all say in the end.'

'Well, I hope that's not true,' says the Little Odd. 'So hullo Vermin, pleased to meet you. If we are just sharing space, I will try to be quiet then, but if you want someone to talk to I'm here, and I might be here for a while.

'You see the people with the screwed-up faces think I am something called a Mutation and when I tried to explain that I was just a Little Odd they wouldn't listen.'

'They said they are going to speak to someone called the Council and get back to me. They said that they would have to find some science tests to do tests on me to find out just what sort of Mutation I am—even though I am not.'

The small creature called Vermin was listening closely now.

'A-ha,' it says, 'then you and me are in the same boat.'

'Are we in a boat now?' asks the Little Odd, puzzled. 'I thought I was in a Lock-Up Bunker.'

(The Little Odd was pleased to show off that it seemed to know what a boat was, for it had watched them from afar).

Vermin looked at the Little Odd funny. 'You really are a little odd aren't you?'

So the Little Odd laughed out loud and wanted to give Vernon a hug because Vermin could see the truth.

'Thank you, thank you… I've never been in a boat before!'

'You are not in a boat Little Odd you are in a Lock-Up Bunker. I was just using a turn of phrase.'

'Oh, that's nice. The Runaway likes using turns of phrase too! She will be looking for me, and I hope she can explain to the people-faces that they have made a terrible mistake… for she knows a lot of things, my Runaway friend.'

Vermin sits quietly rubbing his little paw-things and says,

'Little Odd let me tell you a story…'

'Oh yes please, I love stories. Does it start once upon a time…'

'Would you like it to?'

'Yes, please!'

'Okay then, listen very carefully for I will zay this only once.'

Vermin has a funny way of talking thinks the Little Odd, but that's okay.

Everyone has different ways of doing and saying things—but that doesn't make any one way any better or worse than any other—just different and different is a good thing, the Little Odd thinks inside its own head.

'Once upon a time, I lived in a big white science laboratory…'

What's a science…?

'Dear Little Odd, just listen while I tell the story and if you have any questions save them all up for the end unless it's really vital that you ask.'

'What does vital mean?'

'Ah! It's vital that I tell you that and vital that you ask. It means, very important. The things that really matter. The opposite of trivial.'

'What does trivial mean?'

'The opposite of vital!'

'Oh…'

'Do you understand me?' asks Vermin.

'Yes, um, I think so,' says the Little Odd.

'Okay. Now let me get on with the story…

Once upon a time, in a big white science laboratory I lived with several hundred other members of my species. The scientists didn't even bother to ask us our names, they just called us all Vermin. They gave us each a number and that was the only thing we were allowed to own our number. Look, that's my number…'

(Vermin showed the Little Odd a place on its back where the fur stuff had been shaved and three scribbles were branded in red ink, into its skin stuff).

'Did it hurt—when they did that to you?' asks the Little Odd.

'Oh yes, but not as much as the science tests. Every day, they would call out numbers—at random or so it seemed, and we'd be taken away for tests.

'Sometimes they would put us into Mazes and make us run-a-round and press levers and buttons and things. And if we obeyed, we got scraps of food.'

'Oh dear, why?'

'No idea, but they seemed to know what they were doing and why, and if they didn't really, they just pretended that they did.'

'Most days, some of the other Vermins wouldn't make it back to the cage. Many, many Vermins were never seen again and that went on day after day after day until one day I decided enough is enough!'

'Even if they call me Vermin; for that is just a name, just a label they have put on me, they do not see who I really am, or what I am.'

(The Little Odd looked away, for it didn't know what to say—or if it should say anything. Anything at all).

'You see Little Odd they say we Vermins spread germs and disease and that may be true even if we don't mean to; yet the people-faces are also very good at spreading germs and disease and other bad things too, but they don't see it that way. They just need something to blame for all the problems, so they need to make an escape goat.'

'What's an escape goat?'

'Now that is a good question!'

'An escape goat is someone or something that someone or everyone wants to blame for everything that is wrong in their life or their world, so they pick an escape goat and throw everything they can find at it.'

'They shout abuse and names at the escape goat until it goes away or curls up and dies or runs away. Then they have to find another escape goat to blame for everything that is wrong in their lives or their world. So it goes on and on like that forever because those that make escape goats out of nothing are never strong enough to take a long hard look at themselves and realise that the problem or problems start with themselves. They are too silly to try to do one small thing every day to try to change the problem or to make themselves a kinder person instead of blaming everyone else all the time. It's called taking the log out of your own eye.'

'Oh,' says the Little Odd but was afraid to ask about logs in eyes in case it was just another turn of phrase.

'So,' says Vermin, 'I am an escape goat and so are you.'

'Oh, then if we are escape goats shouldn't we be able to escape?'

'A-ha! Exactly,' says Vermin. 'And that's the next part of my story. Some of the Vermins in the laboratory used their tiny brains to hatch a cunning escape plan. Some Vermins put their heads together and figured out that if we did this and that and the other thing when the scientists were busy, there might just be a way out.'

'So we planned, and we watched, and we figured out patterns and possibilities. We added them all up together and designed an escape route.'

'Oh.'

The Little Odd has looked and listened carefully and says to Vermin, 'You have very funny teeth.'

'Thank you,' says Vermin. 'They are very sharp, and that's how we escaped. Only a few of us made it out, but we gnawed and gnawed and gnawed and then we ran like the hammers…'

'What way do the hammers run?'

'Oh, Little Odd, what will I do with you?' says Vermin, rolling his eyes, heavenwards.

'I have a cunning plan. I am going to get us out of here.'

'Hurray,' says the Little Odd, 'let's get out of here!'

So Vermin explained how he would chew-chew-chew through the ropes around the Little Odd's paw-hand things. Then when its hand-paw-things were free the Little Odd could help Vermin to break the chains. (*Vermin has noticed that the Little Odd's paw-hand things are an interesting design and could help twist the manacles and break them loose. And that's exactly what they did*)!

When the Little Odd was free to jump up and down again, he jumped up and down again. Vermin ran around and round in circles. When they settled down, they realised that this was just the start. They would have to think about how they would get out of the Lock-Up Bunker, for Vermin had been trying for a very long time…

So they put their imaginary thinking hats on to come up with a plan. They called it "Teamwork"!

Vermin asks the Little Odd, 'How fast can you run?'

'Dunno,' says the Little Odd. 'But I am an excellent bouncer! Look—inside the bottom of my misshapen feet things, you will see I have little spring things. I can use them to bounce really big! It's what we use to get around the sky—for we need to leap from cloud to cloud to visit friends and family.'

'Perfecto,' says Vermin. 'Here's how we make our escape… When the people-faces come to take you away—haha—you will start to distract them by bouncing around the Lock-Up Bunker so that they can't catch you. I will scurry around their feet to scare and distract them…'

'Then when we get out through the door you will see me scurry so fast—then just follow me while you bounce, for they'll never be able to catch you. There's a place I know at the crossroads. It's a Burren…'

'What's a Burren?'

'Good question.'

(The Little Odd liked it a lot when Vermin said, 'Good question').

'It's a rabbit warren, only it's for bunnies. It is an underground labyrinth that only some of the animals know about. If we can get you there we can find a way out of the Dump, and get you to a place of safety for I dread to think dear Little Odd, what tests the scientists would want to do on you!' Vermin shakes his head sadly.

'Hurray,' says the Little Odd. 'We are going on a great adventure!'

Then the Little Odd grew sad, for it didn't want to leave the Runaway so soon. It could not imagine life on Earth without the Runaway to run away with. The Little Odd needed her to make sense of things. The Little Odd liked the way they wore their shiniest happiest smiles just for each other.

'What's the matter Little Odd?' asks Vermin.

'I cannot run away without my best friend, the Runaway. It wouldn't be fair to run away without her because she likes to run away.'

So Vermin said not to worry. He had another plan… but first, it was important to get the Little Odd to a safe place. Then he would go find the Runaway, so they could all run away together.

'Hurray! Everything is going to be okay Vermin, isn't it?'

'Yes, Little Odd, it so is, and trust me, because I have run away before too!'

'I'm glad I found you, Vermin.'

'I'm happy to be of assistance, kind sir,' says Vermin.

'What's a kindser…?'

Chapter Four
The Runaway Looks Everywhere

But Finds a Gurney Cat

When the Runaway woke up and realised the Little Odd was no longer curled up in a ball, she wondered if it was just outside looking around. She had warned it about the dangers that lurked all around the Dump, and that it was not to go getting into trouble.

She looked outside the wigwam. No sign of the Little Odd.

She thought maybe it had nipped next door to see Faith and Joy, so she checked with the women, but they said, no, they hadn't seen the Little Odd at all.

Now they were worried because they were the only three people in the Dump who knew about the Little Odd. And Bert, who had a bad memory.

The Runaway started to panic and shriek and throw her arms around in the air.

'My Little Odd could be anywhere; any awful thing might have happened to it Faith. What will we do Joy?'

'Calm down, calm down,' says the wise woman. 'The Little Odd can't be far away, it's probably wandering nearby. It'll be easy to find.'

'But Faith, the Little Odd is so peculiar people will look at it funny. The Little Odd is very curious and will want to look at everything and not know just how dangerous things can be!' cried the Runaway.

So they hatch a plan. The Runaway will go East. Faith will go North and Joy will go South, for they will have to pass through the West first of all. They each come up with a special sound, a whoop, a whistle, a whirling sound, that they will shriek whenever one of them finds the Little Odd. So bravely they set off, in search of the Little Odd.

The Runaway says Thank You to Faith and Joy for all their help. Before they part, they give each other Big Hugs.

The Runaway keeps walking and looks under old cars and inside them. She looks all around the mounds of rags and piles of junk; she lifts things; she whispers its name.

'Little Odd, Little Odd, where are you? Come out… come out… wherever you are. Please, Little Odd; I'm so worried about you.'

People look at her funny, but she can't ask them if they've seen the Little Odd for there is much confusion and fear in the Dump these days about an invasion of Mutations. Some idiots came up with this idea and sowed the seeds of fear in people's minds. Now everyone is looking at each other suspiciously in case the person might be a Mutation in disguise.

So any new creature that arrives, especially one that looks as strange as the Little Odd, is immediately under threat of being a Mutation. The Runaway is annoyed with herself. She'd forgotten about all that Mutation rubbish when she brought the Little Odd to the Dump. She thought it was just a load of nonsense being spouted by the paranoid grown-ups with nothing better to do with their numpty minds, so she hadn't really paid much attention to it. She was too busy going a-wandering every day far from the Dump (which was why she ended up sleeping in that doorway a few nights ago).

The Runaway thinks hard as she searches. What sort of thing might attract the Little Odd? Food—ice cream, cake, candy floss.

The Runaway has been searching and looking everywhere for hours, whispering its name. Then she grows tired and despondent and sits down behind a pile of junk, where no one will hear her cries. The sun is shining high overhead, so she knows it's afternoon. She cries big deep howls; she cries big high shrill sounds, over and over again, until she hears the sounds coming right back at her, like an echo.

'Who's doing that? Stop copying me! Copycat!'

The Runaway looks all around her but sees nothing. When she stops weeping and wailing and is silent, the big deep howls and the big high shrill cries continue. Now she knows for sure it's not her echo, for the Runaway is not stupid you know, even if people try to say she is or make her feel that way.

'Who's there? I said, who's there? Come out come out wherever you are, show yourself!'

She waits a few moments—the sounds start up again. The noise pierces right through her until she can't bear to listen anymore. The Runaway gets annoyed and yells, 'Please stop that noise. Now! What troubles you so, whoever you are, come talk to me! I am troubled too, and we might be able to help each other.'

A few moments later, a Big Orange Cat appears from a gap in the junk pile.

'It's me making that racket, I'm the Gurney Cat. I was getting very annoyed with you being more gurney than me. I am the Queen of Gurns. So who do you think you are? Imposter!'

They eye each other up and down for a few moments, suspiciously. The Runaway thinks that for a Dump cat, this Gurney Cat looks well-fed and well-looked-after. She even has a collar!

'I am the Runaway, and I have lost my best friend, the Little Odd, who is alone in all the world. It has no idea of danger and is bound to get into trouble soon if I don't find it. I can't find my Little Odd anywhere.' She starts to cry again, big deep howls, high shrill shrieks.

The Gurney Cat finds it hard to listen to, and for the first time in her nine lives, thinks, 'Oh my, I must be hard to listen to too.'

The Gurney Cat feels a bit sorry for the Runaway, which is unusual, for usually, the Gurney Cat is too busy gurning over all her own woes and problems—and making so much noise no one ever wants to come near her. In fact, they avoid the Gurney Cat like the Plague, and the Gurney Cat thinks to itself, 'That suits me just fine. The Gurney Cat is quite happy to be miserable all the time.'

'Is your Little Odd about this high? Does it have strange misshapen feet things and strange little paw-hand things and a big happy smile?'

'Yes, yes, that's the Little Odd. Have you seen it?'

The Gurney Cat sits with its two paws straight, so it looks like a triangle of orange fluff. The Gurney Cat looks at the ground. 'I'm afraid that I have, Runaway, and it's not good news.'

The Runaway starts shrieking and shrilling again, and the Gurney Cat joins in and thinks they could be a duet some day if they worked at it.

'Now, hush, shhhsss, Runaway, let me tell you what I saw. If you keep on gurning you'll never hear what I have to say, which is this';

'Early this morning I was chasing mice and rats, for I hate those vicious vermin things, ugh! Then I saw and heard a commotion. The Big Digger was driving slowly and crashed into this odd creature that didn't seem to know where it was—it certainly wasn't looking where it was going—it was too busy looking at the clouds.'

'Then the people-faces all crowded around and talked about it being a Mutation. So they bound its little leg things in chains and its paw-hand things in ropes. They lifted it up, and I followed as they frog-marched to the Lock-Up Bunker and threw it in there, without ceremony. Then they huddled around talking about going to the Council and getting scientists to do tests on the Mutation.'

'Ohhhh noooo,' cried the Runaway, 'I must go to the Lock-Up Bunker. Do you know the way?'

'Yes, but I'm too busy to go with you, I have to stay here and gurn and annoy everyone.'

'Oh well, suit yourself then Gurney Cat, but I could really do with some help right now.'

'I suppose I could show you the way,' says the Gurney Cat, as if this was the most important thing it could ever do, and she should therefore be very grateful.

'Thank you Gurney Cat, I am indeed, very grateful. I don't even mind if you gurn on the way but it would be better if you didn't, for that might attract too much attention to us.'

'Well… okay then, if you insist.'

The Gurney Cat was really quite pleased to be of assistance for no one ever showed any interest in it. This could be a way to prove herself, to be redeemed! So the Gurney Cat ran ahead, and the Runaway ran behind. They did it in such a way that anyone watching would think it was a game, but they didn't make any whooping noises, just ran until they reached the Lock-Up Bunker. They crouched down behind it.

'What now?' whispered the Runaway.

'We should look for a chink, or a tiny gap.'

So they looked very closely all around the rim. The Gurney Cat uses her claws here and there to move the Earth and by some miracle, they find a little gap—a little chink in the wall. The Runaway lies down on the ground and whispers,

'Hullo, Hullo. Anyone in there? Can you hear me? Little Odd, are you in there? Little Odd—knock three times if you can hear my voice?'

Nada.

Then she tries again;

'Little Odd, it's me, the Runaway, I know you're in there. I met a Gurney Cat, and she saw what happened and brought me here. Please, Little Odd, if you can, please knock three times.'

Silence. Then the sound came: One, two, three.

The Runaway heard its voice—so happy to hear hers, and the Little Odd said in such a way that she could see its shiniest happiest smile, 'Runaway, Runaway I thought I'd never see you again! I got into trouble. I got knocked down by a Big Digger, and they think I am something called a Mutation, so they brought me here and threw me in without ceremony.'

'I know,' whispered the Runaway, 'The Gurney Cat saw it all. We have to hatch a cunning plan to get you out of there, so we can run away together, far away, to a new place of safety.'

'I have a cunning plan already,' says the Little Odd. The Runaway was confused, for she knew the Little Odd wasn't very cunning, wasn't cunning at all.

'Oh, said the Runaway, 'What's that then?'

'I've made a new friend, Runaway. I found one in the Lock-Up Bunker quite by accident.'

'Oh!' The Runaway felt a small stab of jealousy, for some reason.

'Yes, his name is Vermin, and he hatched the cunning plan.'

The Gurney Cat and the Runaway looked at each other in surprise and shock.

'Vermin?'

'Yes, Vermin, do you know him?'

'I know *of* him,' says the Runaway. The Gurney Cat looked at her and shook her head. She did the cut-throat sign with her paw and pulled a grimaced face. So did the Runaway. They were not happy that the Little Odd was now friends with Vermin.

'Vermin chew-chewed all through the ropes around my paw-hand things, and then together we figured out how to get rid of the chains around my little leg things and now I am free—but I just have to get out of here. Runaway, Vermin has been really very kind and helpful. This is our plan…'

All the while, the Little Odd and the Runaway are whispering to each other through the gap in the ground, the people-faces are on their way with Council people wearing white coats and fancy suits. They are all a-chatter about the Mutation and "Oh, whatever next"!

What will they do with the Mutation? Do they think there are any more Mutations in the Dump?

We told you so… We told you so. They say all a-chatter and a-rambling on… They are getting closer now…

So the Little Odd explains how when they open the door Vermin will distract them and the Little Odd will bounce. (The Runaway didn't even know that the Little Odd could bounce).

They would bounce and scurry all the way to the crossroads where they would dive into the Burren and find the Great White Rabbit to ask for shelter and help!

'That sounds like a very good plan Little Odd, but I think we can help out further still,' says the Runaway. 'What if, when the door is opened, the Gurney Cat pounces up onto their shoulders and then leaps from one to the other to startle and distract them? Then we all run like the hammers to the crossroads. We could be at the Burren before they even have time to notice or catch up on us.'

'That's a great idea, thank you Runaway! I am so glad you found me again, and this will be the best adventure ever, won't it Runaway?'

'I hope so Little Odd,' says the Runaway—looking at the Gurney Cat with a sense of trepidation. 'I think it will be the best adventure ever. But now we must be very quiet, for I can hear the rabble-rousers and the Council people come closer. Are you ready to bounce as if your life depended on it?'

'Yes, Runaway, my life does depend on it, so does yours and the Gurney Cat's and Vermin's.'

They are all ready. Vermin and the Gurney Cat are aware of each other now, but the Little Odd tells the Runaway to tell the Gurney Cat that it has nothing to fear from Vermin;

and the Gurney Cat tells the Runaway to tell the Little Odd, to tell Vermin that it has nothing to fear from the Gurney Cat.

So the Runaway and the Gurney Cat hide near the door to the Lock-Up Bunker. Inside the Lock-Up Bunker, the Little Odd and Vermin get ready to pounce and bounce;

The rabble-rousers and the council people gather around the door.
Everyone wants to be important,
Everyone wants to watch.
Everyone wants to see what happens next.

Chapter Five
The Little Odd Goes Underground

And Meets Harvey, the Great White Rabbit

'Run, run, run like the hammers,' shrieksthe Runaway.

Vermin scuttles like he never scuttled before;

The Gurney Cat leaps like she never lept before;

The Runaway runs like the hammers;

But the Little Odd bounces in a way no one ever knew existed.

Bong… bong… ping… pong… bong…

The rabble-rousers chase, they holler and howl;

The oldies tire easy but the youngies give them a good run for their money, if they had any…

A few lads, almost grab the Little Odd!

One dives, just as the Little Odd hits the ground, and holds it for a moment, thinks he's got a grip on it—but hey, the Little Odd breaks free with one almighty bounce!

Vermin leads the way—boys-a-dear he can scurry, years of practice no doubt, why he's survived this long no doubt… survival of the fittest and all that malarkey.

Vermin has amazing night vision. He sees precisely where the entrance to the Burren is. The Gurney cat pounces in next. The Runaway dives down the hole and with perfect precision, and perfect timing, the Little Odd's last almighty bounce takes it right down the rabbit hole.

Flip, flap, rustle, skedaddle, plump-blankety-wallop.

The four of them land in a heap. Laughing.

And in the Burren, lots of little Watch Bunnies clap their little paws.

They have landed in a large, dark place like a cave. It is well lit though, with fireflies, there might be ten million fireflies. Or so it seems. They hover, and some cling to the walls; it is really very beautiful as the four of them adjust their eyes to take it all in. Still laughing, catching their breath.

Vermin and the Gurney Cat high-five, then hug; then look at each other funny for they never, ever thought that would happen!

Sitting in an old armchair (how'd that get down here?) is the Great White Rabbit. He wears big round glasses, for he is very, very old. When all the laughing and whooping has toned down, the Watch Bunnies say, 'Shhhh…' and put their little paws to their mouths.

The Great White Rabbit looks at the four of them and kindly says, 'Come closer strange creatures of this night. 'My eyesight is failing me, and I'd like to get a better look. So what have we here? You come closer. What is your name rat?'

'Vermin,' says Vermin as he shyly goes closer with his head hung.

'Ah, of course it is. And you?'

'I am the Gurney Cat—would you like to hear my best gurning?'

'No, thank you, I can imagine! Now you, young human, who are you, what is your name?'

'I am the Runaway.'

'Yes, indeed you are child, but don't you have a name?'

'I do believe so, sir, but I can't recall it now. Everyone just calls me the Runaway.'

'Not to worry, dear, the Runaway you are and will forthwith be known—you are very welcome to our Burren.'

'Thank you, sir.'

They all seem to know the Great White Rabbit is to be treated with reverence, whatever that is. They have all heard tales of the Great White Rabbit before, but no one in the Dump had ever claimed to actually have seen or met him. Or if they did, they were only making it up and everyone knew that.

The Great White Rabbit—everyone knew—was some mystical, secret master of the lower world and should always be spoken of with respect. But now they can see, his face is really very kind, and he is a nice soft voice.

'Now you…' The White Rabbit uses his paw to beckon the Little Odd. 'Do come right up close, so I can have a better look at you.'

The Little Odd slowly goes right up to the Great White Rabbit. The Little Odd is very shy and hangs its head to the side and looks at the ground. The Watch Bunnies huddle closer.

‘Well, look at you!’ says the Great White Rabbit. ‘Please look at me, I don’t bite.’

‘Oh, that’s good,’ says the Little Odd.

‘I heard about your arrival yesterday,’ says the Great White Rabbit. ‘The Watch Bunnies told me all about you. The Watch Bunnies watch everything that’s going on up in the Dump, and tell me so that I can see it’s all in proper order, for my eyesight is failing…’

‘So people are saying you are a Mutation. Are you a Mutation?’

‘No, sir,’ says the Little Odd, and it put on its shiniest happiest smile. ‘I am just a Little Odd.’

‘Ummm, I can see that even with these eyes, ho ho! Well, Little Odd, you and your friends are very welcome here in our Burren. We are happy to be of assistance, we like to help folk in hard times. It’s what we’re really here for. We don’t like it when we hear or see people getting a hard time up on the ground. I don’t see very much anymore, which is why I have sharpened my hearing. Look, do you see these great big white floppy ears…’

(For indeed, they were two of the greatest white floppiest ears they ever did
see; and the Great White Rabbit made them stand up straight
so they could see just how long and wonderful they were)!

‘With these ears, I can hear just about everything that’s going on. I can hear conversations up on the ground, I can hear all the sounds of the Dump clearly for minds around. And the Watch Bunnies of course, always keep their ears close to the ground. It’s essential. That way you can tell who has good in their hearts and minds and who has not.’

‘We heard, the rabble-rousing earlier. We heard everything that was going on up there my dears, but I fear, you really are in extreme danger. They are baying for your blood—listen!’

Everyone fell silent, and up above, you could hear the rabble-rousers rabble-rousing.

It was a horrible cacophony; a terrible racket. There was no music or melody to be heard in its midst.

The Watch Bunnies could see that torches were being shone down the hole. They could hear that spades were being used to dig, dig, dig their way into the

Burren, but they knew it would take a very long time before they got anywhere near.

Then someone up above said, 'Get the diggers, go get the Big Diggers, we'll dig them out alright!'

And in the distance, the Great White Rabbit could hear the sound of the digger engines starting up;

Then from up above, some bright spark said, 'Let's just smoke them out—quick, wrap these rags around these poles, and we'll stick them down all the rabbit holes. That'll finish those odd 'uns off, and all those pesky bunnies that just stand around watching us day after day! They are as bad as Vermin. Let's just get rid of the lot of them in one swoop.'

From down below, they could hear cheers and really loud rabble-rousing.

'We're done for?' says the Runaway, looking at the Little Odd. 'We'll not last more than five minutes max.'

The Great White Rabbit said: 'Dear Little Runaway, do not fear—look around you, do the Watch Bunnies look frightened? Not at all! Those rabble-rousers have tried this one before. In fact, about once a year they try to smoke us out and kill us all, but we are smarter.'

'Come, we have a special place called the Conference Room. It is deep underground. The fireflies will guide our way. Quick, quick. Watch Bunnies, you know the procedures. Tout-suite now boys and girls—vite, vite!'

(That's French, for quick, quick)!

The Great White Rabbit was a bit stiff getting out of the armchair.

'Come Little Odd, hold my paw, this way now. I am a little slow on my old paws these days. Runaway, please take my other paw, I need a little help. I am nine hundred and fifty years old you know.'

'No, I didn't know,' says the Little Odd. 'I have no idea how old I am, or if I am old at all. I don't feel very old.'

(For the Little Odd has no sense of time. No sense of time at all).

The Runaway said she didn't know how old she was either, for she'd forgotten when her birthday was, and how long she'd been a Runaway, for time, seemed to have stopped, for her too.

Odd!

They go down a lot of steps, like going down deep in underground caves. It is very, very pretty, with all the fireflies lighting the way. There is even a little lake deep down underground, with stalagmites and stalactites. It is very, very beautiful and somehow, from the caves, there is the most gentle melodic music humming out, as if by magic!

'Where are we going Great White Rabbit?' asks the Runaway.

'I'll tell you when we're there safe and sound. We don't have much time—just up ahead.'

There was a big red metal door. On the front in big yellow letters were the words:

EMERGENCY NUCLEAR FALLOUT SHELTER

The Runaway said the words out loud. The Little Odd was a little bit worried in case it would fall out. But the Runaway said it wasn't like it.

'Then what if *we* fall out, and aren't friends anymore,' says the Little Odd, hesitating.

But the Runaway said it wasn't like that either, she'd explain inside.

When the last of the Watch Bunnies and all the other animals that gathered along the way were safely in the Nuclear Fallout Shelter, the big metal door was locked, sealed and two heavy protective steel bars slotted into place.

The Great White Rabbit took a large red key from inside his trouser pocket and with a flourish, locked the door. It was very dark but the fireflies were helpful as always. Soon the place was full of light, a lovely orange-red-yellow glow; very pleasant.

There was another special chair for the Great White Rabbit and beside it a second chair. The Great White Rabbit said he had to go into conference with the Bright Badger, and then they would have a plenary session.

'What's a plenary session?' asks the Little Odd, a little worried, for it sounded unpleasant. The Runaway wasn't sure either, she thought it might have something to do with going to the pub. But they were all way too young for that and didn't understand the appeal of the pub for it made people noisy and wobbly-legged.

Some of the Watch Bunnies said the Great White Rabbit and the Bright Badger would confer for a while. This meant they would talk intently about a plan of action. They called this a strategy, which means, what they wanted to do to solve the problem of the day, and what everyone in the Conference Room could do to help solve the problem of the day too.

They would all work together as a team to find a solution. And because all the Watch Bunnies and the other animals that lived underground trusted the Great White Rabbit and the Bright Badger, for they were very wise and showed good leadership (they always had the best interests of all the creatures, underground and over-ground, at heart). The Watch Bunnies said they were benign, and that meant kind and good.

The Little Odd and the Runaway and the Gurney Cat and Vermin all agreed this seemed like a good way to sort things out.

All the Watch Bunnies and the other animals sat in semi-circle rows around the Nuclear Fallout Shelter. There were tanks and containers all around the room—marked "oxygen" and each had a tube coming out of it.

The Watch Bunnies explained that there was enough oxygen in here for about six hours, but after that, they all had to take it in turn to use the oxygen tubes—but no one could ever remember that actually happening before.

'Usually, we are all out of here in a few hours,' says one of the bigger Watch Bunnies.

There was a lot of low chattering in the room, then the Great White Rabbit and the Bright Badger stopped conferring and the Great White Rabbit said, 'Shhhhhhhhh… shhhhhhh…'

And everyone fell silent. He beckoned the Little Odd and the friends to come forward and sit right in front of him and the Bright Badger.

'Dear friends gathered here, once again the rabble-rousers have tried to smoke us out and kill us all. Once again we have survived. And we will live to see another day.'

'However, the Bright Badger and I have been conferring, and we agree that it is our duty, to make sure that the Little Odd and friends must leave the Dump and find another place of safety, for the Dump is not what it used to be. A bad element has got in and taken hold. It is poisoning the minds of those who are easily fooled.'

'They will not stop until they find the Little Odd and put it in a laboratory, then torture it, and that would not be fair, for the Little Odd is just a little odd. It is not a Mutation at all.'

And the Watch Bunnies and the other animals nodded their heads.

☺

'Now as is usual procedure after the plenary session, the great big door is opened, and we all go to the break-out rooms. North South East and West. The Lead Watch Bunnies in your groups will put their heads above ground, look at the lay of the land and decide which direction is safest for the getaway. Then, depending on whether it's North, South, East or West, the Little Odd and friends will make their getaway via that break-out room. Do you all understand?'

'Yes,' they nod.

'Then the Lead Watch Bunnies will make a run for it with the Little Odd and friends. If there is a swift pursuit by the rabble-rousers—and there probably will be, then the little Watch Bunnies will scurry among their feet and trip them up if necessary, jump on them if necessary, and hinder their chase—you all understand the procedure?'

Yes, they nod.

'Good. And now, listen carefully, I have a very important announcement to make. The Little Odd needs our help, and I am very old. It's time I got out of the Burren and went on a great adventure. So I have discussed with the Bright Badger that I will go with the Little Odd and friends for they will need a wise head to help keep them safe. I will return to you someday, in some shape or form.'

There was a whoosh of whispers all around.

'I will miss you all and always keep you in my heart and mind, but I am leaving you in the capable paws of the Bright Badger who will be your leader now. Do you understand?'

Yes, yes they nod and some cry—for they will miss the Great White Rabbit; very much indeed, but they understand he is very old and has always been here for them. He's not getting any younger and it's time he went on a great adventure and had some fun!

'So without further ado… Lead Bunnies, lead the way to the break-out rooms and let us know what direction to take.'

The Great White Rabbit ceremoniously got out of the chair, took the great big key and opened the door, and all the while his great big ears have been standing on end.

The Lead Bunnies rush to their break-out rooms, and the Great White Rabbit hugs and kisses the little ones. His ears flop down. He wipes tears from under his glasses then he takes them off and wipes his eyes with his paws and says,

'I love all my little bunnies. Goodbye little ones.' He makes big sobs.

The Little Odd holds his paw. The Runaway holds the other one.

The Great White Rabbit says, 'Although I am very old and very slow, I have been saving up all my energy reserves for this great adventure. When we have to run like the hammers, I will be fit to run like the hammers with you—in fact, I may even be faster than all of you put together.'

And he laughs.

'Little Odd, are you ready to bounce?'

'Yes!'

'Then follow up, and I will lead us to a place of safety, where we will decide what to do next.'

'Ready troops?'

Yes, they all cry,

The Lead rabbits come back from the break-out rooms and say, 'Go South Great White Rabbit, we will go in all directions and do what you asked.'

The Great White Rabbit hugs the Lead Bunnies and says, 'Right, ready for launching…

Follow me, and run, run, run rabbits, run from the break-out rooms.

Little Odd—you bounce, bounce, bounce as if your life depended on it!'

'Yes, kind sir!' says the Little Odd.

Chapter Six
The Little Odd Goes on the Run

And Meets a Young Buck

It is a miracle, that the Little Odd, the Runaway, Vermin, the Gurney Cat and the Great White Rabbit, make it out of the Dump. What a sight to see, them bounce, run, scuttle, pounce and leap from the Dump, as if by magic!

The rabble-rousers give chase—they have torches and fire on the end of sticks, wrapped in rags. They holler and whoop and make a racket. The Watch Bunnies do their funky stuff and run this way and that among their feet, leap this way and that, on shoulders and heads to distract and annoy. Several Watch Bunnies sustain serious injuries, which isn't nice.

The Five of Them keep going for as long as they can; for they can still hear the rabble-rousers in the distance; gaining ground. Eventually, the Great White Rabbit grows tired for—even though he has special powers—he is very, very old. They decide, breathless, to take a rest in a shuck—which is like a ditch, only it has a little water running by; a small stream, that gently tinkles; as if running fingers along a keyboard.

'I need to rest, for a few moments if you don't mind, young people.'

They say they all need to rest a while;

'…And I need to tell you about my plan…' says the Great White Rabbit, and they are all ears, as is he.

'Not far from here, is the Enchanted Glade—we will find solace there. We will be among friends. I have already sent a thought-by-vibe to the Faerie Queen, and she sent one back to say she knew we would be coming for days now—and is looking forward, to our arrival.'

'We can shelter there a while and will be well looked after—among faerie friends until we can find our feet.'

The Little Odd looks at its misshapen feet things and says, 'But I haven't lost them, Sir Great White Rabbit.'

'My dear Little Odd,' says the Great White Rabbit, 'It is just a turn of phrase.'

'Oh,' says the Little Odd, 'It will take a while for me to understand these turns of phrases.'

The Great White Rabbit's amazing ears prick up, like sentries, and he says, 'Shhhh a moment—one is near. A Young Buck! Be still, my dears… still like statues, hold your breath.'

The rabble-rousers are far behind but the Young Buck has run on ahead. He holds a torch of fire and stops, just beside the shuck. He pauses; holds the fire aloft and in the glint of the light, he sees the ears of the Great White Rabbit sticking up.

The Young Buck steps forward and for a moment, locks eyes with the Great White Rabbit. He takes in the Little Odd and the Runaway.

He doesn't see the Gurney Cat or Vermin for they are keeping their heads down.

… for a moment, he stands there, like a deer in the headlights, like a young buck in the glare, and he is poised with his whistle, just moments from his lips—he stays that way, frozen in time, for he is torn this way and that…

He doesn't understand, why they are chasing these harmless creatures… but then he remembers the Dump is his home and must be protected from Mutations and those who harbour them… then, he looks at their terrified faces and wonders why, and thinks, the Runaway cute, for he is a Young Buck after all and so the Runaway speaks up and says, 'Please don't blow your whistle.'

And she says it in a soft way that is kind and gentle, and he wasn't expecting that;

So he stands, with the whistle poised moments from his lips and thinks,' I will be a hero—a superhero in the Dump if I blow the whistle… Then he thinks again… The dump is the Dump is the Dump… and what did the Dump ever do for me, but make me miserable, make me feel like a loser…

'If I leave, forever, what have I really got to lose? For no one respects me in the Dump, and so if I blow my whistle, I will be a hero for a day, but once they have got what they want, they will discard me like a tonne of bricks for I have seen that day after day all my young buck life…'

'But if I hold fire—and for heaven's sake look at them—harmless—I could save them from the rabble-rousers for I am not really one of them. I was just trying to fit in, for I am a young buck, and I want more than anything, for the rabble-rousers to pat me on the back and say, 'You did good, boy,' but then when it suits them, they will say I am good for nothing…

And at that moment, the Little Odd puts its head above the pretend parapet of the shuck and says, 'Hullo! I am a Little Odd. I mean you no harm. I am your friend.' And the Little Odd wears its shiniest happiest smile.

The Young Buck thinks he might melt, in his guilt, and says, 'Hullo, I am just a Young Buck. I thought I'd be a hero if I turned you in, but I can see, you are not a Mutation and mean no harm to me or the people or the Dump, but they are gaining space, they will be here soon!'

'We are going to the Enchanted Glade,' says the Little Odd. 'I've never been before but it sounds nice, and they have a faerie queen. Would you like to join us? You could be our guest?'

'Dunno,' says the Young Buck, looking at his whistle, thinking…

'Please,' says the Runaway. 'What have you got to gain by being a rabble-rouser?'

And the Great White Rabbit says with authority: 'Young Buck, I can see inside your soul. You are not a rabble-rouser, are you? You are one of us, an outsider—please, come—follow us.'

So without a moment's hesitation, the Young Buck thought, what have I gotto lose but my ignorance and the Dump? This could be, the greatest adventure in history!

He looks at his whistle for a moment. He hears the rabble-rousers draw closer, and he says, 'Let's go, quick, hurry, take me to the Enchanted Glade. Fast as you can, for they are gaining on us.'

Chapter Seven
The Little Odd Seeks Solace

In the Enchanted Glade

In the dark, the Young Buck has put out his torch. For elfin safety reasons, they move quietly like little church mice across the fields.

The Great White Rabbit leads the way, using his great big ears as radars.

They can still hear the distant sounds of the rabble-rousers, their drums, their whistles, their whoops and wallops, but they have no fear, for they sense, the rabble-rousers have lost their way and have changed direction. The animals of the night are distracting them on purpose, this way and that, by making noises and rustling trees and grasses, just for fun.

After crossing several fields and stiles, fences and ditches, shucks and shebeens—deserted cottages where no one lives anymore, but the evil pixies (… and the elfin safety louts, are known to hide out there from time to time…)

***

The Great White Rabbit has grown tired now, and in the shadow of the shuck says, 'Stop a while, while I gather my thoughts.'

The Great White Rabbit takes off his glasses and rubs his eyes a moment; puts them back on and says, 'Good news, my dears. I just got a message from the Faerie Queen. We are almost there. The Enchanted Glade is just this way. They have been expecting us, and have prepared a midnight feast, in our honour, but shhh… we can cheer when we get there!'

So the Little Odd and the Runaway and Vermin and the Gurney Cat and the Young Buck follow the Great White Rabbit across the fields. They can see the Enchanted Glade in the distance.

Ten million fireflies light the glade. They guide them through, like teeny-tiny lanterns. As they make their way through the Forest of the Night, they can see the little faeries and play; their wings are lit in shades of pink and purple and green and blue—luminous hues.

They chitter-chatter the way small flowers do. Giggle-giggle, all a-flutter—'Follow us, follow us,' they chatter, giggling all the while, and in the clearing is the most beautiful sight the Little Odd has ever seen,

Mounds and mounds of semi-hemisphere houses burst from the ground—all the colours of the rainbow, like Music Festival Tents. All around is the sound of music, of harps and guitars and gentle drums. Whistles and flutes and faerie music, like up above, on cloud Ninety-Nine-a-Hundred, and the Little Odd really feels at home, for the first time, since it fell to Earth.

Tears fall down the Little Odd's cheeky cheeks, and it tries to wipe them with its paw-hand things before anyone notices, but it's okay to cry when you are happy and when you are sad and every place else in between.

Giant Sunflowers surround the clearing in the Enchanted Glade. By day, they hold their great big beautiful sunflower heads towards the sun and soak up the rays of golden light. Then at night, when it grows dark, they bend their great big sunflower heads and use the Solar Power and Energy they soaked up all day long to light the clearing.

There are cupcake stands the size of iceberg tops. They are every colour of the rainbow, they have flowers on top. There are tall and bushy trees—strange shapes and sizes. The faeries have tied ribbons to the branches, every colour just for fun.

It's all too beautiful and the Great White Rabbit, the Runaway and Vermin, the Gurney Cat and the Young Buck stand in wonder; then like a vision from the Vault comes the Faerie Queen, more beautiful than any could imagine, in her shades of pink and blue.

'My dear Great White Rabbit,' she says, radiant. 'How long has it been? Two hundred years perhaps?'

The great White Rabbit takes off his glasses and rubs his eyes shyly and says, 'Thereabouts, give or take a few decades.'

'My dear Great White Rabbit, you are all welcome here as our guests. We will give you sanctuary, for as long as you like.'

'My dear Faerie Queen, thank you, kindly.'

The Faerie Queen and the Great White Rabbit hug, and everyone goes, 'Ahhhh!'

'Eat up, eat up! Let the party begin!'

There is music so pure for a midnight feast. There are cupcakes for everyone. There is ice cream and candy floss and chips (cooked in vegetable oil. No animals were harmed, in the making of this party). There are energy swirls all the colours of the rainbow floating up in the air, along with the laughter.

'Dear Little Odd,' says the Faerie Queen, 'We've been expecting you. We've been preparing for you and all of this is in your honour.'

'Oh,' says the Little Odd, 'I am honoured, but I was wondering when can I meet Solace? The Great White Rabbit said we could find Solace here, and I was hoping we could be friends?'

The Great White Rabbit and the Faerie Queen look at each other and laugh and each takes one of the Little Odd's Paw-Hand-Things and says,

'Dear Little Odd, look all around you! You are surrounded by friends. Solace is all around you; Solace is here and now, so just enjoy.'

The music is so beautiful that everyone begins to dance. The Great White Rabbit and the Faerie Queen dance like there is no tomorrow.

The Runaway and the Young Buck dance. Vermin and the Gurney Cat dance, and they might even fall in love for stranger things that have happened.

The Little Odd stands alone tapping its little misshapen feet, swaying this way and that, and filling its face with cupcake—but not too many for its mummy and daddy said only eat what you need, when you need it, and then stop. 'Don't let your belly ache, Little Odd, in case it makes you burpy-burp-burpy or sickly-sick.'

No one has any fear in the Enchanted Glade, for it is a bubble in space and time.

'Tonight,' the Faerie Queen says, 'We party, but tomorrow we must all lend a hand to tidy up and then decide how we help the Little Odd and friends to make their way from here in safety. We need to make sure they come to no harm… for we are your friends, Little Odd, and we are glad you sought Solace here in the Enchanted Glade. Now, time for bed, my dears, time for bed.'

The Little Odd and friends made their way to the Faerie Queen's giant yurt and danced some more, just for fun. Some played the drums and sang until the early hours, 'for tomorrow is another day,' they say.

Chapter Eight
The Little Odd Prepares to Leave the Enchanted Glade

And Hears a Very Special Story

It is a beautiful sunny morning when the Little Odd, the Runaway, Vermin, the Gurney Cat, the Young Buck and the Great White Rabbit wake up and slowly stretch and come to life.

They all fell asleep inside a special mound the faeries had prepared for them, with soft leaves and giant flower petals to lie on. The faeries have laid out lovely fresh fruits, nuts, berries and seeds for everyone to eat.

'Good morning, everyone,' says the Faerie Queen. 'Look how busy and well-behaved the faeries have been, they have cleaned up all the mess and put everything back where it should be. And just look at this beautiful morning! How the Giant Sunflowers have lifted their heads to the sun, so soon in the day.'

'Dear Little Odd, Great White Rabbit and friends, I understand, you will soon have to be on your way for I feel from the rhythm of the forest and the patterns of the plants that the rabble-rousers are chasing you all still. They have scaled down the search, for they know that you will not return to the Dump forever and a day. However, they are still on the lookout for you all and have set traps across the land.'

'So you see, you must be careful—I fear that you have no choice, but to wander from place to place, until they come to realise, my dear, that you are just a little odd, and mean no harm… only good, for I can see, the love shine from your shiniest happiest smile and your cheeky cheeks.'

The Faerie Queen wiped a tear away and then continued, 'I have been sending, thoughts-by-vibes to my friends in high, and low and middle places.

You will know them when you meet, for they will offer you solace and something to eat';

'Just before you go, I will give a special gift to guide you, from above, but first I have to say, it is a school day for the fearies now their chores are done, and they like to start every morning with a story.'

'So gather around everyone,' says the Faerie Queen, 'It's story time.' And in her gentle voice, she began to speak…

This is the story of the hummingbird. Once upon a time, long, long ago, there was an egg. One day it hatched, just a little—then slowly, slowly it hatched a little more until the head of a shy little bird popped out and looked around. It was very, very frightened, for it had been safe and sound in its shell and now that same shell was falling apart and the little bird had no idea why.

Eventually, the little bird saw its mummy and daddy and realised they loved her very much, and even though she was very shy, day by day she grew stronger and happier and eventually she learned to fly. And once she got the hang of it, for she was very nervous and frightened to begin with her mummy and daddy just couldn't keep her in the nest. She loved to fly, higher and higher and higher, and her mummy and daddy loved to watch her soar.

Eventually, she found her voice, and even though she was very, very shy and thought all the other birds her age were better than her, prettier than her and cleverer than her (for they liked to make her feel that way—in fact, they liked the sound of their own voices best for many were show-offs and didn't like the way she did her own thing and didn't seem to want to fly with the flock)!

Her mummy and daddy sang, "Just let her be, for she is a free bird. Every so often, one comes along, and this bird you cannot tame. They should be free, to be, whatever they want to be; or else they grow sad, and many die unless they are stronger than song."

As she grew older, her mummy and daddy thought she might go find a mate someday. So they watched as she hopped from branch to branch and sang her new songs, each day, a different melody.

Down below, at the root of the tree sat a troll each day. It liked to sit there day after day listening to the songbird sing. 'What pretty songs she sings,' says the troll, 'I would like to keep those all to myself,' for it was a very selfish troll.

So one day the troll arrived, and up its sleeve was a cage, with a lock and key. The troll climbed the tree and sat very silently, while the songbird—happy as could be, free as can be—sang her songs so elegantly... Then she saw and troll and sweetly said, 'Oh, hullo,' and she opened her beak to sing some more, but the troll grabbed the songbird round the neck, threw her into the cage, locked the door and put the key in its pocket, then took her home.

*(*The Faerie Queen did all the actions as she told the story. And the little faeries could pretend to be the free bird and flap their little faerie wings*).*

'Sing, songbird. Sing!' roared the troll. But she wouldn't sing. 'Sing, songbird, sing!'

Silence. For she was frightened. How could she sing, in fear?

'What sort of songbird are you! You are useless to me if you do not sing, songbird!'

'Oh, sir, you are mistaken. I am not a songbird,' she said. 'I am a hummingbird. But I cannot hum while I am locked in this cage, so please, open the door, and I will hum for you.'

'Do you think me stupid,' says the troll. 'I sat beneath your tree for many a day, and I listened to your pretty songs and now you are mine, forever and ever. No one else will ever hear your pretty song except for me—so SING stupid bird-brain!'

'I'm afraid I have lost my voice now, for you are cruel and nasty to me.'

'If you do not sing soon, I will kill you, stupid bird-brain, for there are prettier birds out there, and I can so easily replace you with one who sings much better than you.'

But the songbird stood her ground, and refused to sing or even hum until the door of the cage was opened...

So the troll said, it would open the cage door, but it would have to tie unbreakable thread around her feet, so she would not fly away.

The troll opened the door, then tied unbreakable thread around her feet. And just for now, to keep him quiet she would hum, which is not the same as singing, but it was a start. 'She'd soon come around, once she settled in,' thought the troll, who fell asleep and snored all night, every night.

One day the troll said, 'You are a lazy and useless songbird. Make yourself useful! Go make a nest!'

And the songbird was very happy, for she thought this meant the troll was going to let her be free—to build a nest up in the branches of a tree, like any normal songbird but oh No! Ooh no! He wanted her to build the nest inside the cage. It had to be perfect. It had to be a feathered nest, and the troll would inspect, every day, to check that she was making progress.

He said, he would make sure she worked very hard every day, but she could not see the point, in making a nest, inside a cage with no other bird to share it with, but she built the nest anyway. And it was a very lovely nest, not perfect—but good enough, and as nests go, it was really rather fine.

However, the troll never even noticed how nice she made it, or the flowers she placed around it. He didn't care, one bit, for he was too busy going out and about and doing whatever he wanted. When the troll would go out, the cage door was left open.

'Look,' he'd say, 'you are free to go at any time!'

But when she complained that she couldn't really, because of the unbreakable thread around her little skinny bird leg, the troll said, 'Shut up useless humdinger of a bird!' But just to be sure she didn't try to escape, he tied a little bell around her tiny talons.

In time, the songbird got used to being tied up in the cage, and eventually, the troll would let her fly around the house. As long as she hummed away to herself, and in her head, she dreamed day after day of flying far away, of soaring higher and higher to reach the dizzy heights and let her song be heard from up on high, where the church bells ring—or to perch, on the highest branches of the highest trees and sing, songs of freedom and joy.

So the days passed, the seasons passed, the years passed and year after year, the little songbird, could be heard, humming. But soon, the troll grew tired of her rattles and hums, for when she was angry she'd rattle her cage and when the troll would get angry, it would rattle her cage until day after day either one was rattling the cage and making a racket: Cacophony!

The troll hardly even noticed the songbird anymore. He just went here and there and did his own thing, but he didn't want her just flying off around the place, so he clipped her wings and placed a silver ring around her beak for he was tired now of the Humming Bird.

And the Humming Bird—for that's how she thought of herself now—grew tired of being a hummingbird and wanted to be a songbird again. One brave day, she decided she would not waste another minute in the cage at the mercy of the selfish troll, so she gathered together all the strength and wisdom she could gather in her beak and on her wings—then she broke free—for the unbreakable thread was breakable after all! The troll had just convinced her that it wasn't, and she'd believed it.

Once free she was frightened for a while and hid among the eaves and rafters for hours and days. But eventually, she learned how to fly outside again and in time, she spread her wings and felt the wind on her face and the airflow through her feathers. So she flew higher and higher soaring this way and that, swooping here and there until she found her way to the Enchanted Glade, where we gave her solace. She made many friends. She found her voice again and sang songs of freedom and joy.

Look faeries, here she comes...

The songbird swooped down, smiling and bowed.

The Faerie Queen said, 'This is our gift to you. The songbird is ready to leave this place. It is her time. She has been waiting for this great adventure all her life in captivity. She knew, it was only a matter of time…'

The songbird nodded and smiled and flapped her wings.

'The songbird will travel with you. She will fly above your head. She will fly ahead, to look out for signs of danger and for places of safety. She will hum quietly most of the time for it may not always be safe to sing, and when she stops humming she will ring the little bell around her talon, to let you know, there may be trouble ahead…'

Chapter Nine
The Little Odd Finds a Friendly Farmer

Makes Friends with Crispy Duck and the Fantabulous Fish Out of Water

The faeries prepared little nap-sacks for the Little Odd and friends.

They are now a seven-piece band of travellers: the Little Odd, the Runaway, Vermin, the Gurney Cat, the Great White Rabbit, the Young Buck and the Songbird (aka the Humming Bird).

They gathered around the Faerie Queen to say their thanks and say, 'Farewell, Faerie Queen.' She promised she'd always be with them, to send messages of love and support and goodwill through thought-by-vibe, and all they had to do, was close their eyes, be still and listen, and send one back, anytime.

There were hugs and claps and the Little Odd jumped up and down. The Big White Rabbit threw open his arms and said, 'Faerie Queen, we may never see each other until the other side.'

'Harvey, my friend, that may be so, but we will forever be connected, through thought-by-vibe.'

The Little Odds, for that's what the faeries had called them, looked at each other and said out loud, 'Harvey!'

The Great White Rabbit *called* Harvey took off his glasses, rubbed his eyes, cleaned them (the glasses, not his eyes) on the handkerchief in his waistcoat pocket and said laughing, 'But now is my time for a new adventure, so let us go then, You and I…'

And so the Faerie Queen pointed them in the right direction and said, 'Keep walking that way, and you will come to a friendly farm. The farmer is expecting you and will welcome you there.'

The Little Odds walked for the rest of the day over fields and dale, hills and valleys. Sometimes in a row, sometimes in a line. The Songbird flew ahead, flew high then swooped and entertained, with her humming sounds and while she hummed, they knew they were safe and sound. So they chatted and sang songs of their own, or they grew silent and walked in their own thoughts. Sometimes they'd sit beneath a tree and eat a picnic. They were mindful of the Great White Rabbit called Harvey who needed little rests from time to time.

On the horizon, they could see the sun begin to set. They wondered when they'd find the Friendly Farmer. Then down in the valley, on the edge of the hill they could see smoke rise, like signals, from the chimney of a small and cosy cottage;

Instinctively, they knew this was the place. They were glad for they were all growing tired, but they are looking forward to meeting the Friendly Farmer.

☺

Well, the Friendly Farmer isn't at all what they were expecting!

She is tall, about nine foot tall, and really quite glamorous! She has long green hair and it's all bush-whacked; purple lips and big red eyes that twirl in circles. She is really very pretty and the Little Odd is quite in awe—for the cottage is not that tall, at all!

She has a basket of eggs in her hand, fresh vegetables in the other. She jumps up and down when she sees them arrive; which the Little Odd likes, for it thinks, she is a Like Mind. She is not afraid, to show her joy or her happiness, even if people might think her a little odd. She doesn't seem to care.

'Hullllooooo, Little Odds, I am so happy to have visitors!'

She jumps up and down again. So they all join in, while the Songbird sings, and swoops this way and that.

'Omelette du fromage, with salad and creamy mash for dinner. My dears, come this way, to my humble abode. Just make yourselves at home, find a space on the floor. Help yourselves to Berry Juice and Biscuits for starters I've been so excited since the Faerie Queen sent a message to say you were on the way.'

Each time she talked her red eyes swirled this way and that—like kaleidoscopes for the light flashed in and out and hypnotised. They listened to what she had to say, in the pretty cottage, decked with flowers and greenery, and the scents of serenity.

While they sat on the floor, as she prepared their meal, she told them a story, to pass the time… and her voice was like raindrops against the window paene, rhythmic, but mellow and sad at times, but lovely and comforting to listen to.

She said, '*I am so glad to welcome you here, for like the Faerie Queen, I've been expecting you. I was just waiting, passing the time, until the day you came; I have been making preparations, to scale down my farm and leave it ready, for my departure—for I will be joining you on your adventure, if you'll welcome me!*'

The Little Odds nod their heads, for they are enraptured now, and cannot imagine life or a future without the Friendly Farmer amongst them.

I have given away my hens, my goats and cows to Like Minds who I know will respect and care for my animals; I have gathered my small crops and shared them with those who need them more than me, the rest I have prepared for the journey, just as much as we can carry. From now on, this cottage will be our homestead, for the faerie people will protect it from elfin types and the wicked pixies. They will keep it clean and look after it, and we can find solace here anytime we like, for I can make it invisible, with my x-ray eyes. I can divert the glare, of people who cannot, or will not see what's there…

For they do not want me on this land. I am not the sort of farmer they want for I refuse to yield to their ways of wanton greed and land-destruction. They make mutants of the crops, spray stuff on everything and say it's better for everyone—for the good of the people. They make the sheep grow funny, then pull the wool down over their eyes and call it progress. The land cries out for mercy and so do the animals, but they turn a blind eye and deaf ear, from what they do not want to see or hear.

The Little Odds sit there, jaws dropping, then she says, 'Do you follow me?'

And they nod, for they think they do.

Now the omelettes and salads and mashed potatoes are ready. They hadn't even noticed that she worked away, while she talked, for they were spellbound and happy, tummies full, to fall asleep on the soft blankets on the smooth ground of the homestead.

☺

As dawn breaks, the Little Odd can hear the Friendly Farmer up and about, as is the way of Friendly Farmers—early risers, with the sound of the Cockadoodledoo.

The Little Odd stirs, and whispers to the farmer who has put the Singing Kettle on the stove: 'Is it okay if I come help you with your chores?' She says of course, but first, she likes a strong coffee, and she looks the Little Odd in the eye with her big red swirls going this way and that. Like kaleidoscopes.

The Little Odd has a Cirrusoscope on Cloud Ninety-Nine-A-Hundred. It is a favourite toy—quite like a kaleidoscope. The Little Odd loves looking into the Friendly Farmer's swirly eyes.

The Singing Kettle sings—F, F sharp, Geeeeeeeee, until she moves it aside.

(The Little Odd wonders, why the Singing kettle can't do any better than that—surely it could manage a little melody in the morning. Someone should invent a kettle that sings songs, for then, people could sing a long first thing, and it would make them happy. For too many people are way too grumpy at the start of each day when they could be full of joy and wonder at all the possibilities).

The Little Odd watches closely as she makes her strong coffee.

'I'm going to make supplies for the journey,' says the Friendly Farmer, 'to use up all the food that's left so that it won't go to waste. I hate waste,' says the Friendly Farmer.

'Me too!' says the Little Odd.

The Little Odd helps her fill the bags of fruit, seeds and nuts for the journey. She is making egg sandwiches—the last of the eggs, for she has given all her chicks and hens away to the old man who lives nearby.

The Little Odd watches closely as she cuts the eggs with the special instrument. The Little Odd has never seen it used for this purpose before, but down here on this planet, people do strange things. A tear rolls down the Little Odd's cheeky cheeks. The Friendly Farmer notices the sad face and bends down, then kneels to talk to the Little Odd (for she is very, very tall for such a tiny cottage). More tears roll down the cheeky cheeks.

'My dear Little Odd,' she whispers, for the rest are still sleeping, 'Whatever is the matter?'

The Little Odd points at the egg-slicer.

'You don't like the egg-slicer?'

'No, I love it, that's why I'm crying.'

'Oh, I see,' says the Friendly Farmer, but she doesn't see at all, so her swirly eyes close down. For just a moment.

'You see,' says the Little Odd, 'I have one just like that where I come from, on cloud Ninety-Nine-a-Hundred, and when I fell off, I left it behind. It's only when I see yours that I miss it so much.'

Then the Little Odd bursts into tears.

'Dear Little Odd, it's just an egg-slicer, but if it means that much to you, it's yours, forever and ever!'

The Friendly Farmer gives it a little wash and hands it to the Little Odd whose face lights up with its shiniest happiest smile.

'Thank you, Friendly Farmer—can I go outside and play with it?'

'Of course.'

And off it skips… as she watches, and shakes her head, in a kind way.

She gets on with her chores… preparing the cottage for departure, as the others sleep on. She has to step carefully around their sleeping bodies.

Then she stops, looks, listens.

Hey, what's that sound?

She steps outside on the far side of the farmyard stands the Little Odd, making music on the egg-slicer… The Little Odd weaves its little paw-hand things this way and that across and between the wires, in a way she never thought humanly possible. The music that flows from the egg-slicer and the Little Odd's paw-hand things is the sweetest she ever heard in her long life;

It's like nothing she ever heard before. Who'd have thought, a simple egg-slicer could sound so good? And she can see the Little Odd is lost in time and space. She hears, behind her, the others stir, and one by one they step outside and stare at the Little Odd across the farm yard who is oblivious to them all; caught up only, in the notes that flow, that float in swirls and staccato balls, into the ether and beyond—a melody, the likes of which was never heard before about this neck of the woods.

The music stops suddenly. Something has disturbed the Little Odd.

Hey! What's that sound?

There seems to be a commotion coming from the pond… splash, splish, splosh!

Something is doing a lot of squawk, squawk, squawkkking. And something is doing a lot of splish, splash, sploooooooshing!

A duck appears to have jumped into the pond and a very strange fish indeed, appears to have leapt out of the pond.

What's going on?

The Little Odd stops and stares. The fish that has jumped out of the water is golden and glitters in the early morning sun. The fish holds a fancy hat in one fin and a tap-dancing stick in the other. It has big fish eyes and a mouth in the shape of a Big O, and in the early morning sun, the fish out of water starts tap-dancing, just for fun. It makes a rhythm on the ground, the likes of which, the Little Odd had never heard before.

'Oh, Hullo!'

Oh—tap-tapety-tap-tap—oooohhhhhh

Tap-tapety-tap-tap

The fish moves its body this way and that; twirls this way and that in a way the Little Odd thought not humanly possible. The fish does somersaults and flick flacks and cartwheels and arabesques. This fish can do the crab! How weird is that—then dances again, throwing the hat and cane in the air and catching them in its fins!

The Little Odd stands like a statue and stares. It makes O shapes with its mouth too for it is in awe! The Little Odd has never seen a Fantabulous-Fish-Out-of-Water before, because there is only one, in all the world. *'Show-Off! Show-Off!'* says a voice. '*Show-Off! Show-Off!'* says the voice again.

But the Fantabulous-Fish-Out-of-Water doesn't care. It just keeps on dancing, without a dare and yes, it knows, it is a show-off! So what!

'If ya got it, flaunt it!' laughs the Fantabulous-Fish-Out-of-Water, and he winks at the Little Odd who tries to wink back, but can't quite get the hang of it.

'Hullo there, I am the Fantabulous-Fish-Out-of-Water, and you must be the Little Odd. Pleased to meet you!'

The Fantabulous-Fish-Out-of-Water waves, and explains he can't shake fins for he has a top hat in one and a cane in the other, and he can't stop dancing, when out of the water, or he'll die so the Fantabulous-Fish-Out-of-Water keeps on movin' and says, 'Just ignore my dear wife, she is always grumpy in the morning. It's why I call her Crispy.'

The Little Odd looks towards the pond to see where the rather squawky squawky duck has gone.

'Show-Off!' sounds were coming from the pond, and there the Little Odd sees a rather proud looking duck swimming about, duckbill in the air, snooty-snooty-high-fallooty;

'Squawky,' says the Crispy Duck, 'Isn't he just a big show-off?'

'Ummmm…' says the Little Odd, 'He is theee most Fantabulous-Fish-Out-of-Water, I think him very talented.'

'Ha! He is so full of beans in the morning, he should count himself lucky I don't have him for breakfast. Sqwaaaaack!'

'Is a Duck and a Fish not an Odd Couple?'

'Indeed, indeed! We are the Odd Couple, which is nice, for folk just leave us alone, to dance and swan around, as we please, which suits us both well. I am of course a swan, stuck in a duck-body. You must see that,' she said, turning her duckbill high and to the right and the Little Odd says, 'Of course.' 'You are a very fine duck-swan indeed.'

'Thank you,' says Crispy Duck. 'And as we are the Odd Couple, we'd like to be your friends! May we join you on your journey? We fancy some adventures for we've been stuck in this small pond for far too long. Fantabulous is always complaining about being a big fish in a small pond, show-off that he is!'

'Of course, you can! It will be wonderful to have a Fantabulous-Fish-Out-of-Water and a Crispy Duck along the way.'

So the Little Odd jumped up and down and wore its shiniest happiest smile. The Fantabulous Fish just kept on dancing, then leapt into the pond to hug his wife, who splish-splashed around. The Fantabulous Fish did leaps and somersaults until it was time to go.

And now, there are ten…;

Chapter Ten
The Lovely Little Lion Man

The Friendly Farmer is very organised and efficient. She packs all her belongings into a rucksack. She packs baskets of food and fills flasks with juice, herbal teas and strong coffee (for it might be a few days before she gets a fresh one).

She gives each Little Odd a basket or bag to carry, so the weight is spread evenly, to each according to their strength and ability. Now, they are ready for the next adventure.

'Where are we going now?' asks the Little Odd.

'It's still not safe Little Odd. I got a thought-by-vibe from the Faerie Queen. We are to go to the Land of Wonder. It will take a few days, but it's mostly a safe route, and we'll have some fun. We might have to sleep beneath the stars tonight if that's okay,' says the Friendly Farmer.

All the Little Odds jumped up and down and said, 'Hurray,' except for the Great White Rabbit who just smiled and said, 'Perfect!'

It was one of those glorious mornings in early autumn—the sort you want to package up and pocket, to look at in the dark days. Everyone is happy. The Runaway and the Young Buck laugh and chat. The Gurney Cat and Vermin Play I-spy. Crispy Duck waddles and holds her beak up high. The Fantabulous-Fish-Out-of-Water dances, this way and that, tappety-tap.

The Friendly Farmer walks behind, keeping a watchful eye. Beside her is the Great White Rabbit, who gives a little sigh of happiness, for he is glad to be out in the fresh air this fine morning. The Songbird flies high and swoops, this way and that, humming all the while, keeping a watchful eye;

The Little Odd steps out in front—not in an "I'm the leader look at me" way but just because that's the way it is this day. He plucks on his egg-slicer, and the Little Odds look at each other and nod, smiling. They like the sound but ask no questions, for that's just the day it is.

They stay this way for many hours. The road is winding, but flat, and there is no one for miles around. The hedgerows smell delicious, and if they like, they pluck blackberries on the way, but only what they need and when, leaving the rest, for the wee birdies. The juice is delicious and colours their fingertips, like henna.

They pass sparrows and swallows (packing up for their long-haul flight). They see squirrels and rabbits and honey bees. They see trees, many trees, that nod and acknowledge the Little Odds passing by, for trees, are polite that way (they woodn't have it any other way). They whisper well-wishes, as does the grass.

They cover many miles and to pass the time, the Young Buck sings and my, oh my, who'd have thought this thorny youth, could sing this way!

The Runaway—well her jaw falls open, wide, then she smiles, bashfully. She turns bright pink. The Young Buck notices this, and likes her smile—her feisty-shy style.

So he keeps on singing the songs inside his head that come from places he knows not where; and the Songbird, on high, picks up the harmonies. Then the Little Odd, joins in and makes the egg-slicer ting in ways that somehow seem to match, the tap-tap dance of the Fantabulous Fish. The Gurney Cat, stays silent, which is a relief to all; for this is music, that could fill the Albert Hall (*but they don't know about the Albert Hall and all the holes in it*).

This travelling band grows weary and tired—happy-tired. Up ahead is a Grand Old Oak Tree that beckons them hither and says in a deep voice, up from the roots so long and strong, 'Dear Little Odds, I've been expecting you. Tonight, I give you shelter and protection. Tomorrow, I give you strength for the road ahead. Come, sit with me. Come, dine with me. It will be nice, to have the company. 'Don't worry—I don't bite, but I may bark from time to time.'

Then he laughs, a deep jolly laugh and says, 'My little joke, for I too, am a Little Odd!'

The Friendly Farmer spreads out the picnic. The Young Buck helps, and Crispy Duck flaps about and squawks a bit. The Gurney Cat opens its mouth, for it is hungry, but thinks better of making a noise, so purrs instead. The Fantabulous Fish goes in search of plankton, for there's a small pool over there and Crispy Duck goes join him for a splash about.

Everyone else gets stuck into breads and cakes, berries and nuts, fruits, all set out, higgledy-piggledy, on pretty plates and bowls.

Afterwards, everyone chills—play games like tig, statues and catch-that-fish. The Friendly Farmer and the Great White Rabbit don't join in. They smile at the others, having fun and think, inside their own heads, wouldn't it be good, if it was like this all the time?

Then the Grand Old Oak Tree says, 'Ahem, may I tell my life story?' So they are all ears—especially the Great White Rabbit, and they listen very carefully.

'Three hundred years I've stood here, he says, *and there's not much I haven't seen since I was a small acorn. All the comings and goings, the too-ing and fro-ings but still the sun rises over there and sets just over there, each day, majestic, like before, so much so that we all, just take it for granted—same as it ever was. Yet don't they fully see how I shed my leaves this time of year? Look—see how they're coming on!'*

And the Great White Rabbit and the Friendly Farmer agree the leaves are looking very fine, in their first throes of change.

'And each year, I make this glorious display of colour—I'm not boasting you understand, it's just I have so many thousand leaves each year. Each one is a work of art—and the colour changes under the sun's direction, to gold, then brown, until I shed them down, so daintily—ha—a big awkward oak like me!'

'Then for 300 years, I turn indoors and re-charge myself, for spring, that's just my thing. I don't mind the cold, even though I'm old. I am protected, by the sun and the planet—for spring comes, around again. That's just the way it is.'

The Friendly Farmer and the Great White Rabbit nod in agreement and say, 'That's just the way it is, some things will never change.'

Then way up high, in the lofty branches, they hear a stirring—a sound so simple, a movement, in fluent flute, and say, *'Stop! What's that sound? Everyone look what's going down!* Where is that melody coming from? The leaves?' they ask. The Oak just laughs and says, 'No, no. That's my visitor, my special friend. He's very shy, and when he's ready, I'll introduce you. He'll give me a sign when he's good and ready, like I say he's very shy, but I was happy to give him solace here—for my tree, has many branches, and moves, as the wind blows… Music Maestro!'

From the leaves and branches comes a sound, like Bach's Badiniere Suite Number 2 in B Minor. Two eyes hiding in the branches and leaves have been watching the Little Odds play from afar, and would very much like, to join in…

The flute notes float up into the air. They twirl and spin up into the ether, higher and higher, like curls of spinning energy…

And down below, the Fantabulous-Fish-Out-of-Water just can't help himself—tap dances; and everyone else joins in, even the Grand Old Oak Tree sways his branches and leaves. It's all too beautiful—the way the Friendly Farmer's red eyes twirl this way and that; the fish tips his hat, and Crispy Duck dances with a rat (*she never thought she'd do that)!*

Then down from the branches, comes Ludwig, the Little Lion Man and everybody claps, but Ludwig is very shy and takes a shallow bow, so they clap some more, then shy Ludwig takes another longer, lower bow—and smiles his shiniest happiest smile.

The Grand Old Oak Trees says, 'That was wonderful Ludwig. Now say Hullo to the Little Odds.'

'Hullo…'

'Hullo! Hullo! Will you be our friend?' says the Little Odd.

'Yes, thank you,' says Ludwig the Little Lion Man.

'Would you like to come on a journey with us?' asks the Little Odd.

'Dunno…'

'Please!'

'I wouldn't like to leave the Grand Old Oak Tree. It might be lonely without me here, to shake its branches and leaves and sway to the music.'

But the Grand Old Oak says, 'Little Lion Man it has been my great pleasure to have you in my leaves, to listen to your songs, but now it is your time to leave—for I gave you solace when you needed a place of sanctuary. You have been so lonely up here without any playmates.'

'I know this, for I would hear it in your notes. Here we have a group of wee dotes who want you to go with them. You will find courage there for they will make you feel at home, even as you wander far and wide.'

Ludwig wipes a tear from his eye. Then gives the Grand Old Oak a great big hug.

The Little Odds are all tired now. The stars have filled the heavens, so they settle down, beneath the Grand Old Oak to look up at the stars and wonder…

Chapter Eleven
The Little Odds Take Pity on a Puzzled Penguin

An early autumn dawn, soaked in dew—the Little Odds stretch and rise in dribs and drabs like happy zombies rising from silent slumber beneath the stars, which have all gone to bed now. The sun climbs between two hills in the distance and the Grand Old Oak tells them that's the direction they are going today.' Go east,' he says, 'and you have two more sleeps, until you come to the Land of Wonder!'

'I wish I could go with you all,' says the Grand Old Oak. 'But I've taken root here, and here, I will stay. When you hear the whoosh of the wind in the trees, that will be me. I am your strength, I am the Grand Old Oak Tree, for that is what oak symbolises in mythology.'

The Little Odds enjoy a great big picnic breakfast before each one hugs the oak and garners strength for the days ahead… Promises of mystery and adventure and everything under the sun in the Land of Wonder, just two days away, where they will be safe from the rabble-rousers. Free to be, whatever they want to be! Before they set off the Grand Old Oak gathers them around and says words of wisdom…

'The Land of Wonder is full of special, magical things but never take your eye off the ball…'

The Little Odd asks what the ball looks like, so they will recognise it—'Is it like the ball I curled up in?' But the Grand Old Oak says that's just a turn of phrase.

'Oh, I see,' says the Little Odd, for it's beginning to understand such things now.

The Grand Old Oak says, 'The day after tomorrow you will go through a very dark place, but I will guide you from afar and so will the Little Lion Man from up close, for he knows this place well. He's journeyed there, it's what brought him here to me, seeking solace in my branches. Now his purpose is clear, to go back that way, with strength and courage, with dignity—to protect and show you the way.'

'Today, you have no fear, but I hear through the whispering grass someone needs your help out there. Just over the hill, beside a lake is another little odd, just waiting, to be found.'

'Now I wish you well, Good Bye Little Odds and someday, if you pass this way again don't be a stranger!'

So they say they won't be strangers, and hug it one last time, for now.

But the Grand Old Oak is at that age in life, three hundred years or more, whereby it's happy, to be left alone in thought, yet to keep a watchful eye on all around, to infinity, and beyond.

***

They set off up to the top of yonder hill, then stop for a rest at the top, a few hours after setting off. The view is breathtaking from up here! A three-hundred-and-sixty-degree panorama of the planet, as far as their eyes can see (*but for the Great White Rabbit that's not too far*, b*ut he says, he can imagine, for he's seen it all before*)!

There are stone circles on top of the hill, so they play there awhile and do spinnies—over and over until they are dizzy and have to lie down to make grass angels, but only the Runaway and Young Buck make grass angels that make sense—the rest come out all odd, but that's okay. Who cares up here in a place of the free? Where the air is pure and the wind roams, and no one sees, but those who open their eyes to the beauty all around them, to the natural world, so simple so pure so untouched all around them!

Then when their tummies have settled after all the spinnies the Friendly Farmer serves up lunch. The Fantabulous-Fish-Out-of-Water is flaggin' and says he needs to find some fresh water soon or he might take one of his dizzy spells. Over yonder, they can see a freshwater lake, so when all are fed and watered they make their way downhill to a place of clear water; called Anahorish.

There, they see a creature, and they know not what it is! It is black and shiny and scared. This strange black shiny creature can see these Little Odds coming towards it but it knows not what they are, so it dives in the water, and disappears…

Whatever can it be?

'It's a baby lake monster, there are tales afoot. Everyone hasheard of lake and lough monsters? Haven't they? I heard there's one in Bonnie Scotland they call Nessie,' says Crispy Duck and the Fantabulous-Fish-Out-of-Water nods his head sagely.

'Uh, no,' says the Little Odd and the rest are glad, for they did not want to show that they had not either, except for the Friendly Farmer and the Great White Rabbit who had heard, such tales before, in childhood.

They sit by the water's edge and take refreshments while the Fantabulous-Fish-Out-of-Water dives in and leaps out—giant carp! Full of Joy! So happy to feel the cool of the freshwater against its scales. While the others watch, Fantabulous does somersaults and leaps and splashes! 'Show-off!' shouts Crispy, but that's okay, for she means it in a kind and loving way really.

The sun is high in the sky now. They decide to rest awhile and let the Fantabulous Fish and the Crispy Duck, who has waddled to the water's edge—and is swimming along nicely (duckbill in air), have some fun, and chill time in the water. For it can't be easy, being out of your natural habitat, for long periods of time. Yet they never complain, much, well Crispy Duck does, from time to time—like when she says, she's feeling a bit dried out, at her age…

The Great White Rabbit is glad for the rest and lies looking at the sky. The Little Odd takes out its egg-slicer and twangs. The Little Lion Man plays his wooden flute made of twig and the Young Buck sings, while the Runaway does harmonies. The hummingbird keeps an eternal watchful eye from above and Hummmmmmmmsssssssss.

In the distance, a little black head has come out of the water and watches, still as a bush-beetle (whatever that is). Crispy Duck and Fantabulous swim towards the black head, and say, Hi! But the little black head disappears again, underwater.

They shrug at each other, Crispy Duck and Fantabulous Fish. They are used to meeting creatures of the deep, who chose to be left alone, but they reckon not so on this occasion. They will wait until it raises its head above water again.

So they bide their time but the music, underwater sounds even more mysterious and so the black creature can't help but put its head above water again to see what's going on and why?

Crispy Duck and Fantabulous Fish say, 'Hi! We are your friends!' But the black head disappears underwater again. This time, so do Crispy Duck and Fantabulous. They swim underwater. They swim around it, and show that they are no threat; then up for air, and together they laugh—the Fantabulous Fish leaps out and shows the black-headed creature what it can do out on land!

Crispy Duck shakes her bill and says, 'Never mind him, he's a show-off.' Then black-headed creature smiles shyly for the first time. Crispy smiles back and says, 'Look over there, we are your friends. Do not be afraid. We mean you no harm.'

But it disappears again, comes up flapping and splashing this time and says, 'Hi! I am shy!' Then disappears again.

Crispy Duck squacks and says, 'Hullo Shy!' And this time, just a little flipper comes above water and waves—then swims on. Again, another little flipper, waving—then disappears.

But next time, the black head and the two flippers appear. Crispy Duck and Shy do a high-five, wing to flipper just for fun! Again. And again!

Next time Crispy Duck says, 'Come join us—are you hungry? 'But Fantabulous shudders and shakes its head towards Crispy Duck, who just laughs and says, 'Come join us, by the water's edge, you are most welcome.'

Shy shakes its black head, and disappears again. Crispy Duck and Fantabulous ignore it and say, Let it come to us in its own time… eventually, it does,

Slowly the black head paddles across the water's edge, and when it is close by, for all to see, raises one flipper and shyly, waves. Everyone waves back all at once, so Shy disappears again, in ripples and waves, but they all laugh for they know it's coming back. Next time, a flipper wave and splash. And next time, everyone waves…

So it disappears again and now it is a game, until eventually, the black head of Shy! Pulls up by the water's edge and says, 'Yelp-urk-yelp-yippety.'

They don't understand a word, so they just say Hullloooo and Hiiii! But they beckon and everyone understands that, so the black head and flippers of Shy! Come out further still until it stands before them and says, 'I know this much—I am a penguin, but I am puzzled. I don't know why I'm here, how I got here, where I came from or how I can get back. Can you help?'

The Little Odds look at each other confused and say they are not sure who it is, why it's here, where it came from or how it can get back, but if they did, they would surely help.

Shy, the Puzzled Penguin, thinks for a minute and thinks at least they speak the same language. At least it can understand them, even though they sound funny and so Shy the Puzzled Penguin decides to get out of the water and stand before them and say, 'Here I am. My name is Shy, the Puzzled Penguin. I did not come from the sky that much I know for I have watched and wandered; 'I know this much—I need water to stay alive and although there is water in the sky, in the clouds—it is not enough! So I have to stay down here yet I know this much: It is too warm, and I like to be cold; it is too green, and I like it to be white. I am far from home, but I know not where home is, and I have no idea, how I got to be in this place. I have a memory, that I sailed away from my family… I got confused—there was a big storm one night that gave me such a fright and the boat fell to pieces and everything fell apart and somehow I ended up here, the rest, I don't recall.'

'Aw poor Shy!' they all said, 'No wonder, you are a puzzled penguin! How long have you been this way?'

'No idea; that is just one of many puzzles,' says Shy! 'I have no idea what age I am or if I am a boy or a girl penguin. I know nothing, so I stay here day after day, trying to figure things out.'

'Poor Puzzled Penguin, we can help if you like, for we are all mixed up and confused too.'

'That would be nice,' says Shy the Puzzled Penguin, 'for I know one thing—I am not meant to be here, all alone, forever. It would be nice to have friends.'

'Then, we are your friends,' says the Little Odds, and that night, beneath the stars again, to try to help the Puzzled Penguin remember, they took it in turns to tell their own stories, about who they are and who they think they are and stories, of times past, before, they became the Little Odds.

So the Puzzled Penguin felt very much at home with this Motley Crew. Far, far from home in the company of these Little Odds.

'Achoooo,' sneezed the Penguin. Achooo, for it was chilly now in the early autumn evening air.

Chapter Twelve
The Little Odds Enter the Valley of Dark

But Meet an Elegant Elephant There

As the day moves on the Puzzled Penguin is one of the Little Odds, welcomed and confirmed. It shows its toys, the conkers and puzzling things it has gathered along the way, and so they give it a little bag to put everything in, for they are still not sure if it is a he or a she, and the Puzzled Penguin knows not either. But that's okay, that's just the way it is.

The Puzzled Penguin is happy. It eats and jumps up and down, splashes around with the Fantabulous Fish who no longer feels under threat—he married Crispy Duck, didn't he? And she's a pain, in the duckbill, but has a heart of gold, nonetheless. He could have got stuck with a whiny shiny goldfish, who wanted gold-carped this and gold-carped that but Crispy's just happy the way she is, as long as she's top-duck, and he gets to tap-dance and show off, and she gets to tell him he's a show-off and a pain in the feathers.

So they travel on a while, Penguin in tow, one of them now. Gurney Cat and Vermin make it at home, flipper in paws. They travel; until the sun sets, and they look to the Friendly Farmers for advice. She says, 'Look over there! Shelter! A play park for the night! A place to play and not get in the way.'

She guides them there, for she knows, tomorrow will be a long and arduous day. Provisions are running low until they get to the Land of Wonder… They will have to make do, with what's left but tonight, there is enough for everyone to eat and drink coffee and berry juice (note to self, says Friendly Farmer, almost out of coffee, so she saves the rest for morning).

'Look,' she says, 'Let's take shelter here. Tomorrow will be a long day, but I have to say whatever happens we leave no one behind, we stick together, and we tread the way like warriors until we come to the Land of Wonder. Understand?'

They nod their heads. They are gathered around in a circle. Someone lit a campfire and no one noticed. The stars are out now, as if by magic, but no one noticed.

The Little Lion Man raises his hand and says to the Friendly Farmer, 'I'd like to tell you a story for I have been through the Valley of Dark before but no one seemed to notice, so if you don't mind I'd like to tell you what it was like for me. That way, I can tell you all, that everything will be okay—even if it hurts at the time.'

The Friendly Farmer nods. The Little Odds gather round wrapped in each other's arms for warmth to hear the story, that the Little Lion Man has to tell, for he's been through it all, and he says, this…

It pains me to tell this story, for while I sought solace in the branches of the oak tree and played my music no harm could come to me. Now I know, the reason. I was taken to that place to be there for you—to guide you through the Valley of Dark and into the Land of Wonder, for if you have not known one you will never know, the other.

The Little Odds, nod sagely as if in understanding so Ludwig the Little Lion Man continues:

To the west of the Valley of Dark is Wild-er-ness, where I was born free, the first of three.

My mother was the Queen of the Pride. I was her firstborn, and she was so proud then came, my sister and brother. Within days and weeks, it became apparent to my parents, up close and beyond (my father—a watchful eye from the head of the pride) that their firstborn was a Little Odd. They kept a watchful eye on me. I did not, interact, in the way they'd like and showed no signs of leadership they said. I wandered, here and there and constantly, got into places of danger—an innocent, among the pride and soon the other mothers laughed at me and encouraged their cubs to do the same, but my sister was the warrior, and she chastised and fought my corners, this way and that and said, 'Hey Brother, what are thou? Not one of us?' for the younger was the fighter and pride of watchful eyes. It only takes a minute in a crowd, to figure out the fighters from the fools, and the fools from the wise…

So to cut a long story short, I lost my mind. I was cast out from the Pride for crimes against Nature. 'Firstborn, born free off ye go!' they teased. 'Make your own way, not one of us, shame on you.'

And so I left, tail between legs. My mother cried, but I promised, no matter what lay ahead, in life or death, I'd make her proud, and she said she knew—then she whispered in my ear: 'They say, we are born equal, but that's not true. Some are born, less but more, to seek out their place in the universe, but first comes scorn and ridicule. You, Little Lion Man, are the bravest of brave, in my view. I am always with you, through the Valley of Dark, she whispers, for Iam your Mother, the Lioness, the Protector of Cubs. Go, leave this place and come back, to save it someday for you, have been born with poetry in your soul and so you will always be a Little Odd.' Then she nodded and said, 'That will make sense someday.'

And so here I am, with you, and I am, self-confessed, a Little Odd.

'Wow,' says the Little Odd, 'What happened after that?'

'Well now,' says the Little Lion Man, 'cast out from the pride for I didn't fit in I spent years, wandering, from dark place to dark place. I took the beatings everywhere I went, punishment, for being different I suppose. But that's just the way it was, back then. Things are different now!'

'Then what?' asks the Young Buck and the Runaway in unison for they were keen to hear:

'Well, my sister became the warrior and my younger brother the alpha male. They were not proud of me which hurt. For if you can't rely on family, then who can you?'

'You can rely on us,' says the Great White Rabbit as he wiped his spectacles.

'I know,' says the Little Lion Man, as he wiped his eyes discreetly. 'You are my family now. But I have to tell you the rest of my story. When I was in the Valley of Dark, I met an Elegant Elephant who pulled me from that place. She is still there, as far as I know. I hope we meet her for I feel the Oak will guide

us to her. She is wise, like he, and beautiful, the most beautiful Elegant Elephant you ever did meet!'

'When I was cast out from the pride for being a poet, and musician, it was the herd that took me in, even though, they knew I could threaten them. They saw through me and could see I'd never hurt, those who gave me solace, which they did. Through the bad times, they took me into the centre of the herd, and I walked with them, a lion along elephants, and yet, in the Valley of Dark, they showed no fear. I asked them why. They said, you have the music in your soul, the poetry in your open ear, the universe has sent us you Little Lion Man, so we have no fear, now... Music Maestro.

So I played my flute for them—the elephants heard. They said even though I looked like a lion I had the soul of a Man, so they called me Ludwig Little Lion Man, and somehow it stuck, and here I am—Little Lion Man—at your service!

Tomorrow is another day, but I know the way the wilderness works. By the way, just so you know, I really am that odd—a vegetarian lion! The elephants taught me how!

At the end of this strange story, the Little Odds fell asleep for tomorrow, is another day. It will somehow see them through to the Land of Wander and all through the night, the Little Lion Man kept watch for he was more brave than those who take the name.

***

Into the Valley of the Dark went the Little Odds the next day—hands in paws and flippers in fins; hand-paw-things in wing-things. What a motley crew they looked! They marched fearless and brave until they could see nothing up ahead. In the dark, they could see the outlines of trees with spooky faces and branches that moved in strange places. They kept on walking,—eyes wide open, ears alert for signs and sounds of danger. Before long, they are in the thick of it and can no longer walk in a row, so they double up in partners: Crispy with Fantabulous, Young Buck and Runaway; Vermin and Gurney Cat; Friendly Farmer and Great White Rabbit; Little Odd and Puzzled Penguin. Up ahead, Little Lion Man behind, the Humming Bird—a watchful eye from above, swoops, in and out the branches and trees. She has an overview, as far as her eyes can see. She hums, a sign, that there's no concern for now.

In the hollows, of the trees creatures, poke their goblin heads out—cackling, screeching, sticking out tongues—but the Little Odds, walk straight ahead. Owls coo, branches snap, cries in the night from distant spaces in the dark forest which seems to go on forever.

Shadows and sounds from underground. Small creatures that scuttle, this way and that between their feet and up their legs until they shake them off: Beetles and the size of balls! Spiders that come from Mars, long-legged and twitching, cast shadows, size of halls;

No one breathes a word. They think the Little Lion Man very brave for he walks ahead, not a sound he makes, just guides them on—even though they fear, it's close to the brink or at the end of the dark forest is a cliff, steep and stark, and there is only space for them to carefully slide, one by one, along the place twixt the edge and the trees,

'Don't look down,' says the Lion Man. 'This doesn't last long, here is the most dangerous bit.'

And at that, The Little Odd slips!

Those misshapen feet things the wrong size and shape—Little Odd loses balance, and trips over the edge, but quick as a flash turns and grabs the edge with its paw-hand things that are the right shape to hold him there.

Terrified, wide-eyed, doesn't make a sound
Doesn't dare and carefully, it dangles there
Until, with ease and courage, the Little Lion Man
The Runaway and the Young Buck, ease the Little Odd up
To safety…

Shhh, it's okay, Little Odd. We're almost there, a few yards more, then a clearing where we can rest and talk awhile.

'Phew,' they say, when they are all safe and sound in the clearing, that was a close shave, but the Little Odd is silent and shaking, so they hug it and keep warm but the Little Odd is not cold, just traumatised, by the scary things it saw down below, had it fallen, into the pyre.

It is still dark, but at least it's flat and the creatures of the Forest of the Night keep their distance. They all eye each other suspiciously. The Friendly Farmer says, 'We have each other, huddle round, huddle round. We have to walk, through this night, to get out the other side. We'll be fine!'

***

The valley is dark and ominous as they continue, two by two. There are bones of big beetles. Skeletons of super-spiders. There are fires burning. Grey-faced folk, stare at them. Eyes hollow, faces fearful or grey. Giant fruit bats swamp the night sky. No air, stifling, hot then cold, alternate. Goblins and gnomes, pixies and elves, full of hate for the creatures that pass by,

On Life, On Death

Cast a cold-eye

Headless horseman

Passes by…

Screeches in the night. There might be Pterodactyls! Yikes! Then in the distance—a strange sight—a herd of elephants take fright, raucous, trunks in the air, distracted!

The Little Lion Man says, 'Come, quick, this is my herd.'

So they rush that way. Little Lion Man asks the head of the herd, 'Sir, what's wrong?'

'Little Lion Man, it's you, come back in our hour of need. Oh, Little Lion Man, my beloved daughter is missing. We haven't seen her for days, we've been looking everywhere. We fear the Hairy Mammoth has got hold of her, my beautiful Elegant Elephant, my darling child.'

Mrs Elegant Elephant caterwauls and the other females, aunts and cousins, try to comfort her, with trunks and kindness—but to no effect; for an elephant, is an emotional thing.

Little Lion Man stands up tall and says, 'We'll find her, won't we guys?'

Yes, of course—then the Little Odd says, 'Excuse me, Sir Elephant, but I heard a cry, from over there as we were walking over here. It was a painful cry, not the same as all the other sounds I heard. Let us go there, you and I…'

So Sir Elephant lifts the Little Odd onto his back and walks to the place where it said it heard the pained sound. There she is, trapped in a ditch, up to her neck in it—dirty dank water, and so Sir Elephant raises the alarm. The whole herd and the Little Odds hurry that way. There she is, the Elegant Elephant in a terrible way.

The Little Lion Man leaps down, to the ditch and hugs her, says, it will be okay, and she wraps her weary trunk around his neck and says, 'Hi, Little Lion Man, I always knew you'd come back someday. And here you are, in my darkest hour—how did you know?'

'I didn't—but the Little Odd did.'

So they ease her out and wash her down and soon she is back on her feet. Her colour returns, her beautiful luminous indigo blue, her diamonds and gems, of many hues, sparkle, and glow; and the herd is happy again and now, it can accompany the Little Odds, for the rest of the way, in the bosom of the herd, to protect them from elves, trolls and all the rest, vixens and vipers and fools.

As they walk in the bosom of her herd. Elegant Elephant's eight tusks sprout out again, and they say, 'Surely, only boy elephants have tusks?'

But she giggles and says, 'I too am a Little Odd! I am a Multi-Tusker!'

'What's that over there?' asks the Little Odd, for it can see a skyline of colour and light—like fairy lights, all the colour of the rainbow.

'That,' says Sir Elephant, 'is the Land of Wonder. We will see you safely there, for you saved our only child from the ditch of disaster.'

He wraps a fatherly trunk around his girl, the Elegant Elephant, 'Just like her mother,' he says 'Always up to something, poking her trunk in where it's not needed.'

Then nudges her affectionately and Mummy Elephant smiles, knowingly; she bows her head towards the Little Odd who blushes, in that shy way it does.

'May the goodness of the universe travel with you and when you are in need, and when you are in trouble call us, 0800 Trunk Call for united we are strong, steadfast and safe, if a little clumsy, but that's okay.'

'Thank you, thank you,' says the Little Odds.

'Look, it's almost dawn,' smiles the Great White Rabbit, who is wiping his glasses, again!

'Come, we will walk you all to the gates and see you safely into the Land of Wonder. Many adventures await you there!'

'The Elegant Elephant can stay with you one day and one night only then she must return to the herd, for it is her time soon, to fall in love for it only takes a minute, dear Little Odd, to fall in love!'

The Little Odd blushes bright pink, then looks at its little misshapen feet. Sir Elegant Elephant smiles and bestows many blessings in Elephantese.

The Little Odds stand before the glistening gates of the Land of Wonder—so full of promise and pretty things.

'Mañana'

'Tomorrow.'

'A new dawn.'

'A New Era.'

The Little Odd steps forward and says, ‘Thank you, one and all; my friends. Let us go then You and I, into the Land of Wonder. And all you Little Odds out there, well, you are welcome to join us. Just walk this way…’

***

☺

Part Two

Chapter One
Enter the Land of Wonder!

It is a new dawn in the Land of Wonder. The Little Odds can see the pinky-blue hue—over yonder, just breaking through, as the bright colours of the night—the neon lights amid the darkness—pale in comparison to this clear day.

Three Little Birds hop this way, singing sweet songs—melodies pure and bright. This is their message to you: *'Don't worry, about a thing*, for *every little thing, is gonna be alright. Welcome, to the Land of Wonder,* where *you will see, many beautiful sights.'* Then the Three Little Birds chirped and flew away.

The Elegant Elephant led the way, still glowing, indigo blue. And what a Motley Crew followed behind, with eyes of wonder—every kind, from green saucers to red swirls, taking in the sights, of this wonderful world.

The Elegant Elephant elegantly turns around and says, 'Look, what do you see? Listen, what do you hear? Feel, what do you feel?'

So they stop. Look. Listen. Remember what it's like to feel alive, for all these Little Odds have known a wilderness, a dump, a dive, but in this moment, they are alive in the Land of Wonder. So they smile their happiest shiniest smiles and jump up and down, for it's all so beautiful—the colours, the sounds, the sights—so taken for granted day and night.

There are giant yellow birds in the sky, so huge and feathered—big eyes and beaks, swifting, drifting this way and that. There are dragons with wings, like soft things, gentle, in the dawn of the day. The Elegant Elephant says they are the Fluff Dragons that guard this place for fear of the Top Hats—those big black marshmallow clouds that gather from time to time to cause thunder and fear! But not today, for the Fluff Dragons are high in the sky, and that means sunshine and dreams of candy floss.

She says she's looked at clouds from both sides now, and it'll be okay today. 'I have only one more day to be with you, then I promised my father I'd go back to the herd so let us go then, you and I; Let me show you around, for there is nowhere on Earth quite like the Land of Wonder!

'I'd like to introduce you to my friend Eunice, the unicorn, and she's been expecting you. She's teasing us now, with her horse hoof-prints in the sand—look! Let's follow and see where they go, if anywhere at all!'

So along the Main Street of the Land of Wonder, on a glorious brand new day the Little Odds follow, as the Elegant Elephant leads the way—past the hoof-prints in the sand until they stop at the end of the Main Street, the shops closed up still. Where can she be, this Eunice Unicorn?

Here she comes! Gliding down, great white wings and hues of pinky-blue-purple, so graceful. She lands like a lady and says, 'How was that for grace and poise then, Dear Elegant Elephant my friend?' And they nuzzle trunks and uni-horn.

'So look at these Little Odds. How glorious, this motley crew! All mixed up together, like jars in a candy store!'

'Yes, indeed,' says the Elegant Elephant, 'and I am to leave them in your custardy, for tomorrow I return to the herd. We have one day to play here in the Land of Wonder. My friend, please, lead the way!'

Each Little Odd is introduced to Eunice who is very pleased to meet them. She nods and says, 'Na-na-na-nah, way-hay, na-na-na-nah,' to which the Little Odds sway, for she has a lovely way with her.

'Hey, Little Odd,' she says, 'You and I are colour-coordinated! You can ride on my back, but I see the Great White Rabbit, is weary, so come join me.'

The Little Odd and the Great White Rabbit get on her unicorn back, and she shows them around the Land of Wonder.

***

Rainbows and roundabouts; Swings and slides; see-saws and rides. Apple trees and angel hair; pears and fruits for free. Children in fancy dress; butterflies and bees; candy floss and ice cream—even Mexican cheese! Angel Fish of indigo kiss, as if to please; fishermen and faerie tales; innocence and peace—that is the flavour of the Land of Wonder.

A Leopard, who changes her spots to colours of the breeze; a Hippo with a bow on top, giraffes who sip from trees; a pond with boats that sail like yachts; a place for folk to play, for Crispy Duck and Penguin to slip in and display—for a tap-dancing fish to feel at home; for the Little Odds, to roam…

A Mermaid pops up from the lake and says, 'Helloooo,' to the unicorn. She asks, 'Who are these friends of yours, and what is it they do?'

'Ahem,' says the unicorn, 'you know, I do not know, for they are all new to me. But everyone has a talent or two, so let us ask them, you and I?'

'Indeed,' says the Mermaid, 'for this is the Land of Wonder! Everyone must do or say something to make you wonder, or else they wander lonely as clouds, way up on high.'

Then the Little Odd speaks up and says, 'Hullo Missus Mermaid, but we are not lonely at all—those of us who live with our heads in the clouds.'

'Oh, I say,' says the Mermaid, 'and who are you and what do you do to make me wonder?'

'I am a Little Odd, and I play the egg-slicer. Would you like to listen, to a tune or two?'

'Absoooluuutely!' says the Mermaid, for she fancies herself as high-fallutin.'

So the Little Odd plays the egg-slicer, in bars of eight or twelve. The Mermaid raises an eyebrow—for she hadn't quite expected that and fancies herself, as a talent judge (for she'd heard of such things, even underwater).

'So you can hold a tune or two Little Odd, that's what you can do in the Land of Wonder. A song, on an egg-slicer, who'd have thought!'

But the Little Odd looks at her funny and thinks her vain and frivolous—not like the Runaway or the Friendly Farmer. Just 'cause she has golden tresses, doesn't make her any better than his favourite misses. *Shame on her and her vanity* thinks the Little Odd inside its own head.

'Well then,' she says all matter of factly, 'you Little Odd have shown that you have a talent but what about your friends, who are a motley crew; what can they do, if anything at all?'

The Little Odd looks at her funny and says, 'They can do many things for they have talents, talons and other things even *you* would be amazed at in this Land of Wonder!'

The Mermaid locks eyes with the Little Odd and says, 'Well then, that's wonderful for everyone in the Land of Wonder, but they must show what makes them wonderful; that's just the way it is!' (Then she slicks her tail out of water, to show her displeasure).

The Elegant Elephant and Eunice the Unicorn look at each other in that way, between friends, who sense the same…

'Come now, Little Odds, let us go, you and I…' they say, in unison, Elephant and Unicorn, but by now, a crowd has gathered by the lake and wants to know, what things of wonder, the new arrivals can bring, to the Land of Wonder?

Chapter Two
The Little Odds Put on a Talent Show

And It Makes You Wonder...

A huge crowd has gathered now around the lake, and this was not what was planned;

It just turned out that way, but the Elegant Elephant and Eunice the Unicorn sense unease

Among the Little Odds, who look this way and that, at the scene unfolding around them;

Then the Mermaid, rises out of the ripples and claps her hands, high above her head as if summoning something, and here it comes, snorting, its snout above water.

It's Slapper the Sea Lion, come to sit in judgment. Then, bob-bob-bobbing along the surface, a head above water until it rises, from the ripples is Octave, the Octopus who waves its tentacles in the air. Everyone cheers. Slapper slaps her flappers some more, and everyone cheers again—louder and louder as if baying for blood, but this is the Land of Wonder—that wouldn't happen here.

Slapper and Octave say the Little Odd can stay for the egg-slicer was novel and new, but they want to see more from these Little Odds turned up upon these shores.

'Next,' shouts the Mermaid, bossily. 'Who's next?' The Little Odds look at each other and sigh.

Ludwig, the Little Lion Man steps forward. His mane tumbles down around this head, and they think him handsome and say, 'So Ludwig, is that a wig?'

Ludwig says, 'No, I'm for real,' looks them in the eyes the way, only a Lion Man can do. They shift in the waters and say, 'Music Maestro!'

With a flourish Ludwig, puts the flute to his lips and lets the notes float into the ether. The Mermaid gasps, and Slapper slabbers. Octave taps its tentacles on the surface to make waves and soon, the crowd, roars for more. So Ludwig gives them more until the Mermaid rises from the water; shushes the crowd and says to Slapper and Octave, 'What did you make of that?'

'It was okay, s'pose.'

The crowd goes wild, in disbelief—and chant Ludwig, Ludwig, Ludwig. So they say, he can stay.

Next!

The Little Odds look at each other uncertainly. They are not sure, about these shenanigans but the Fantabulous-Fish-Out-of-Water is a natural performer and a show-off. He can't wait to get in the water and do his funky stuff, so he steps forward and before those who sit in judgement can say a word he says—rather grandly—'I am the Fantabulous-Fishy-Out-of-Water, and this is my wife, Crispy Duck. We sing and dance!'

Fantabulous jumps in and does his aquabatics for starters. Slapper likes and claps her flippers. Octave waves, tentacles in the air. Mermaid, mumbles to herself—hits the buzzer but the crowd goes wild so Crispy Duck gets in on the act and squawks, squawks in time to the music and then they leap onto dry land where the Fantabulous-Fish-Out-of-Water does his tap routine, then waves his cane and top hat, to perfection for this is his moment—this is his time! Crispy stamps her webbed feet in time, and waddles like a duck, with her head held high, for she is really a swan in a duck-body. The crowd goes wild and chants, 'Crispy, Crispy, Crispy.' She plays to the crowd; shakes, and flaps her wings then sings,

Oops, mistake…

It goes quiet now…

…the judges talk among themselves;

Fantabulous Fish gives her a dirty look, so she gives one back and says, 'Show-off,' but they say, they can stay, for the crowd liked the wild duck and the swish fish; and they call them a Novelty Act, which puzzles the Little Odds, who thinks that's okay but what if one is not allowed to stay. What will they do?

Next!

The Puzzled Penguin thinks, *Might as well get it over with*, and steps forward. The judges ask, 'What's your trick?'

The Puzzled Penguin looks at its feet for inspiration and says, 'I do tricks, with conkers and twigs and sticks!'

So it juggles with conkers and twigs and sticks; throws them high in the sky and twirls expertly as it catches each one, in perfect time, but the judges roll their eyes and look at each other and say, 'That's not that wonderful, we see stuff like that every day on every street corner; so goodbye, you have to go!'

The Puzzled Penguin looks at its feet and cries, saying bye-bye to the Little Odds who cry in unison. 'That's not fair. If Puzzled Penguin has to go, then we all go; we leave no one behind.'

The crowd goes wild and chants with anger. The judges confer and say after a while, 'Okay, it can stay, so long as it stays in the background.'

The Puzzled Penguin says, 'That's okay.'

But the Little Odd says, 'Your time, to shine will come, Puzzled Penguin,' and gives it a big hug for it feels, the pain.

Next!

The Little Odds look at each other, uncertain. Who will have the guts to go next?

The Gurney Cat steps forward, and says, 'I have the guts to go next, after that and show them what I'm made of for I may be a Gurney Cat, but I have guts, cat guts, and I can sing gueeee-taaaarrrrr!'

Gurney Cat steps forward. The judges look at each other funny and say, 'So what's your trick?'

Gurney Cat says, 'I sing guitar, from my guts; for I have, the music in me! Meeaaaaaoooowww!'

'Oh my,' says the Mermaid, 'show us what you're made of then.'

Gurney plays guitar from her guts, all the way up from her soul. The judges lose control—they do air guitar with tentacles and flippers held high. The crowd joins in, and everyone is doing air guitar while Gurney Cat, caterwauls, in a way, no one thought possible, but the sound, of air guitar, lifts their souls, in a way no one thought possible!

The Little Odds look at each other, for they never knew the Gurney Cat had this music in her for she'd taken to purring these days, now that she is happy, with a band of misfits and make-believers.

The crowd goes bananas for that was an electric performance, and the Gurney Cat takes a bow and waits for the comments. The judges are blown away, they must say, 'You can stay!'

Next!

The Young Buck steps forward and says, 'Hullo, I am the Young Buck, and this is my friend the Humming Bird, she sings harmony, and I sing the song.'

'Okay, sing,' says the Mermaid, dismissively. The Young Buck sings—a song from the sea, about mystery. The Mermaid, Slapper and Octave go dewy-eyed; while the Humming Bird sings in harmony, about the air and the land and things to see. The crowd, goes silent, with dignity so that when the Young Buck and the Humming Bird have finished their song, there is no sound—just the sound of silence. The Little Odds look around to see what's wrong, but nothing's wrong. Everything is right. When the judges have wiped their eyes, the crowd—stunned in silence goes wild. The Young Buck gives a bow, and the Humming Bird swoops this way and that. The judges say they have never, ever, heard anything so beautiful, so they can stay, in the Land of Wonder, for now, until something better comes along The crowd stamps their feet and reap applause;

So far, so good, think the Little Odds.

Who's left?

The Great White Rabbit is too old and says so but the judges say no one, is ever too old, yet they recognise, his dignity, in age and faded glory. The Great White Rabbit says, 'I have a poem I learned when I was a wee bunny at school. It goes something like this.'

'Run rabbit, run rabbit run, run, run; don't let the farmer get his gun, gun, gun… but I can't remember the rest.' The Great White Rabbit takes off his glasses, wipes them and says with shame, 'I am too old for this, I never, in my wildest dreams, thought, when I entered the Land of Wonder, I'd have to prove myself, after all these years!'

For once, the judges felt ashamed and said, 'It's okay Great White Rabbit, you can stay.' They felt, a tad embarrassed that he had to go through these shenanigans, just for a passport to the Land of Wonder, after all he'd done, this past thousand years or thereabouts,

The crowd got to their feet and gave the Great White Rabbit a standing ovation, for they knew who he was but it didn't make it any easier, after all these years to be put through the mill at the will of those who sit in judgement. This wasn't what the Great White Rabbit thought he'd find in the Land of Wonder, so he sat down in despair and wiped, his glasses, with his handkerchief and his eyes, with his great white paws.

The crowd had gone silent again. The judges felt uneasy for they cried,

Next!

Who was left?

Just the Friendly Farmer and the Runaway who look at each other in alarm!

'What can you do,' asks the Little Odd, who is not, happy, about this whole thing. This wasn't what it had been expected in the Land of Wonder either that his friends would be judged, before such a crowd.

The Runaway says, 'When I was a little girl I played the viola, and I learned a song my mummy taught me, about running away.'

The Friendly Farmer says, 'Long ago, and far, far away I had a cello. I wasn't very good, but I learned a song, and I taught it to my daughter And that song, was about running too; Do you think it was the same one?'

They hummed and it was, so the Little Odd asked the judges if could they find a viola and a cello for the next one. So a cello and a viola appeared. The Friendly Farmer, eyes swirling, and the Runaway, hair flowing, stepped forward and explained that it'd been years since they played this song, but they'd give it a go, just for show. Frankly, they didn't have a choice and all they both wanted to do was run, like the hammers.

The Friendly Farmer steps forward—stammers, they have never seen her nervous—always self-assured. She says, this is a song I used to play with my daughter, long ago and far away and oddly it turns out, this Runaway, used to play the same song with her mother, long ago and far away. We are going to try, to play it for you, but please be patient and kind for we have never played it together before…

The judges look hesitant. They nod sagely. 'Give it a go.'

The Friendly Farmer looks at the Runaway and nods. 'One two three.' They play on viola and cello—then it hits them both like the hammers, but they can't stop now!

Somehow they make it to the end, tears streaming down their cheeks as it dawns on them, who they are and what they are to each other.

The crowd goes wild again. The judges jump out of the water but the Friendly Farmer and the Runaway just look at each other in wonder as all around applaud until slowly they set aside their strings and bows, falling into each other's arms, oblivious, to all around!

'Mamma!'

'Baby, you're found!'

***

When the judges have composed themselves they look around the Little Odds, oblivious to what's just gone down. The Mermaid says, 'Is that it?'

The Little Odds say, 'Think so,' and look at their feet but the judges say, 'Nah, one more, the little guy—over there! What's he done, for the Land of Wonder?'

Vermin looks at his paws. He doesn't have an act. All he can do is run around a maze and press levers; might as well get it over with—if he's a loser he's a loser, that's just the way it is. He throws himself into the loop for there is one he can jump through—a hula-hoop, and that gets a whoop. So he does it a few times, but they lose interest. He runs up trees and flowers and jumps here and there until the buzzers sound, and he knows he's a goner.

The Judges say, 'What sort of act was that?'

Vermin says, 'It's all I know. But if you taught me new tricks, I could learn them, I don't want to go or leave this place, I have friends here.'

The Mermaid says, 'What's your name?'

Vermin says, 'Vermin.'

Then the judges gasp, the crowd gasps and run riot.

Someone says, 'Catch that rat!'

***

The Little Odds look aghast. 'Let's run, like the hammers—no one, gets left behind!'

'Yikes!'

Chapter Three
Eunice the Unicorn and the Elegant Elephant Save the Day

In the chaos, they get away. The Young Buck says, 'Quick Vermin, jump this way!' He holds open the pocket of his tatty-old jacket for Vermin to leap in and hide, for they are baying for blood—this crazy crowd and not for the first time!

'What is happening to the Land of Wonder?' Eunice says to Elegant! 'Quick Little Odds, wings ready for flight; Elegant, propeller ready for flight? Meet you on the Heights! Jump this way Little Odds—half of you to Elegant, the rest take on me. Quick before they notice, for they are headless chickens! look at the lot of them, shame on them! What is the Land of Wonder, coming to.' She shakes her unicorn head and says, 'Humph,' then scraps her hoof on the ground.

As the Little Odd, Gurney and Crispy and Fantabulous jump on board with Puzzled Penguin behind on Elegant, who has sprouted her many tusks—a natural reaction in times of danger. From her head, she has propelled a huge propeller and a large umbrella to lift her high into the sky with the Friendly Farmer, the Runaway, the Little Lion Man, the Young Buck and Vermin on board (in his pocket). The Humming Bird doesn't need a lift.

All aboard and off they go—but the Little Odd cries, 'One of our crew is missing!'

The Great White Rabbit has been left on the ground! Too slow, too tired to jump on board he stands there, looking bewildered. Elegant can't go back to Earth, for her propeller just keeps on making her rise, higher and higher; and it's too late for Eunice, who has soared on beyond for she knew, Elegant would know where to go, and meet them on the Heights!

The Humming Bird rings her bell, then swoops down for she is stronger than strong. She cries to the Great White Rabbit, 'Grab my talons, hold on tight! You'll be alright—I am stronger than strong.'

The Great White Rabbit wonders, 'How can such a little bird, support a big lump like me?'

'Oh, ye of Little Faith.' Laughs the Humming Bird, as she lifts him high into the sky. He holds on tight, in fear of flight, for he's never flown before, a land bunny—all his life, he explains, but she says, that's okay, she won't let him fall.

She follows the Elegant Elephant who floats like a barrage balloon, Led Zeppelin; and the unicorn, who flies like a bird in the sky. Way up, into the dizzy Heights at the centre of the Land of Wonder where they can see all, for miles around on a clear blue day like today.

***

Down below they barely notice the Elegant Elephant and Eunice the Unicorn make their getaway for they are still running around like headless chickens, creaming.

'A rat! A rat!' Rat-a-tat-tat, this way and that. Some say they smell the rat. Some say, 'Something is rotten in the Land of Wonder since those Little Odds arrived showing off like peacocks,' say the women in their fancy frocks.

The Mermaid is foaming at the gills. She says, 'Attack, attack! Give them a smack!'

Slapper says, 'Catch the humming pigeon for she's just vermin with wings!'

Octave says 'Amen to that!' But all a-flap they do not see them rise. They rise above the trees to a place of safety for they are the Little Odds, and they have done no wrong. Just sing, a new song; to the petty minds who clog up this Land of Wonder.

The Little Odds leave them far behind in disarray, sorry to say, of their own making; for the Little Odds are innocent. Sing songs of innocence.

And… down below the people around the lake are confused and divided now. They wonder, how did this come to pass?

Some say all around the Land of Wonder the Mole Hills will get bigger and if we don't do something they will turn into mountains that move the land, this way and that which can only mean one thing. When the Mole Hills turn into mountains, people are displaced, and confusion reigns—which paves the way for the Underlies—and no one wants the Underlies to rise up again, or do they?

For they'd seen it all before in the Land of Wonder… and surely no one wants to go back there ever again, but give an Underlie a foot and it will take your smile.

***

Chapter Four
The Little Odds Find Love on a Mountaintop

Down below there may be chaos, but through no fault of their own, the Little Odds are safe on a mountaintop, thanks to Eunice the Unicorn and the Elegant Elephant who are happy, to be of help. The Little Odd, confused, asks, 'What was all that about?'

And nobody knows for sure, but they suspect they are scapegoats for something rotten in the state of the Land of Wonder. But hey, they are all safe and sound and look around and think the mountaintop the most beautiful place they've seen, for a while, for each have their beautiful places, wrapped up in their hearts and minds and souls;

But just for today this is their place of wonder—so high, you could touch the sky and the wispy clouds float by and whisper, 'Well done, Little Ones…'

One by one the Little Odds disembark, from Eunice and Elegant and hug, for that was horrible—the whole shenanigans they were caught up in through no choice of their own.

Vermin, pokes his head out of the Young Buck's pocket and asks, 'Is it okay to come out?' They laugh when the Young Buck says, 'Freedom up here, friend, but you are welcome to share my pocket any time.'

Vermin laughs back and says, 'I am your pocket rocket then!'

'Anytime'; smiles the Young Buck with affection, for it can't be easy being Vermin, despised, taking beatings, everywhere you go, when you are just a rat, misunderstood and all that.

The Humming Bird lands gently with the Great White Rabbit who takes off his glasses, wipes them and says, 'Wow, what a ride! Who'd have thought, I'd glide like a bird in the sky!'

One by one the Little Odds hit solid ground and feel the dizzy Heights beneath their feet as they climb down from elephant and unicorn, who were happy to oblige.

Crispy and Fantabulous coo-coo at their moment, in the sun which shines, majestically on the moment but over there, is another scene, they dare not share for the Runaway and the Friendly Farmer have wandered off where they hold hands and look at each other. They hug, then jump up and down and wear their shiniest happiest smiles. No one knows, what's going on, or if this is their moment alone, under the sun, oblivious and the unicorn wishes, she had her Aztec camera for the Mother and child reunion is only a moment away—just over there.

A moment in the sun, then everyone claps and shouts hurray as the Friendly Farmer and the Runaway take a bow, and walk their way and say, 'We are one, Mother and child! Who'd have thought this possible, one week ago? But a week, is just a drop in time, and we lived in hope this day would come!'

***

Well, those that have jaws fall open and drop! The Friendly Farmer and The Runaway! She is her mum! So they jump up and down with their shiniest happiest smiles and everyone, hugs everyone, for some things that are really worth celebrating in space, and time…

Love on a mountaintop. Who'd have thought… Then the Friendly Farmer says, 'Sit down, while I tell you a story…'

So they sit in a circle (a magical stone circle). The Friendly Farmer and the Runaway sit in the middle wearing their shiniest happiest smiles and all the Little Odds, and Eunice and Elegant smile back and say, 'Tell us a story, in your moment, of glory!'

'Would you like it to start Once upon a time?'

'Yessss!'

'Okay, when I'll begin. Are you sitting comfortably?'

They nod, eagerly…

Once upon a time, there was a travelling circus, and we belonged to it. It had a big top of candy colour stripes, and when the circus came to town, there was much excitement and mirth. At first, life in the circus was fun for me and my little one, but in the end we ran away—you see, the Ringmaster turned very nasty.

He turned me into a circus freak show—for I was the girl with kaleidoscope eyes. I had to wear these x-ray specs that made my eyes go all swirly. I was blinded by those big top lights, night after night. People would come and stand there gawking at me and the little ones would say, 'Look look at that lady with the funny eyes.' My little one had to run around selling kaleidoscopes, and I wasn't happy about this. That was every night—and at the end of each show, we'd have to play viola and cello until all the people were out of sight. Then every morning, we'd get up at dawn for our day job was to look after the farm animals that went along with the circus as a travelling zoo. There were goats and lambs, cows and cart horses, chickens and hens and squawkyadoodledoos, and we loved them all, and they loved us too, but we didn't like the way the Ringmaster treated the little farm animals. Sometimes he was mean. He would crack his whip and startle the poor things. He gave them hardly any food until one day, I took off my x-ray specs and said, 'Little One, I've had enough,' so we decided to run away.

In the dead of night, we got the old horse and cart and filled it up with all the farm animals, very quietly and then we ran away. When the Ringmaster discovered we were gone, he gave chase with the creepy clowns who followed him around sycophantically. The old cart horse couldn't go too fast, but my friend the Faerie Queen sent a message via thought-by-vibe to say she'd heard our plea, and had a lovely farm for us to stay in and look after the animals. I thought my little one was sleeping somewhere in the cart with the animals, but when I arrived at the farm, she was gone!

I looked everywhere, and the Faerie Queen got the faeries out as a search party. But she was nowhere to be seen. What happened or how she disappeared we do not know, only that she was gone, along with the song that we used to sing.

My kaleidoscope eyes were failing me, and I was left with these swirly whirly eyes of mystery. People still look at me funny, and I see the world funny but every day, I'd go looking for my Little Runaway—I was so worried, although I knew she was tough and sassy and could look after herself—I never ever gave up hope. I'd find her some day and guess what? Here she is—my Little Runaway returned.

The Little Odd gets up and hugs the Runaway and the Friendly Farmer like there is no tomorrow. Over its shoulder, the Runaway, sees the Young Buck wipe a tear, and smile her way, which makes her happy, inside.

'Wow,' says the Elegant Elephant. 'What a story! I guess, we are tired now.'

'Yes,' says Eunice, 'We should cuddle up and sleep. For tomorrow is another day, and Elegant has to go back to the herd.'

Chapter Five
Sleep Under the Stars and a Funny Thing Happens

To celebrate the Little Odds do spinnies on the mountaintop until they get dizzy and tired. There are flowers the size of trees—all the colours of the rainbow, swaying in the breeze. They have never seen flowers, this big before—even bigger, than the sunflowers in the Enchanted Glade.

They watch the sunset sitting in a row and go "Oooh" and "aah", at its splendour. They are not cold, even though they shiver. They are not hungry, even though, there is no food. Mañana, they will worry about that, and figure it out for the Elegant Elephant, must leave at dawn.

You can see 360 from here. They can see the lights of the Land of Wonder twinkle below, and they wonder at the neon glow, what's going on, down there, but here, they are safe in the afterglow of a sunset, so natural, so pure. Although they cuddle up to sleep no one is all that tired, and then they see a tall figure, emerge from the trees. He has a long white beard and a wise old face. He says kindly, 'Come, journey with me…'

'Where are you going?' asks Eunice, politely.

'To the stars,' he says. 'I will keep you safe. You may never, get another chance in this lifetime.'

Eunice knows this true for she has been before; and so has the Elegant Elephant. The Little Odds, sit up and take notice of what's going on around them. Tall men with long white beards and gowns surround the mountaintop, women too, with children looking on, smiling and wide-eyed. One by one, they go toward The Guide who says, 'Trust Me, I am Conscience, I am the Dru. Follow me, and I'll take you to the stars, and promise a safe return.'

As they pass through the passageway, they soar, all the Little Odds, soar, up into the cosmos, and it's the most beautiful thing they ever saw.

The Runaway and the Friendly Farmer hold hands and laugh. 'Do you remember,' she says, 'when you were small, I'd sing this song… Bend and stretch, reach for the stars—there goes Jupiter, there goes Mars?'

'Yesssss!' shrieks the Runaway. 'Let's go to Jupiter, they have many moons there';

So all the Little Odds follow, as the Dru leads the way to Jupiter. Indeed, it has many moons—which turn into trampolines! So they bounce, from moon to moon, laughing, all the way for its funny, to jump the moons of Jupiter.

'It's lovely out here,' says the Little Odd, 'Even though, it's dark and spacious. It's very pleasant, I feel at home.'

'Indeed,' says the Dru as they travel in space and time; 'But this is your space, this is your time. You need, to go back down to Earth.'

Sky rockets fly by. They wave at the astronauts who wave back. Flying saucers spin by. They wave at the aliens, who wave back.

'Be careful of the Black Holes,' says the Dru. 'Don't go too near, case you tip over the edge. He says, 'Stay, in this universe, that's as far as we're allowed for now.'

Everyone is having so much fun but it's time now, he calls, 'Time up! Back down, Little Odds,' and because they are law-abiding, the laws of the universe, the speed of light in the darkness; they do what's told by the Dru.

How much fun was that! Who'd have thought, trampoline-moons and search-machines could be such fun?

The Dru says, 'All hold hands for descent. No one gets lost.'

The Young Buck holds on to Vermin in his pocket just in case he floats away, for the atmosphere was lovely up there (even though there wasn't any).

Everyone yells, 'Weeeeeee!' as they float, back down to a mountaintop, shrouded in darkness now. The big flowers nod their heads in sleep, but everyone is giggling, and they won't get much sleep…

But, eventually, space travelling catches up on them. Soon, they are all a-snoozing under the watchful eyes, of the Dru.

'Night, night Little Odds, God bless,' he says.

***

Chapter Six
Band on the Run

At first light, the Little Odd awakes. It is always the early riser. It feels both happy and sad. Happy, because last night reminded it of home. Sad, because it missed home.

The Dru is standing there with his staff *(that's his big stick, not his people-helpers)* and says, 'Little Odd, come, take a walk with me before the others wake; we need to talk a while, alone.' He takes the Little Odd's paw-hand thing in his to watch the sunrise, and the giant flowers lift their heads to the sun again. The Dru says, 'Little Odd, I sense you are troubled, yet glad. It's okay, to be sad, but look at the friends you have made!'

The Little Odd looks Dru in the eyes and says, 'I know, I am very lucky, but I get confused you see. What's happening to me? My comfort zone is up there, and I'd like to go back someday, but I can't imagine not having my friends with me!'

So the Dru says, 'There's something you need to see. Look over there, your great-grand-uncles…'

'Oh my!' says the Little Odd, for there, in the clouds—giant clouds, perfect, 'I see the three great-grand-uncles, looking down on me!'

The Little Odd jumps up and down and wears its shiniest happiest smile. It waves, 'Uncles, it's me, it's me!' But they just smile, a while, then float, away…

'Sir Dru, what's to become of me?'

'Dear Little Odd, you are fine, and you will be fine, but there are dark times ahead and many dangers. Many battles to be fought and won, but good is on your side. These friends, you've made, are the poetry in your soul personified. It is no coincidence that you have found each other. Together you are rhyme and reason, for there is treason in the Underworld, where the Underlies are rising up, and trying to take over the Land of Wonder one more time; with their evil greedy ways…'

'You and these Like Minds, dear Little Odd, are the rhythm of the Earth. Take up your drums, and follow me for here's what you have to do… Are you listening carefully?'

'Yes, Dru.'

'Then I'll begin. Make music, Little Odd. Everywhere you go, you and the Like Minds show the way, light the way, with your voices and your sounds; lead the way, with music in your hearts, and those who hear your song will follow you, to the ends of the Earth, but I fear Little Odd, you will have to go under, and that's where you will be in grave danger. Can you cope?'

'Yes, sir.'

'Correct answer, Little Odd Solider. We will send you Warriors of Light. You will know them on sight. Your Travelling Troupe is brave and bright; filled with the Light. You are the Little Odds, and the Land of Wonder is full of Like Minds who have lost, or are losing their way, for the Underlies are a-stirring and a-filling the lost minds, with paranoia…'

'What's paranoia, Sir Dru?'

'Fear, Little Odd, fear and loathing. Ignorance and prejudice, and other destructive things.'

'Oh, not nice!'

'No, Little Odd, not nice.'

The Little Odd is thoughtful for a while. The Dru goes silent. They wait for the words to follow…

'So, Sir Dru, what do we do next then?'

'Ah, that is the question! How do we change the state of things when they start to go rotten? How do we make people see what's wrong when they won't hear your song? For it's easy to sit in a comfort zone where you feel safe and warm and dry; it's much harder to put your head above the parapet and ask the question, why?'

'Sir Dru, what sort of pet is a parapet? It is like a ghost pet?'

Dru smiles kindly. 'No, Little Odd. It is the wall around a castle, like a fortress.'

'I know what a castle is. What's a fortress?'

'It's like a big castle with big strong walls built all around it to protect the wealth within; to keep invaders out.'

The Little Odd smiles and jumps up and down 'Oh, Sir Dru, I know what space invaders are. It's a game I used to play, it's so much fun!'

'The same but different, I've played space invaders too—thousands of years ago, but it wasn't fun, many people got killed for it was for real.'

And the Dru grew sad,

The Little Odd looks at its misshapen feet things and says, 'Oh, I'm sorry.'

'Do you know what war is Little Odd?'

Little Odd looks into the sun and says, 'It is the opposite of peace.'

'Correct answer, do you know what hate is?'

'It is the opposite of love.'

'Correct again Little Odd. Do you know what greed is?'

'It is the opposite of kindness.'

'Indeed and do you know what fair is?'

'Yes, it is when something is right; for when something is wrong you say, that's not fair, out loud!'

'That is all correct Little Odd.

Now do you know what a bully is?'

The Little Odd is thoughtful for a while and says, 'Yes, Sir Dru. It is someone who is mean and cruel to someone else. It is someone who makes someone else feel bad about themselves.'

'That's right and do you know what makes a bully bully?'

'I think it's because they are jealous. Or because they are just mean. Or because someone has made them that way, because they were not jealous or just mean, to begin with. And so it mightn't even be their fault, you have to forgive them, for they know not what they do.'

'That's a very hard thing, isn't it Little Odd.'

'I expect so,' says the Little Odd. 'I've never known a bully, but I've watched them from afar, and I can see the damage they do; that was when I sat in my comfort zone with my cirrusoscope, and even though I'd get cross and shout—Hey you! Bully! Leave that kid alone! They didn't seem to hear, or if they did they just ignored me.'

'How did that make you feel, Little Odd?'

'Sad and helpless.'

'Maybe, that's why you fell out of your comfort zone when you least expected it—to do something about the bullies, in a kind and gentle way; to do something about what's not fair, in a kind and gentle way; to do something about greed, and hate and war, but in a kind and gentle way.'

The Little Odd stopped and looked at the sky. It turned all the way around in a circle and looked at the beautiful Land of Wonder. Then the Little Odd looked the Dru in the eye and said, 'Maybe, Sir Dru, but why me? I am just a Little Odd!'

'Maybe, Little Odd, because, your heart is pure. Maybe Little Odd, because, your heart is in the right place.'

The Little Odd put its paw-hand thing over the place where its heart should be and could feel, the pump-pump-tickety-tick where its heart should be and so it smiles at the Dru and says, 'Yes, Sir Dru. My heart is in the right place after all—phew!'

The Dru smiles, and says, 'You'll never forget, what we said this day.'

And hand in paw-hand thing, solemn but calm they walk back to the camp on the mountaintop where all the Dru people—men, women and children have emerged from the earth-mounds and the Little Odds are all awake. The Dru people share their food and a great breakfast feast prepared, for their departure. "These people are so kind," thinks the Little Odd, inside its own head.

***

'How will we get down the mountain this time?' asks the Young Buck—for he has noticed the Elegant Elephant, anxious to return to the herd (but how on Earth will she get down from the mountaintop)?

The Dru says, 'I have asked the charioteer to prepare one of our finest chariots to be harnessed to Eunice who loves to chariot-fly (Eunice snorts and stamps her hoof and says neigh, which in unicorn means, weigh-hay). A hot air balloon will carry Elegant down.'

One by one, the Little Odds prepare to get on board the chariot, fuelled by fire, which has just been lit. Nearby a huge pink and blue air balloon floats down from the sky with a big wicker basket attached. The Dru says, 'Dear Miss Elegant Elephant, your own chariot awaits; may you return to visit us soon,' Dru bows and flourishes, his arm in gesture and one by one, the Little Odds bid her farewell. She wraps her trunk around each one. They wipe a tear from their own eyes, from hers. Last up comes, the Little Odd, followed by the Little Lion

Man, and she says, to all, as she waves her trunk, this is not A Dieu Dear Dru; just Au revoir! 'Goodbye, farewell, and thank you!'

As the air balloon floats off, she waves her trunk elegantly and flaps her big beautiful ears. As she drifts away the Dru says, 'Gather round my dears. Lend me your ears! This is my message to you all. Don't worry, about a thing. Stick together and always do what's right. Never do anything wrong. Use your gift of song. Each one of you has a talent, even if you didn't know it until this moment, in the Land of Wonder.'

'You have already had to prove yourselves at the water's edge. Now, go—spread the word, Love and Peace is all they need to know; and if they ask, what Love is… say it's patient and kind. And if they ask what peace is, well, it's just a state of mind.'

The Little Odd hugs the Dru, who whispers in the place where its ear should be, 'Remember, what we talked about, I am with you, until the end of time…'

As they board the chariots the Dru says, 'You will have to sing for your supper from now on!'

He laughs, 'Raise the roof, for you are the Band on the Run. You know what must be done! The Little Odds will capture hearts and minds. Your friends are called the Like Minds, they follow through. It's the lost souls, who will challenge you.'

***

Chapter Seven
The Master of Ceremonies Wants Them to Headline

At the Festival of Things to Do for a Fistful of Squiggles Each!

Eunice Unicorn glides the Little Odds safely to the Land of Wonder's pearly gates. On the other side, they can see the herd of elephants. They see the big pinky-blue balloon land the Elegant Elephant, so they wave at her. The herd wave their trunks as they wander off into the great blue yonder.

The Little Odds suddenly feel a bit lost now. They wonder what they should do now they are back down in the Land of Wonder. They are not sure they want to stay here anymore and think maybe, they should leave this place and find a new adventure.

Just then, a very tall skinny man walks towards them. He wears a pinstripe suit and a bowler hat on his head. His shoes are pointy and polished, and so is his nose. He wears dark sunglasses. He has big flap ears. His bow tie is really a camera. On one hand, he has a long pointy umbrella, in the other he carries an officious-looking briefcase. His black moustache is long and swirly—his beard a little goatee.

His voice is loud and booming, and he shouts, 'What's this, what's this I see before me! A pack of geeks trying to sneak out of the Land of Wonder unannounced. What sorcery is this, you cheeky crew? Don't you know, this is the Land of Wonder? You can check out anytime you like, but you can never leave!'

'Now, line up—against these gates and show me your passports—on the double, quick you miserly bunch of misfits,' he shrieks.

The Little Odds are very confused. They don't have any passports and nobody said they weren't free to come and go from the Land of Wonder anytime they pleased!

'I—I said I—am the Master of Ceremonies in the Land of Wonder. Everyone must answer to me, do you hear!'

'Yes,' say the Little Odds in unison.

'Yes. What?' gulders the Master of Ceremonies.

'Yes, sir,' they reply—although the Great White Rabbit looks him in the eye. The Little Odd looks at the sky, and wonders, if it might see its cloud passing by, or maybe the great-grand-uncles.

Eunice neighs and flaps her great big unicorn wings, which annoys the Master of Ceremonies who tells her to fly away, fly away home. But Eunice stays and neighs, snorts and stamps her unicorn hoof.

'Soooo,' shouts the Master of Ceremonies. 'I catch you just in time, trying to sneak out. Now here's the plan—listen up, stand up straight—look at the shape of you lot.'

Then he stops, smiles, laughs out loud and says, 'A-ha, I got you! That was just an act, I was only teasing you. Everything is fandabydooozy—in fact, I have wonderful news for you.'

'Remember the talent show—oh yes, it was a wonderful thing to see and hear. I watched you from afar, you see—the Vain Mermaid, Slapper and Octave—they work for me! They are my minions—their task is simply to find new talent in the Land of Wonder and what talent they have found in you.'

'Now, here is my wonderful news. I have chosen YOU lot to headline at the Festival of Things to Do. The Festival is the highlight of the year in the Land of Wonder. It takes place in the Pleasure Park and people come from all across this land, from near and far, from yonder and beyond to be entertained at the Festival of Things to Do.'

'There is everything you can imagine going on—the circus comes to town, there is music and singing and dancing in the streets. There is every type of tasty thing to eat—candy-coloured sweets and all sorts of treats. There are fireworks to light up the sky in the grand finale.

'It would be a tragedy if you were all to leave now and miss this sensational spectacle wouldn't it dear Little Odds? Of course, it would. So I've made arrangements for your band to headline at the Festival of Things to Do.'

'You see,' he sobs into his hanky, 'my headline act has let me down, and I will get the sack as Master of Ceremonies if I don't come up with a new and exciting headline act as soon as possible. So I thought, they'll do… I mean, I thought the crowd would go wild for the Little Odds for they saw what you could do at the lakeside.'

'You are superstars. I will put your name up in lights so big the sky will be bright. I can see it now… The Little Odds headline the Festival of Things to Do,' says the MC flourishing his arm in an ostentatious gesture.

'Now, sign this contract.'

And with that, the Master of Ceremonies whips open his black briefcase and waves a very official document in the air.

The Little Odds look at each other confused.

The Master of Ceremonies pulls off his dark glasses.

'Why look so perplexed Little Odds. Here's the deal. You cannot leave the Land of Wonder without your passports now can you?'

'Ummmm…' They shuffle and look at each other.

'Well, you can but the Land of Wonder security will seek you down, and they WILL find you. You can leave the Land of Wonder any time you please, but it will cost one hundred squiggles each. However, here, in this carefully put-together contract, you will see, that your precise fee for performing at the Festival of Things to Do is precisely… one hundred squiggles each. And you can have a super supper and all the loveliest food and drink, ice cream and sweets that you can eat—we'll throw that into the contract as an added bonus, for I am the Master of Ceremonies, and I am soooo generous and kind of course.'

'So sign here, it's a done deal.'

'What's a squiggle?' asks the Little Odd.

'Why you fool, I mean, my sweet Little Odd, the squiggle is the currency in the Land of Wonder. Now, sign here…' and he hands the Little Odd a golden fountain pen.

'We need to confer,' says the Great White Rabbit.

'Well, hurry up… hurry up… I don't have all day. I am the Master of Ceremonies. I am a VIP—a very important man. I have places to go and people to see. I need to organise the Festival of Things to DO for heaven's sake. I can't waste my time on this mullarkey.'

The Little Odds gather round and talk among themselves.

‘What else can we do?’ they agree. ‘The Master of Ceremonies has got us all confused.’

The Great White Rabbit speaks up after a long sigh and his eyes roll heavenwards.

‘We should do this Festival of Things to Do. We should put on an amazing show and leave right away. The Land of Wonder has lost its gloss and glory. I think, we are tired of it now and should earn our squiggles and then make our getaway, with our dignity and self-respect intact. All agreed?’

‘All agreed.’ So they put their hands in the centre, to cement the deal and unannounced the Master of Ceremonies comes into the huddle and slams his big hand on top.

‘Agreed. Right—sign this contract then we can all have a nice cup of tea to celebrate. And some candy.’

But somehow, the Little Odds don’t feel happy inside, but they will do the best they can, then leave the Land of Wonder, without ceremony. That is their plan—surely there is a new and happy adventure waiting to happen, somewhere else?

Chapter Eight
Sing for Their Supper;
Then Someone Gets the Sickliness

The Master of Ceremonies parades down Main Street like he owns the place. The Little Odds follow after, and there is this weird adulation; misplaced, unsanctioned, peculiar! They only arrived here, quite by accident, some days ago. Now they are local heroes, and everyone wants to know and be their friend!

They feel a curious mix of confusion and wonder. The Fantabulous-Fish-Out-of-Water and Crispy Duck play to the crowd, but they will need a dip soon, as will Puzzled penguin who does some tricks to amuse. Gurney plays air gueee-taaarrrrr and whines—she thinks she's Hendrix. In between the Little Lion Man plays his flute, and the people say, Look, The Little Odd plays a flute! This confuses the Little Odd for it's not sure that's the right word for the egg-slicer, but it sounds good. The Little Odd nods its head and smiles its shiniest happiest smile for it's very kind of the people of the Land of Wonder to show such appreciation so soon, after arrival.

The Humming Bird flies this way and that—hums and waits for the Young Buck to join in, so she can do harmony, but he seems a bit distracted—hand in pocket. She thinks he is saving his voice for later, no doubt;

At the back come the Great White Rabbit, the Friendly Farmer, the Runaway who just nod and say, Thank you; thank you!

The Runaway nuzzles into her mum and says, 'I don't feel so good.'

***

The Master of Ceremonies leads the way into the park. He leads the Little Odds to the back of the main stage. All the people follow into the Pleasure Park, ticket holders and new arrivals,

'Room for all, space for all. Pitch your tents, pay your rent,' shout the helpers, smiling—for these are the greatest days of the year in the Land of Wonder, even though every day is wonderful. There are regular feast days and festivals; carnivals and holidays, but this is the best of the rest! The autumn equinox, when it's half light, half dark.

All around the Pleasure Park, there are glorious things to see. Performers, circus acts, acrobats! Jugglers and stilt-walkers. Puppets and poets, pictures and pretty things; flags and bunting, food vans and fabulous things to make and see and do. Everyone is welcome—families and foreigners, insiders and outsiders, the meek and mild, the bold and old; the young—just about everyone! Such an atmosphere!

The Little Odds look this way and that. They would like to spend some time in the Pleasure Park among the people, soak up the atmosphere, to join in the fun but the Master of Ceremonies says, 'Sorry, that's not in the contract. It will take away, your air of mystery! You must stay behind the stage, until it's your turn to shine, Little Odds, that's the rules, that's just the way it is!'

'But,' says the Lion Man, 'It's hours and hours until you want us on stage!'

The Master of Ceremonies quips, 'Don't matter, he who pays the piper, calls the tune, and I pay the piper, geddit!'

'Now, there are lots of nice things to eat and drink and enjoy behind the stage before nightfall, you are free to eat and drink and do whatever you like for the rest of the day, but you can't go out there!

Look, it's in your contract!'

'Grrrr…' says the Little Lion Man; for they hadn't noticed that bit.

'Never mind,' says Puzzled Penguin. 'We can play games, like I-spy.'

But they all sit down, a little down-hearted, for it wasn't meant to be this way…

***

The sun is shining, and they eat nice things, and it's not so bad. They meet new people and make new friends and acquaintances, who sing, play strings and other things. The atmosphere is good like it should be, but somehow the

Little Odd is confused and says, ‘So what are we going to do on stage to earn our squiggles? We haven’t really figured it out. The people might shout if we don’t get it right, and I’m a bit afraid of the Master of Ceremonies! He might turn nasty!’

They all agree, sitting in a circle, that this is a possibility. He might turn nasty and refuse to pay the squiggles. He might wave the contract and say, mean things!

Fantabulous and Crispy say, ‘Let’s just do what we did by the water’s edge, for they seemed to like that.’

The Little Odds look at each other and consider this a fair idea, but the Great White Rabbit says, ‘You make a fair point, Crispy and Fantabulous. You do just that for it’s what you do best. Puzzled… I suggest you stand at the edge of the stage and do your tricks in time to the music?’

These three nod, agreed;

‘But the rest of the act we need to co-ordinate, so we are all singing from the same hymn sheet.’

‘Which Hymn Sheet?’ asks the Little Odd as if it understands;

But the Great White Rabbit says, ‘It’s just a turn of phrase.’ So the Little Odd nods knowingly.

‘We all have our instruments, with us or within us,’ says the Great White Rabbit, nodding at the Young Buck and the Gurney Cat. The Humming Bird hums on high—she can turn her tune, to whatever is required for the harmonies. The Great White Rabbit says, ‘That is deeply appreciated, Humming Bird, we can rely on that, I know—but we need to get hold of a viola, and a cello!’

The Friendly Farmer takes control, asks some questions and lo and behold, viola and cello appear, along with some other gear—amplifiers, keyboards and other things attached to wires!

The Little Odd says, ‘We need some drums, We need a row of drums and drummers to the rear,’ and somehow they appear, a row of drummers in neat red uniforms, nodding heads. So that’s sorted. As if, my magic.

‘At your service,’ says the head of the red drummers, ‘we are the thread. We will move to the rhythm and make it up as we go along.’

‘Well, that is good news,’ says the Great White Rabbit.

So between them, the Young Buck and the Little Odd and the Little Lion Man discuss the music in their heads, the songs in their souls, and somehow they know that it will hold together and when it gets tough, they can rely on the Gurney Cat for a heavenly gueee-tarrrrr solo, to cheer the crowds, before they bay for blood (for they are doing this on a wing and a prayer).

But no one has noticed. The Friendly Farmer and the Runaway sit aside, astride, the cello and viola. It's been such a long time, since they played together, and they are unsure, how it works!

The Little Odd comes over to console but is sad when the Runaway looks it in the eye and says, 'I feel bad,' Then she cries and snuggles into her mummy for she has the sickness…

(And that, wasn't in the contract…)

***

The time grows near when they are to appear, but the sweat runs off the Runaway. She cries inside for she doesn't want to let them down yet she feels so bad, so sad, and the Ringmaster might get mad!

Her mummy says, 'Don't worry dear, I'm here—that's one bully you won't have to stand up to, for I'll give him a piece of my mind!'

The Runaway says, 'Mummy, you were always so busy giving people who didn't deserve it bits of your mind—be careful, you may run out of bits to give away!'

The Friendly Farmer chews this over and says, 'Blagh, there's enough to go around! Just wait, 'til he hears, the sound of my voice! Then he'll know, what's hit him!'

So she whispers in her baby's ear, 'Get through this, dear. Do the best you can. Do it for your friends, who love and care for you. Then we'll run far from here, but no one gets left behind, Understand?'

She understands, 'I can do this Mum, for you and me, and for the Little Odds, but after that, may we go then, you and I? Can we leave this place, for it is losing its sense of wonder now?'

The Friendly Farmer held the Runaway close to her chest and said, 'Of course, we are all in this, together.'

'I'll muddle through then Mum, for you.'

The Friendly Farmer whispered in her ear, 'Let's muddle through, babe, it's what we do; best.'

***

So the time has come for the Grand Performance. They can't believe they are the Headline Act, and as far as their eyes can see are the people of the Land of Wonder, and they don't want to let them down. They come on stage and look at each other anxiously.

'Music Maestro,' says the Little Odd. The blinking blinding lights come up and the row of red drummers start the beat. Fantabulous and Crispy and Puzzled take control in front of the stage and the crowd go wild before a note is sung or an instrument played; Little Odd takes centre-stage and plays to the crowd, and they go wild. The Little Odd makes it up, as it goes along, but they cheer and hear the words and music as if by magic—la-la-la, la-la-la ….la-la-la-la.

When it's clear the Little Odd is tired, the Young Buck sings harmony with Humming Bird and in between the songs the Gurney Cat struts her guts. The crowd go insane to the sounds of the Little Odds, each goes solo, but combined it's alchemy—whatever that is;

And now it's time, for cello and viola. They take over—centre-stage and the notes float in ecstasy but it's all so scary. The Runaway gets carried away with each beat, she's weak, but tweaks the strings as the Little Odds sing … she grows uneasy and gets queasy;

Her knees tremble, crowds assemble, she sees the lights
She feels the fright; the notes float by, and she wonders why…

She falls
She calls
Mummy!
Then it all goes dark;
Hark!

The crowd is a frenzy. The child is lost, in space and time. The Master of Ceremony takes centre-stage and lifts a leg as if to kick the faltering child but the mother springs to her feet, flings the cello aside and sings

Falsetto, liberetto, soprano, operatto!

'Hey! Leave that child alone!'

So the Master of Ceremonies loses control,

In front of all these people!

And screams

'You are the Headline Act;

You fail me, and our contract!'

He sings, operatto rigoletto!

He cracks his whip at her,

To make her feel bad, even in front of all these people, she sings Liberatto, operatto;

'No! No! No! Your royal nastiness—I know who you are! You are the Ringmaster. The cruel Ringmaster of the circus, and here, you are in disguise as the Master of Ceremonies! Shame! Shame on you bad man!'

The crowd gasps. They think this is all an Act—the highlight of the Headline Act—High Drama!

So they go wild with wonder. Who'd have thought—this in the plot!

Until the Little Odds intervene and say, 'Show over!'

The crowd goes crazy. 'Wasn't that the Best Headline Act ever,' the people say—for they hadn't expected opera, high drama.

They think it is all part of the act, but we know, that it wasn't like that.

Chapter Nine
Rescue the Runaway and Seek a Safe Place to Stay

(For She Needs Medical Treatment)

The crowd, thousands and thousands as far as the eye can see are delighted with such high drama on stage. The Master of Ceremonies—who turned out to be the circus Ringmaster also thinks this the best thing ever and plays to the crowd.

He cracks his whip and lifts his hat—what an unexpected grand finale at the Festival of Things to Do. Vainly, he thinks himself as the star of the show. He lifts his hat again and bows dramatically—once, twice, thrice.

He takes the squiggles from his pockets and thrills, as he throws them in the air.

Squiggles and squiggles and squiggles tumble everywhere. They float, like notes, around the stage;

The Ringmaster steps forward centre-stage and flamboyantly waves and bows to the adulation he considers all for him and takes more squiggles from his pockets and floats them in the air.

Behind him, the drama unfolds—but the crowd still think this is all part of the act!

The Friendly Farmer and the Little Odd tend to the Runaway—collapsed on stage. The row of red drummers gather up the notes, the squiggles and stuff them in their pockets…

The Little Odds scoop the Runaway's fragile body in their arms for a getaway. Exit—stage right, speed of light and as the Ringmaster continues to bask in his moment of glory the Little Odds make their getaway.

There is a carriage out back. They lay her gently in that, and the red drummers give chase in an old ambulance…

Nee-naw, nee-naw.

They catch up, then say, 'Hey! You'll need these to pay for medical attention for it doesn't come cheap in the Land of Wonder. The drummers hand over fistfuls of squiggle notes, all they could gather, they say.'

The Little Odds say, 'Thank you, we sang for our supper like the Ringmaster said. We earned these squiggles fair and square. We need this, for it's an emergency…'

Nee-nah, nee-nah, nee-nah, follow our ambulance, we know the way to a place of safety!

***

They can't go to the hospital for the Ringmaster will find them there. The lead drummer says, 'Take her to The Elbow. The innkeeper and his wife will know what to do—they are wise and very, very nice.'

'Where is The Elbow—how far?' asks the Friendly Farmer, terrified.

'It's next door, to Filfthy McNasty's…'

So all the Little Odds are in the rickety carriage. The Friendly Farmer cradles her child.

In her arms, and sing sweet child of mine, but the Runaway is weak, maybe dying and all the while the Ringmaster stays centre-stage, taking bows for adulation that is not earned and the crowd begins to wonder and shout, 'Where are the Little Odds? Bring them back out!' They are expecting them back on stage for an encore?

The crowd chants Little Odds! Little Odds! Little Odds…' over and over. The Ringmaster looks over his shoulder and realises they have gone! Forsaken him! How dare they? Thieves and rogues; scoundrels and sinners! They have stolen the squiggles he so flamboyantly paid out to them! Shame on them! Shame on them! He rages on stage, 'I've been robbed, I've been robbed by those pesky Little Odds… robbed, I tell you—robbed! They took the squiggles and ran!'

But the crowd are baying now.

Little Odds!
Little Odds!
Little Odds!

We want
The Little Odds!
When do we want them?
Now!

Over and over. The Ringmaster can't comply. He says that the deceitful mob have done a runner! Shame on them, shame on them!

The crowd bays, and the lights go out. The Ringmaster has had enough! His blood boils, he is fit to be tied at the injustice of it all! So security takes over—they turn the lights back on and say, 'Show over, show over, please make your exit peacefully and quietly, safe home, good night!'

The Ringmaster predicts a riot. When they hit the streets, the people bowed and prayed to the neon god they'd made. They say, 'Wasn't that the most amazing show on Earth!' Who'd have thought, it would end in high opera, sure you couldn't make it up, and they hailed the Ringmaster, as a Genius!

'Three cheers for the Master of Ceremonies,' they sing, all the way home.

***

The Ringmaster—who is aka the Master of Ceremonies—goes ballistic. High on adulation, he wonders why the Little Odds did a runner when they were all on to a winner!

The creepy clowns gather around the Ringmaster and say, 'Oh yea, you're amazing. You were fantastic. You are a god! Wow wow wow wow woooooowwwww. Unbelieevveeabole.'

With a flourish and a nod he says, 'thank you, thank you—I know… yes, I do know, but where did those thieving cheating scoundrels go!'

Security looks around and says, 'We do not know! Well, catch them dead or alive,'

He waves the contract before their eyes, 'Failures, failures—what sort of security are you! Let them pass by, before your eyes!'

One security man speaks up—for they have diverted their eyes to the floor.

'Sir, Ringmaster or Master of Ceremonies—whatever you call yourself these days—if they are to be believed, the young girl was taken ill—she was turning blue. They all left in a carriage, with blue flashing lights, for fear, she might die Sir Ringmaster!'

The Ringmaster flies into a rage and yells: 'Lies; Lies, and storytelling; I have never seen that woman before in my life! Dramatic effect, all part of the Act I tell you. It was all rehearsed backstage—just for show. We just wanted to show off—how we could put on the Best Concert Ever at the fantastical fabulous Festival of Things to Do, in the glorious Land of Wonder!'

'No more, no less; that was just a dream, that was just a dream I had, to put on the greatest show on Earth and my oh my, did we do just that!'

***

The carriage pulls up outside The Elbow Rooms. It's on the crook of the arm of a high hill overlooking the beach and the ocean, but that is the least of their worries right now. They have to get the Runaway to a place of safety. They need a doctor, they are assured, one is on her way.

The Little Lion Man, carried her frail body, from the carriage to the attic room, dimly lit and cold. They light a fire, they huddle around. She drifts in and out of sanity. She recognises them. She speaks their names, one after one, and they try to make her laugh. She manages a smile. The doctor comes and says her heart is weak, she is dehydrated and she is underweight. She is malnourished, she has something called malnutrition mixed with exhaustion which is not a good look (all that time, living in the Dump, cannot have done her good).

'Oh! How do we make her better?' ask the Little Odds.

'Rest. Good food. Soups and stews and salads. Love, affection, attention, gentle words. Patience, kindness and understanding. Plant medicine—I'll leave you some. Flowers and light and fresh air when she's well again. She is gentle and fragile and fears the night. She needs love and understanding, your time most of all.'

They think this doctor, a miracle. This doctor is patient and kind. She checks the Runaway's eyes. She talks in deep, low tones to the Friendly Farmer and says, 'This child, is exhausted, depleted and weak. This child needs rest, at least a week in a warm bed in a safe place. She has no voice; her throat infected; she has a virus. She is fit for nothing, she could die, for I cannot tell a lie.'

The Friendly Farmer sobs. 'My baby, my child! We will pull her through. She is surrounded by friends, by love and love is all she needs. The rest will follow through!'

The kind doctor says that she'll come every day for a week. Her job is to tend the weak, and she wants no payment, but they say, 'We will pay you for it's your job to make her better.'

She sighs and says, that would be good for things are tough in the Land of Wonder these days. She says, she'll only take what she needs and give the rest to those in more need—to help them get better for her job is to heal.

The Little Odds say they have squiggles—they earned them fair and square, and she can have half and the rest will go to the innkeeper and his wife for they will all have to stay there for a week, then they will be glad, to leave the Land of Wonder behind.

***

Chapter Ten
The Runaway Gets Better and the Little Odds Have a Holiday

In an Unexpected but Happy Way

The Little Odds took it in turns to sit with the Runaway through that first night. The room was dark and lit with candles. The kind man with the nice voice who owned The Elbow with his wife, made a giant pot of healthy soup for everyone's supper, to sustain them through the night that hissed and twisted in her mind, as she tossed and turned, sweating and shivering…

The fire burned. Sometimes, it hissed and spat. One by one, they took turns to sleep—all except the Friendly Farmer who sat by her pillow, wiped her brow and gently wept;

No one talked. They just shared glances and hopeful smiles. They shared sighs and some held hands, or hugged from time to time as if to say, 'It will be fine, everything will be fine,'

'She's young and strong inside, she has the will to live,' says the Great White Rabbit sagely, as he rubbed his glasses clean…

And then, as if by magic, through the crack of the curtains the light streamed in. The Friendly Farmer had fallen asleep with her child in her arms. They stayed that way pretty much, for the rest of that day. The next few days passed in a bit of a blur. Each day, she got stronger and stronger. The soups and stews were delicious. Fruit juices, freshly baked scones, oat biscuits, chocolate cake and ice cream, by the bucket load, arrived every day as if by magic for the Little Odds to share.

It made the Runaway very happy to get ice cream for her sore throat. She'd get to pick the flavour each day, but the wise man who ran The Elbow with his wife didn't tell a soul, who passed that way that the Little Odds were here to stay, hiding in the attic room.

The kind doctor came each day too. She said, 'Now she is getting stronger, she needs fresh air, but how?'

The wise man who ran The Elbow says, 'There is an attic door, that leads to a window that takes you onto the roof. No one knows it's there and no one can see from down below. I'll bring up some deckchairs. Don't worry—it's safe, for there's a railing. No one can fall off. You can sit out there in these fine autumn days. The views, are stunning over the ocean.'

Everyone thought this was a wonderful idea. They could relax and pretend they were on holiday! 'Hurray,' says the Little Odd, so the innkeeper brought them up to the attic and onto the roof: deckchairs, umbrellas, tables, board games, card games and even a little fridge freezer for their fruit juice and ice cream. Chocolate cake, cupcakes and all sorts of yummy things—but they decided it best not to play their instruments or sing in case someone down below heard them and called the Ringmaster (aka the Master of Ceremonies).

***

The Ringmaster had put up "Wanted" posters all around the Land of Wonder. Some wanted posters just had a picture of the Little Odd who was easy to spot for it looked like nothing on Earth. Others had photos of all the Little Odds, for photos were taken before they went on stage, all smiling at the camera, so they didn't look like a dangerous bunch at all. Yet The Ringmaster wrote:

Wanted—Dead or Alive! Reward—
Lots and lots of squiggles!

So now there were Bounty Hunters all over the Land of Wonder, looking for the Little Odds and all the people thought this odd. They said they didn't look like thieves and scoundrels; they looked nice and soft and cuddly. They had big happy smiles.

Then others not so sure said, 'Appearances can be deceptive. You should never be taken in by friendly grins,' but the children liked the Little Odds and thought grown-ups are very odd. Very odd indeed!

***

Each day the kind doctor would come and fill them in on what was happening. She said it might not be safe to leave this place just yet. She said that the Runaway was almost fully fit. She looked lovely and healthy. Her autumn-leaf hair tumbled this way and that. It shone in the sun so much so that the Young Buck thought it quite intriguing.

They invented a game they played day after day called Cloud Bursting. All the Little Odds lay on their backs and watched the clouds float by, then they made shapes and animals and invented stories.

The Little Odd loved this game, most of all. Sometimes, it would see clouds it recognised but didn't say that out loud. One day, the Little Odd saw Ninety-Nine-a-Hundred—right up there, floating by. The Little Odd felt a twang inside, on its heartstrings, and longed for home…

Every day, they looked at the ocean and wondered at its cool, blue beauty. The Runaway took the Little Odd's hand-paw-thing in hers and showed him a line far, far away.

She said, 'That's the Horizon! It's as far as the Eye can see!'

'Wow!' says the Little Odd, for it had never seen a line quite like that before—so straight and long and simple, as far as the eye can see. The Little Odd thought it was the most amazing horizon it had ever seen. Then they jumped up and down and wore their shiniest happiest smiles. They were very, very happy, for they both knew, the Runaway was well again!

***

However, for now, although it missed Ninety-Nine-A-Hundred, deep down inside its heart and soul, the Little Odd was happy and enjoying all these wonderful new experiences with these special, beautiful friends, who it loves with all its heart and soul.

***

One day, when the Friendly Farmer was making ice cream cones for everyone she stuck a chocolate flake into the Little Odd's Pink One and said, 'This ice cream is now called a Ninety-Nine!'

The Runaway smiled at the Little Odd. She found some hundreds and thousands (that the innkeepers wife had left up on the roof, having heard of their passion for ice cream). The Runaway sprinkled the ice cream cone with rainbow colours and said that it was now called a Ninety-Nine-with-Hundreds-and-Thousands!

The Little Odd, jumped up and down, for this was heaven. It felt more at home in that moment than since it fell to Earth, which seemed like an awful long time ago, now…

***

Everyone was happy for these days of rest and recuperation, this gentle holiday to catch up on sleep and good food, to bond more closely after all their adventures, these past few weeks. Who'd have thought they'd find each other, in such a strange and mysterious way?

On the seventh day, they decided to hold a meeting. They asked the doctor, the innkeeper and his wife to join them; they had to plan their next steps—how to get away and where to go. They needed advice and guidance, they needed to pay their bill! They needed to show appreciation and recognition. They needed to give thanks, to the doctor, the innkeeper and his wife! So they all sat around and everyone took it in turn to say their thank you and goodbyes, for there might not be time later. The word on the ground was that the Ringmaster, his cronies and the Bounty Hunters, were roaming near… yet they had no fear.

The Little Odds sat around in a big circle on the roof. They watched the clouds float by. The Great White Rabbit and the Little Lion Man counted up the leftover squiggles and said, 'That should do the trick.' The Little Odd got confused. It asked the Puzzled Penguin if it knew the trick. But it just flapped its flippers and shook its head and said, 'Nope, but I am always willing to learn new tricks!'

The Great White Rabbit and the Little Lion Man counted out the squiggles so that everyone got an equal share of what was left over, just in case something went wrong, everyone had enough to survive!

The Fantabulous Fish and Crispy did a little dance and said, 'Hey! What could go wrong? The Runaway is better, and we have each other?'

The Great White Rabbit said, 'We stick together, no matter what! Even poor Vermin has had to hide in the Young Buck's pocket for fear he's found out here! We are a team. We go forward together. We defend, each other. We would go to the ends of the Earth for each other, that's understood?'

They all nod;

The Little Odd studied its misshapen feet things for a moment and said, 'Please, Sir Great White Rabbit, where do we go, and how do we get there?'

'Ah, good question, Little Odd,' who always liked it when someone said "Good question", especially the Great White Rabbit!

'I was communicating this morning, at dawn through thought-by-vibe, with the Faerie Queen…'

'Wow, did you send her our love?'

'Yes, of course, and she returned it. You may have felt it.'

And they agreed. They all felt free and happy somehow…

'This thought-by-vibe mullarkey is a wonderful thing,' says Crispy Duck and everyone laughed; so she tossed her duckbill high and mighty for they just took her as she is; loved her all the same, a swan, insane.

'What did she say?' asks the Little Lion Man; his face intent and worried for he fears the Ringmaster is closing in. He has this thing called Instinct, he's a lion after all; albeit, a gentle one. The Little Odds, are his pride and joy, he wants no harm, to come their way. He is a manly Little Lion Man, despite, what the cynics say… He flicks his mane and strokes his chin then begins, the begin… for there is this vision, in his head of the road ahead, many dangers lie therein. He goes into conference, tete-a-tete, with the Great White Rabbit. Together, they read the road ahead, and the dangers therein, but they cannot share for fear, they may not win!

Then the Great White Rabbit says to all assembled, 'Prick up your ears. Let me tell you what I have seen in a dream, and then we will ask the innkeeper and doctor for their interpretation. They know the lay of the Land of Wonder, while we do not…'

'It goes something like this: in my dream, we are all together, in a long boat. We row, row, row the boat gently down the stream. Merrily, merrily, merrily for life is like a dream…'

'Then the long boat, hits a waterfall. We tumble down, but we are all safe and well. It's like white water rafting! It's fun, we shriek and scream and are soaked to the skin but everyone is fine. At the bottom of the waterfall, we realise that we are in a strange place. The river is long and winding and dark. There is a forest, left and right. The animals howl; wolves and bears with strange eyes poke at us, follow us… yet we are safe and calm for the boat is steered, front and back, by two fine young men. Two young women with long dark hair hold our hands and say, "Don't worry, everything will be okay"!'

And oddly, they realise, over the past week that they have all had a similar dream, some vision, of the days to come.

The doctor, the innkeeper and his wife look at each other, for they know this place and it's precisely, what they were going to suggest…

The innkeeper says, 'That's Odd! We have an idea we plan to suggest. There is a river that runs behind The Elbow bend. It is shallow and safe before the rains, but when the rains come, it is a dangerous place! If you follow the flow of the river downstream you will eventually come to an island—just before the river meets the ocean. They say, there is a goddess there who guides the way, the Star of the Sea!'

'Not many have ever seen her, some sailors say so. They say she is just an illusion for the lost and lonely. We believe that is not so… We have asked our friends, the tribesmen and women of the deep forest to lend us their boat to guide you there—but beware the waterfall, and as long as the rains don't come the river won't swell, and you will all be safe and well. Please, don't forget us, when this tale you tell!'

Everyone hugs and kisses, for they have all had this dream
In one form or another, over the past week:
The long boat, in the long river, with the tribesmen

Front and back, and the two pretty girls, who take their hands and say
'Everything will be okay…'

Chapter Eleven
All in the Same Boat

The Humming Bird has an idea. She suggests that in the dawn, before they leave, she should fly ahead and test the water and check out the river—at least as far as the waterfall. This is agreed to be a good idea. 'Well done, Humming Bird,' says the Little Odd out loud.

The Humming Bird was the only free bird this last week, to fly high, above the Land of Wonder and with her eagle eye was able to see what was going on down yonder.

She is happy to help and flaps her wings, which seem bigger somehow, unfurled. And her hum transcends when she flies high into song, that only the skies can hear. All week long, she took a flight out over the ocean. She flew high up into the mountains where she says, she met a condor. She'd never met a condor before and thought it the most beautiful bird she'd ever seen—its wing span, the way it could glide. They made friends and promised to meet again someday.

(The Little Odds tease her, and say, haha, a holiday romance, but she just tucks her head under her wing, to hide... so they don't see her smile).

***

The innkeeper and his wife need to journey by road, across the hills, to ask the tribesmen to bring the long boat upriver, to The Elbow, where there is a little jetty hidden to the rear (for The Elbow man loves to go fishing from time to time, but he has to keep that quiet from Fantabulous and Puzzled in case one wants to swim-run-away, and one wants to join in too...)

The tribesmen, are friends of the innkeeper and his wife, and are happy to help, for they have helped the tribesmen out of danger many times in the past. The tribesmen want to repay in kind, the kindness shown to them, in times of fear and danger.

The innkeeper says they will be back before nightfall. Then they will celebrate one last supper before they leave. It will be a feast fit for a king; for the innkeeper's wife has everything prepared in her big kitchen down below. Tonight they will party and sleep sound, and before they rise, the Humming Bird will be back, with news.

The innkeeper insists and says it's the least they can do. He tells them to enjoy the rest of the day, the last of their stay *(he's going to miss them when they go, they were such pleasant attic guests).*

The Little Odds while the day away. They have nothing much to pack, having made a quick getaway, so they just chill, and look at the ocean, or play, Snap, Jack Changes, and other games, to pass the day…

I-spy
I-scream
We all scream
For ice cream…

***

The Little Odd wishes it had the cirrusoscope for far, far away, on the horizon it thinks it sees a pirate ship—bounty hunters perhaps! The Little Odd thinks about asking the Great White Rabbit if he can see the pirate ship too, but then realises, he can't see much beyond his white rabbit nose.

The Little Odd thinks about saying to the others but doesn't want to worry them. It's so far away that it will take at least a day, for the pirate ship to get this far. However, the Little Odd thinks inside its own head, that it will tell the innkeeper and wife, to be on guard, just in case, pirates are coming in search of treasure, squiggles and Little Odds… for there is a price on their heads, alive or dead.

***

As night falls the innkeeper and his wife return with the long boat and the tribesmen, one for front and one for rear, to steer and row. Two young tribeswomen to help—one for each side, in case it would capsize... The Little Odds are all shown, where the boat is for the dawn in case they have to make—another getaway but tonight, they eat, dance and be merry, so they can go, merrily, merrily, merrily, merrily down the dream, for tonight, is like a stream of laughter and joy that they will never forget, as long as they all shall live...

***

The two tribesmen are tall and good-looking. They wear traditional tribesmen dress as do the two tribe girls who are young and good-looking. They are shy, and sit by the fire making dolls out of straw—gifts for the innkeeper and his wife, plus one for each Little Odd. They offer the gifts with shy and gentle smiles. They bow, and each bows back as they accept the hand-made gift with good grace, and thanks. There is no shared language in words—just the language of gesture, of kindness and of truth.

One by one, in the glow of the embers, the Little Odds fall asleep. At first light, the hummingbird returns. The tribesmen have prepared the long boat. They set sail, silently, in the gentle river. They wave quiet farewells to the innkeeper and his wife, who stand on the jetty, in the still of the dawn. The river takes a turn and meanders on without a sound, in silence—just the occasional ebb and flow, of ripples on the side of the long boat, that glides alone through the misty dawn.

***

Just before they left, as they hugged farewell, the Little Odd, whispers to the innkeeper about the Pirate Boat. The Innkeeper nods—he knows exactly what this means. He says, 'Don't worry Little Odd, we have fought them off before, we can do it again! We do it with love, we call their bluff, and they don't know how to handle it, haha!'

***

Onwards glides the long boat in the cool of first light. It is pleasant and fine. Up ahead, they see a big sign on the riverbank:

'Welcome to Cheerie Vallee'

On either side are giant flowers, as if reaching to the stars, all the colours of the rainbow. Bushes and shrubs flank the river bank. Up on the genteel slopes of Cheerie Vallee are the biggest fanciest houses they ever seen! Spaced out in their grandeur, each has chariots parked outside. Stallions stand by. Eagles perched on gates keep a look-out, eyes flash this way and that. These eagle eyes see the Little Odds in the long boat approach. They sense so much fear so have no need, to react—just ignore, for in the big houses the people snore, for they have servants, maids and lesser folk to do their chores.

In the gardens, some children sit in neat little rows, with their fingers on their lips (for children should be seen and not heard). They should know their place and sit quietly so as not to disturb the sleep of the grown-ups. The Little Odd thinks something is not right in the state of Cheerie Vallee. The Little Odd whispers, 'children should be seen and heard, they should run around and shriek and play and learn all about life, in this Land of Wonder should they not?'

Gliding past, they see people, sitting at garden tables, pouring tea and reading newspapers, There are big bowls of fruits, juices and breads on the tables. Behind them stand the nervous servants, stepping forward on the click of finger command, to fill a teacup, to pour some juice, to spread butter on scones, then discreetly they step back, for they know their place and don't try to rise above their stations. For the foolish folk in Cheerie Vallee think that is the natural order of their world… Of course, they don't say that out loud unless they have to—unless some pesky upstart challenges and roars outside their doors, uncouth, ignorant, uneducated. They tut, shame on them!

They think, *We have all the squiggles to ourselves. We earned them fair and square off the backs of our workers, our business deals, our banks, our clever appeals. We are smarter therefore we are greater and deserve to be so; for that is the natural order of this Land of Wonder.*

As the long boat glides by they see more and more fancy folks sitting in their fancy gardens eating fancy things. The Little Odd decides to wave, so they decide to wave back and say things like: 'Oh my! Look, a tourist boat this early in the morning! Tally Ho, Tally Ho tourists!'

The Little Odds wave back politely but the tribesmen, look straight ahead.

'Good heavens, good heavens—aren't they the strangest bunch we ever did see!'

'Look harmless enough,' some say. 'Let them pass this way.'

'Have a nice day,' wave some (*secretly hoping, that they are admiring* their *very fancy houses and chariots).*

'Jolly good show,' say some for nothing much happens in Cheerie Vallee from morning until night. The children are bored. The women are bored. The men are bored.

But they never say that out loud for they would be told: 'How dare you! You have every material thing anyone could possibly ever want! The most expensive toys, the fanciest phones; servants to serve your every whim. The fanciest foods, the fanciest gyms, hairdressers and people to inject your chins! How ungrateful is that!'

So they keep their heads down and think, whatever you say, say nothing, for they would call it a sin if you were to say, 'It doesn't mean anything!'

The Little Odd thinks, *It is one thing to be good, it's another to be grateful but where there is no love, or truth or wonder at the world, there is no joy in privilege.*

'Ah, you read my thoughts,' says a voice from the river banks of the Cheerie Vallee.

'Oh, hullo,' says the Little Odd for there is a nice man, strolling along this fine dawn... 'I'm a Little Odd, and these are my friends. They are all a little odd too, pleased to meet you' (for the Little Odd, senses this a kind man).

'Good morning,' says the kind man. 'This is my morning pleasure. Each new day I stroll these river banks and think about what's in my head. Each evening I return to greet the remains of the day.'

'That's nice,' says the Little Odd, 'but what do you do in between?'

'Ah, I lock myself away, each day, in my imagination. I stay there from dawn until dusk for it is filled with wonder which is something I feel now lacking in the Land of Wonder. I grew up not far from here. When I was a boy, I'd roam these fine streets and was filled with the wonder of being a small boy;

the joy at seeing each new thing, like a bird's nest, or one season rest just to rise again, anew.

'Now I am old. My greatest pleasure is to walk these paths anew, to still wander with nature, in all its hues and glory. I wonder how it all came to be—each tree, each flower, each rain shower…?'

Then the man went quiet for a while. He is wearing the attire of an old-fashioned gentleman—a waistcoat and a watch, but his shoes are worn. The Little Odd wonders if that's why he looks at his feet now so to make conversation the Little Odd says, 'We are going on another adventure! We've had so many since we came to the Land of Wonder.'

This makes the old man chuckle, and he says, 'Little Odds, may you have many adventures. May you be safe and sound, I will think of you and join you in my head, good luck and have fun. Here's where our paths stop, I turn around now and walk back. It has been a pleasure to have your company this fine morning.'

'This is the end of Cheerie Vallee. Up ahead you will see many interesting things on your way to the island. Are you going to see the Earth goddess?'

'We hope so,' nod the Little Odds.

'Ah, send her my love, and my best regards,' as he waves his hand.

'We will,' says the Little Odd 'What shall we say is your name?' but the kind old man has turned around. He walks away, with his eyes, cast to the ground.

Chapter Twelve
The Tribesmen Take Them to the Island

... and trace their footprints in the sand

On and on, they sail past Cheerie Vallee where the trees curl their branches over the river until they meet overhead to make natural arches.

Farther on, the trees become thicker and larger; darker and dense; magic faces are etched on the bark. Some light gets through, to twinkle, dappled on the river bed, but now it seems swollen and brown for the rains start to tumble down.

The Little Odds get wet, wet, wet but the tribesmen don't flinch. They just stare right ahead and paddle their own canoe. The tribegirls look at the river and dangle their hands in the water. The Little Odds, wet and sodden, can't take their eyes off the river banks for there are creatures that stare back at them, eyes bright, in the darkness of the thicket.

Owls. Coo. Birds take flight even though up above it's daylight. They take flight like birds in the night, with fright; the heavy, flutter of wings, in plight. The caw of a crow; the cackle, of a magpie; small creatures stand and stare—trolls, elves, goblins, even wicked pixies.

The Little Odds lock eyes from time to time with these strange creatures. No one dares breathe a word. There are all thin ghost-like figures—spectres of shadow and light, limbs like long bones, heads shaped like toads.

There is a wolf!

Another one;

A bear—another one!

They walk along the darkened banks, deep in the thick of it, but close enough to see their majesty, and though they make no contact, the Little Odds, believe the wolves and bears are there as protectors on either side. As the journey passes this way, for what seems like hours (but it may be less) they are suspended in space and time in motion, slow motion.

Then up ahead, on a branch that stretches out over the water they see a majestic blue peacock, who cocks its head to the side as if to be admired. When it's satisfied that everyone can see its tail feathers, so long, they trail into the water, it jumps down just as the long boat passes. The peacock turns its back and shows the most spectacular display of peacock features. Slowly it turns around to show them off.

Crispy says, 'Oh my,' and the Humming Bird, who until now sat quietly at the helm of the boat with the tribesman, flies up and over, to take a closer look. She nods acknowledgement at the peacock, who nods back in approval.

The Young Buck says, 'Hey Vermin' (in a whisper). 'Come out and look at this.' For Vermin hides now, sleeps a lot, in the pocket where he feels quite safe and at home, just popping his head out from time to time to see what's going on.

Vermin keeps his head down passing through Cheerie Vallee and then gets scared when he thinks he has seen some ghosties but the peacock is worth a look surely.

The peacock hops on ahead then stops suddenly—turns and says, 'You are not far from the island now. You will see the light up ahead, and the river will widen. Just round that bend yonder…' He bows his head. 'You will find the Earth goddess. Good Luck my friend—here—have a feather,' and he plucks one from his tail and hands it to the Great White Rabbit who despite his ailing eyesight is able to see clearly now, with this fine feather in his paw.

***

There is the island in all its glorious beauty! The river widens. The sun twinkles on the river and lights the way out of the darkness. The tribesmen, paddle into a little inlet—then tie the long boat to a wooden totem pole.

The Little Odds are safe and dry and warm, for the sun is basking over the island. Farther along the shore are the island people who dance and sing and play drums to welcome the Little Odds (who jump up and down and wear their shiniest happiest smiles).

The Little Odds join in the dance, for the people are very welcoming, and wear their shiniest happiest smiles too.

Here is the leader of the Tribe. He is the father of the two tall men. He welcomes them and explains the ritual which is very simple, for they love to have visitors and to be able to remember them forever when they leave. They trace their footprints in the sand, so their imprint is on the land forever and a day, even, when the tides have washed them all away…

One by one, the Little Odds line up and present their feet for tracing.

Ladies first.

Crispy Duck waddles right up for she is very proud of the shape of her webbed ones. Next, for fun, the Runaway and the Friendly Farmer, side by side, foot by foot—same size now, when once the Runaway's was the size of the inside of the palm of the Friendly Farmer's hand.

The Humming Bird glides down. She only has little talons for tracing; then the Gurney Cat who has been quiet for a long time, presents her paws, as if she is a tiger, for she struts her funky stuff now that she is feeling so much better inside herself and has forgotten what all the gurning was about anyway…

Then the Puzzled Penguin presents for it is not sure if it's a boy or a girl but it'll take its turn now anyway—does a little twirl, and taps those penguin feet, the way small penguins do.

Not to be outdone, fantabulous, dances up the sand and says out loud, 'I am a Fantabulous-Fish-Out-of-Water. Therefore, I don't have feet for you to trace in the sand, but you are welcome to capture the tap-tapety-tap of my dance when I leave prints in the sand.'

The chief tribesman nods and smiles.

Here comes the Great White Rabbit, who rather shyly presents his feet for tracing. The chief beckons him over—whispers, in another language that they both understand, 'You are a chief in your own land. You are welcome to the island. I understand rabbit feet are lucky!'

And in that moment, the Great White Rabbit understands and gives the peacock feather to the chief as a gift. Then they embrace like brothers for it is always considered good manners to bring a gift when you visit to show goodwill and the gentle art of kindness…

Next, the Little Lion Man presents. They trace his majestic paws. After the chief beckons him over, embraces him and whispers in his lion ear, 'You were born to be a chief of your pride. I prophesise, that someday you will return to take your rightful place, for you have the heart of a lion, the wisdom of a bear, but the soul of humankind.'

The Little Lion Man nods and takes his place beside his traced paws.

The Young Buck hesitates unsure then steps forward, and they trace the feet of a man, for he is almost that, and a fine young man he's growing into. The chief says, he is welcome to join the tribe for he can see this is a fine young man, but the Young Buck says, 'Thank you for the kindly offer, but my place is with the Little Odds, for we are all one people under one sun.'

The Chief nods and says, 'Right answer!' Then unexpectedly, the Chief calls him back and indicates—

'The little visitor in your pocket, we need to trace his feet even if they are only little, for it's all part of the ritual.'

For the first time in over a week, Vermin pops his head out and runs down the Young Buck's trouser leg to have his feet prints traced, in the sand and for the first time in… um… for the first time ever…

Vermin, feels like an equal, for the Chief says, he is very welcome!

Now, bashful, for the Little Odd studies its misshapen feet thing and wonders what the tribe's people will make of them, but then they have had to trace the feet, of all the Little Odds, no two even remotely the same, insane!

The Little Odd thinks, inside its own head, there are more things between heaven and Earth but it still stands there, shy, until the chief says, 'Little Odd, your turn.'

And so the Little Odd steps forward, to get his footprints traced in the sand. The Little Odd thinks, inside its own head, that this the strangest, but most beautiful ritual in all the land, for no one gets hurt, and just feels special, valued and welcome and loved.

***

There is a celebratory meal which involves sitting around in a circle and eating a soup-stew thing which the chief explains is made only from the gifts of the land. 'No animals were hurt in the making of this meal,' which is how the Little Odds like it.

The Chief says, 'The goddess awaits. The drummers will lead the way.'

The Little Odds follow the chief, his sons and the young tribes women along a path that leads to a clearing. They are blinded by the light—for there she is standing on a stone that makes her taller than tall—like a statue that shimmers in the prism of light, all the colours of the rainbow—the full spectrum, around this sight. She wears her shiniest happiest smile. She doesn't jump up and down for she's too serene for that, but she laughs and holds out her arms. She says, 'My cutest Little Odds,' but they just stand there, don't know what to do—so they wear their shiniest happiest smiles. The Little Odd looks down at its misshapen feet things and says, 'Hullo,' which makes her laugh again. She is the most beautiful creation the Little Odd has ever seen, and from her beaming face shines love, everlasting.

'I have something important to say' (the drums fall silent, and everyone is all a-hush).

'Little Odds, I have followed every step of your journey here, but you've only just begun, for there is much work to be done.'

'I am Mother-Earth. I love, all creation with all my heart and soul, but there are dark forces at work here in paradise. They have taken what is not theirs to take, all for the sake of squiggles and greed and corruption. It makes no sense, for they are blinkered and blind and will not see—they package the beauty of the planet, in plastic wrappers and call it progress.'

'They destroy the planet for their own ends, for their own gluttony. They take more than they need, when no one, should ever take more than they need—for that way there is always enough to go around if everyone plays nice and shares what the planet provides. For the sun feeds everyone and it hurts the sun and the Earth to see this dearth, this dire, state of affairs—the wars, the death and destruction, the wilderness of empty struggle when there is no need, for any need!'

'Yet it is those in need who hurt the most. It doesn't have to be that way if people would open their hearts and minds to simplicity; to love and peace man; to patience and kindness instead of wanting to live on a planet, devoid of these things, where every man lives for himself, an island, a bit lost—and lonely.'

Then the Goddess of the Earth looks sad. She turns her eyes, to the ground and weeps…

The Little Odd says, 'Please, Lady Goddess of the Earth, I don't like to see you sad, what can we do to help?'

She lifts her beautiful face to his and says, 'Just be yourself for your heart is pure, and your love is crystal clear. Just show the way, every day, in what you do and say. You light the way, Little Odd.'

Then she shines her happiest smile into its eyes like laser beams… and says, 'Dear Little Odds, there are three parts to your story. You are almost at the end of the second part. So you must depart this island, but I have to tell you that Part Three will be no picnic in the park for you have to go down to the Underworld for it was written long, long ago that the Little Odds would journey into the centre of the Earth, to take on the Underlies.'

'Oh,' says the Little Odd, 'that sounds a bit scary!'

The Earth goddess says, 'Have no fear. We will be near. You will have a whale of a time. Mark my words, this will be the adventure of a lifetime, a roller-coaster of cosmic dimension that will see you sink to the under-belly of the Earth and soar to the highest elements of the universe and beyond.'

'Oh my! After that, can I go home to Ninety-nine-a-hundred for I miss my cirrusoscope, my kaleidoscope, my music toys and my friends and family?' says the Little Odd counting on its hand-paw-things.

'Of course, you can, baby,' she says, smiling beatifically.

'Well then,' says the Little Odd, 'bring it on! Where is this whale you talk of?'

'She's a beached whale. Blue is her colour, deep-sea diving is her game; quite the expert, I'd never place my precious cargo with an amateur!'

'What's her name?' asks the Little Odd.

'Levi. Levi A. Thon, but they call her the lovely mummy whale for short. Long live all who sail in her. Now go, Little Odds. Let the story unfold, and let it start from the belly of our lovely whale!'

She laughs her Earth goddess laugh. She is funny and very kind. They bow, before the glory of the Earth goddess then make their way behind the chief and the tribesmen to the beach where they see, before them Levi A. Thon—her face pointed out to sea, as if, she knew all along, she was meant to be a beached whale, precisely at this point in time. A man with a picture-taker machine records the moment for history.

The Little Odds form an orderly queue. It seems the right thing to do. The chief goes to have a word with the big beautiful mummy whale *(who is forever blubbering for she feels the pain of the planet)*.

The drummers, drum. The women and men sing, in adulation to the majesty of the sea beast, a gentle guest comes to visit them. They agree it's been a special day, one that will go down in the history of the island as recorded in the imprint of the sands, for destiny, and those with the wisdom, to interpret it, years from now…

The whale flaps her giant tail. The chief beckons the Little Odds, 'Whale, meet thy Little Odds. Little Odds, meet thy whale.'

One by one, they climb on board, through the mouth of the whale and into her belly. As they go they sing a song the Friendly Farmer used to know when she was a child, and they soon catch on:

'*We all live in a yellow submarine; a yellow submarine, a yellow submarine*
We all live in a pot of margarine; a pot of margarine, a pot of margarine
And we sail under the sea, in our beautiful submarine…'

The Blue Whale is not yellow, but she is mellow and likes the song. She hums along, so they feel no fear. She hopes, they feel at home in her belly of hope and love and understanding where they will be her babies, for her babies have grown huge and floated far, far away, but they still pass her way—for whales make wonderful mums, and their children never forget that.

She says, there is no need for seatbelts, but they might want to hold on to each other for the descent, which can be bumpy. 'Hold on to your hats,' she yells, as the tribesmen go "Heave ho, heave ho, heave ho" to push her and the precious cargo out into the ocean waves for the adventure, to beat them all—that takes them to the pits of the planet, to the core of the cosmos, in one almighty roller-coaster of a trip.

Hold on to your hats!

Part Three Coming up!

Yikes!

***

Part Three

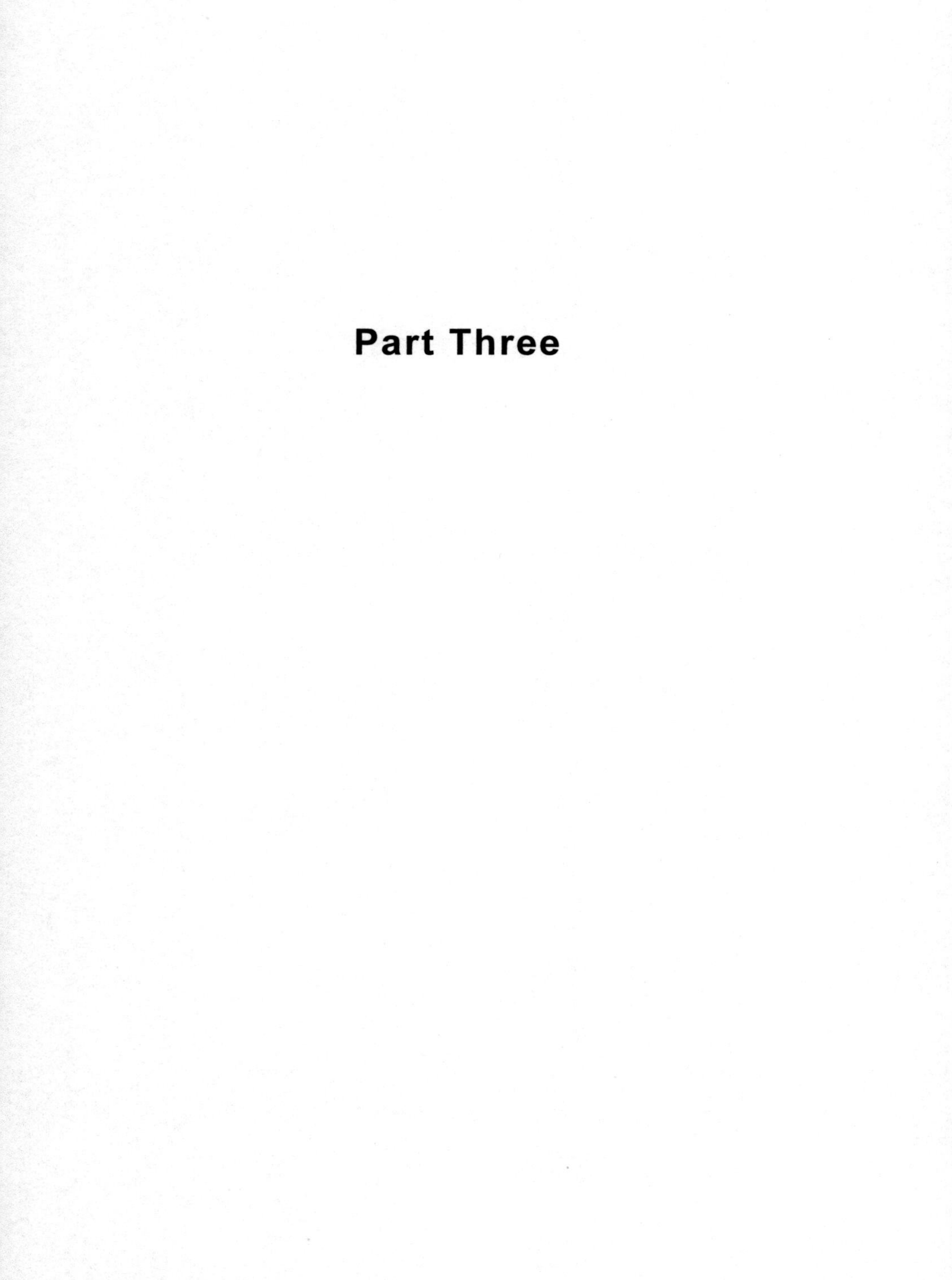

Chapter One
Somewhere Beneath the Sea...

'So,' says Levi, 'is everyone sitting comfortably…?'

'Yes, ma'am,' shouts the Little Odd, for it's not sure she can hear;

'I can hear,' she says, 'Then I'll begin. The first part of our descent should be calm and uneventful. Just sit back and enjoy the views. The trolley fish will be along soon to serve you seaweeds and sea stew—all on the house, so to speak, for you are my first class passengers.'

'Oh, thank you,' says the Little Odd 'What is a first class? Is that like kindergarten?'

'No,' says the mother whale, 'it's just a turn of phrase.'

'Ah,' and the Little Odds laugh and the Little Odd smiles, bashful but it likes when its friends laugh with it, not at it for they are used to the ways of the Little Odd, for they are one and the same.

As she glides—leaves land behind she says, 'There are six flaps on either side. you can lift these and then you can see out my sides. Look, do it now, the tribe's people are waving from the sea shore!'

So they flip up, the little windows of her soul and wave to those who showed them kindness and warmth, appreciation and love.

The Little Odds will never forget the island, for it was paradise. Before they know it, they are under the deep blue sea. The light still filters down, and there is so much to see.

They sit, silent passengers watching the beautiful flowers of the ocean—wafting along; entwined, with shells and small sea creatures—shrimps, mussels and whelks. Crabs of all sizes, lift heir claws and wave. Lobsters, look intently at the cargo of the whale and say, 'Shoo…' for they don't like to be disturbed—rock lobsters get embarrassed—go bright red! The damp squids and octopi get very excited and wave octo-tentacles, so they all wave back. The sea horses, follow, in herds.

'Oh my, look at those skates,' shouts the Fantabulous Fish who feels at home, somewhere, beneath the sea, and he hums under his, ahem, breath (if he had some)!

'Well, hullooooo, skates!' He shouts, for he used to have a best friend who was a sea skate, in fact, could it be, could it possibly be? Stranger things have happened at sea!

'Cedric is it really you!'

Cedric presses his nose to the whale—nods, laughs and says, 'Yes. It's really me!'

So Cedric swims to the mouth of the whale and asks, 'Can I come in, just for a swim, for my best friend from childhood, is in there?'

'Ah, who might that be?' asks Levi, knowing the answer already.

'Why! Fantabulous of course!'

'Go right ahead'; she says, 'but be out in an hour, or I digest you.' She laughs.

Cedric the sea skate, sails in and says, 'Fantabulous—it is really you!'

'Cedric—it is really you!'

They embrace. Do a little dance; then Fantabulous says, 'Oh, Cedric, it's been a long time. So much water under the bridge since then.' They hug and laugh;

'These are my friends, the Little Odds. And let me introduce you to my beautiful wife, Crispy… um, duck…'

There is an awkward moment. Then they all burst out laughing when Cedric says, 'You always were a little odd, Fantabulous!'

Cedric shows sepia photos of his wife and kids, for sepia comes from the sea you know, from the squirt of the squid… and they all agree, this a fine family of cute sea skate.

'You got kids?' asks Cedric.

'Nah, wrong species, but hey, who knows. Anything is possible, these days,' and they high-five, fin on fin. Cedric says, 'I must be on my way, so where are you going?'

'To the Underworld!'

'Ah, I hear, things are bad—dark ages, you sure you wanna go there? You could leave now, I could take you and Crispy to my plaice, she'd like it there?'

'Nah,' says Fantabulous, 'We stick together, we are on a mission, somewhere, beneath the sea!'

So Cedric says he has contacts in the deep. He will radar, and give details in case they need help! The Little Odds say that's appreciated but Cedric says, 'Seriously, be careful down there; I'll do what I can, to radar ahead. If you see my mate Manitou, say hi!'

'We will!'

They hug again for the skate has amazing hug-wrap abilities and then off he goes and waves again, from the outside in. Levi opens her mouth to let him out but warns, 'Mermaid Alert! Mermaid Alert!'

She says this means he'll have to keep her mouth closed for they are such vein creatures, sneak up and in when they know there are passengers… How many sea men got caught out this way by these Sirens of the Sea—all long hair and strategically placed sea shells, all poise and promises, just slippery slither.

'Give me a porpoise any day, at least they have purpose! These mermaids are nothing but trouble! Give me a dolphin any day—actually, we're close to Dolphin City—would you like a quick detour—I think we have time?'

'Yes, please,' cries the Little Odds.

'No problem, they call it Atlantis where you come from, I believe.'

Before long, they are sailing through the dark streets of Atlantis; lit up by little neon fish—a million little lights like the Blackpool illuminations! It's the most amazing Aquarium you can imagine, like the inside of a tropical tank but multiplied by ten million! There are shipwrecks all-a-glow. There are fish restaurants and seafood bars; sea florists and sea weed sellers on every corner; sea salt shakers and movers; sponges and plankton-bars—all the creatures of the night create a beautiful sight, from afar!

The whale doesn't want them to disembark for Atlantis ain't what it used to be. The shadows of the deep and the dark have taken hold, since the days of the Ark when it sank to this place, after the storms and the floods. It's such a long time ago now, but still within collective living memory. Oh no, she says. She doesn't want them to get out for there are dangers in the deep, and her job is to deliver them safely to the Underworld, as best she can. She says this—solemnly as if she'd taken a vow.

'If it's okay, I'd like to pass their way for there are things, I need to say…'

The Little Odds say that's okay. They are taking in the sights of this underwater city at night. This far down, it's always night. Levi says, 'Thank

God for the neon fish and the others that carry light, for without them we'd be lost at sea. They are like candles, in the night.'

They meet a school of Angel Fish who say, 'Dolly and the Dolphs, heard you were in town. Follow us, we won't take long.'

Levi follows the Angel Fish who lights the way, through the back streets of Atlantis. The Dolphins have prepared a display for they heard she was coming with precious cargo, but they understand, she can't stop long.

Levi has a chat with Dolly the Dolphin Lady, who promises to do anything she can to help. They just have to send the word. Underwater radar is usually good, failing that, resort to sea text, she says.

The Dolphins agree that things are bad underwater but it's nothing compared, to what's going on in the Underworld, which has a bad habit, of filtering up when conditions, are right, or rather, wrong…

Dolly and Levi nod in mutual understanding. She knows she can call on the Dolphins for help any time for they go back a long way to those dark days of a dim and distant time. Dolly says, 'They are fighting again—the dinosaurs of the deep. They went to sleep centuries ago but some rumbling has awakened them. They fight to the death, these dinosaurs of the deep, and it disturbs every living thing beneath the sea.'

Dolly heard through the sea vines that there is a battle down below to stop them from getting to the Underworld. Two great sea creatures, one good, one evil—will fight to the death, and they may have to witness it on descent, for the forces of evil don't want the forces of good to infiltrate that place and disrupt, their wicked plans…

The Little Odds don't have a clue what's going on, but they're here now—somewhere, beneath the sea.

Chapter Two
A Crash Landing and the Skanky Sea Spectres

They sail back out through the gates of Atlantis. Levi—the lovely mummy whale, is quiet. She is a worried whale and wonders what lies beneath. She will have to prepare her precious cargo for the darkness of the deep, for the horror that lingers there. She thinks for a while as she listens to the chatter of the Little Odds inside her belly and wonders what words to choose to create the right balance of courage and concern.

'My dear Little Odds I need to tell you some things; are you sitting comfortably? Then I'll begin… We are about to begin our final descent to the ocean floor. From here on down, it will be pitch black. You will be under a lot of pressure. Those of you with ears may feel them pop. You may experience sea nausea, and you may have mild or horrendous headaches, depending on your species. Some will be more acclimatised than others. There is a high chance of sea turbulence. We may hit sea black holes, in which case there will be a sudden drop. When I say Brace! Brace!'

'What does Brace mean?' asks the Little Odd.

'Ah good question,' says Levi. 'It means, curl up and hold on to your head. Understand.'

Uh-huh, say the Little Odds, worriedly.

'Now listen very carefully for I will say this only once. There may be trouble ahead, there is a high chance of a crash landing on the ocean floor. This may be accidental, or it may have to be on purpose. I won't know for sure until I read the road ahead. We will have to play it by ear, for those of you who have them; I will be using radar, but as we are many leagues under the sea, radar can be rusty, or faulty. In the dark, it is easy to lose one's direction.'

'However, my mission is to get you to the other side. The door to the Underworld doesn't open easily. There is a closed-door policy, for they don't want anyone to know what goes on behind closed doors.'

'However, there is also a high chance that the Underworld is aware that we are on our way. The dark powers that be may be expecting us. They snigger and cackle and think us fools of the highest order to take on this mission willingly. I hear they call us Lightweights, and can't wait to play games with us—and Little Odd, before you say a word, this is not games in a nice way. Be strong, be brave, be careful. Whatever happens, we stick together. Understood?'

'Uh-huh—but what happens if one of us gets lost, or stolen? Do we go to Lost and Found?' asks the Little Odd.

The lovely mummy whale says, 'Everyone in the Underworld is lost. They live in despair, which is not a nice place to be. So many lost souls, have lost hope.'

Levi sighs, for she is frightened too that she may not see her children, her grand-children or great-grand-children ever again, but when she was given this mission what sort of lovely mummy whale would she be if she turned her back and swam away, which would have been the easy option.

***

Suddenly
There is a sudden drop
It lasts for a lifetime
But in the darkness of the deep
No one knows, how long that is
In clock time.
They gasp and scream!
Then the whale is viciously knocked sideways to the left
Then right again, then up and down and what the hell is going on?
Outside, as their eyes adjust
They can see two huge sea monsters
Dinosaurs of the deep, and they fight
To the death.
Dinosaur sea monster blood sprays from one or other
One is purple, one is grey, but they look much the same way
Huge bodies and flippers and dinosaur heads, in voracious battle
The evil one is intent
On killing the whale and cargo

Determined, to earn its place
In the hierarchy of the Underworld
The other is a force for good, sent to protect
The whale and her precious cargo
And they will fight to the death, and they do
Both perish, somewhere, beneath the sea.
No one screams;
The Friendly Farmer and the Runaway hug
She cries, into her mummy's arms, and she holds her tight
And says, it will be okay.
They huddle;
The bird and cat and rat
The Young Buck wraps
His strong arms around;
The Little Lion Man
Takes care of the Great White Rabbit
Who has a gash, across his forehead and the blood
Trickles into his eyes, so he has to wipe his glasses
Fantabulous and Crispy
Hug, for they have each other;
And Puzzled cuddles in.
Levi asks
'Is everyone okay?'
And they say
'Aye, aye captain'
For they heard that said before
Somewhere, above the sea.
'Are you okay, Missus Whale?'
Asks the Little Odd. She laughs and says
'I will be. That really hurt, but it's okay';
'I've had bumpier rides than that before.'
'I think I have some tail damage,'
which could cause problems
With my sense of direction;
'A few cuts and bruises—
I may be leaking blubber, but hey

Will live!'
She sighs,
She plays down,
The extent of damage;
For now she knows,
A crash landing is
Inevitable.

***

'Oh my, oh dear
Little Odd, I am taking a tumble
Out of control,'
She plummets
Down, down, down
Deeper and deeper and deeper
Into the abyss
She says
'Brace!'
So they try
To brace, but
It's easier said than
Done, as they tumble
This way and that
Nobody
Screams
For in lower-space
No one can hear
So it seems…
They are tossed
This way and that
Beneath the sea
In the belly of the whale
For what seems
Like eternity
Then crash
Bang, wallop!

They hit the ocean floor
And they don't know what's hit them
But this almighty cloud of brown dirt and ash
Flows up around them, then gradually disappears
As they ask
Are you alright?
Are you?
Is everyone okay?
Any casualties?
Some have cuts
But no one seems
To be seriously hurt
The Great White Rabbit is dazed
The Little Lion Man takes care of him
As they all pinch themselves to check they are alive
And comfort each other…
Comfort each other
Then the Little Odd asks
'Levi, are you okay?'
Nada
'Levi, are you alive?'
Nothing.
'Missus Whale, Missus Whale'
Silence
Then out the cabin windows
They scream, for they have never seen
The like of this before
All around, spindly skanky sea spectres
The ghosts of the deepest, darkest depths
Emerge from the brown dust, and dirt which has
Calmed now
So they can see,
These ugly scenes,
Tall, small and in between
Spindly shadowy creatures of the deep
Dead, but alive—zombies that glide, sinewy

Despite their awkward angularity.
Ugly and gaping and mocking and obscene.
They surround, the body of the whale
Who still, makes no sound, no guidance
Of what to do next.
Then she gasps, opens her mouth
And lets a visitor in, who says his name is
Manitee, the Manitou
He looks very worried, frightened
He says he is a friend sent with a message
For the Little Odds… but they must listen very carefully.
'Hullo Manitee the Manitou
We are very glad to see a friend
For we are very frightened and don't know what to do…'
'Manitee the Manitou, please tell us, is Missus Whale dead or alive?'
She lives
They all gasp and say, 'Hallelujah!'
'But she is seriously injured,
As she let me in, she said through radar
Which is thought-by-vibe beneath the sea—
To tell you that she will be okay, she is tough as old boots!'
'But her work is finished for now,
For she has delivered you safely this far
And that is half her work done, but now
She must go away to lick her wounds and heal
And when the time is right, she'll be back to take you all
Safely home.'
'She said, tell them this:
"I won't give up on you, my most precious cargo"
But she is in a bad way, oh! And she said, tell them
"I love them so"!'
And in this moment
Many tears are wiped away;
The Great White Rabbit cleans his glasses
Which are broken now, so he can't see through them
Anymore.

Outside, the Skanky Sea spectres
Start howling and making ugly gurgling noises
And Manitee the Manitou looks alarmed…
'We must be quick—can you all gather yourselves together;
If you thought that was bad, the next bit could be really scary.
Be strong, be vigilant, look out for each other—
Those skanky sea spectres, are to be feared!'
Manitee the Manitou looks very worried,
He says his message comes in two parts—
'Part one—We are all under threat;
The Underwater ecosystems, that's our way of life
Are being destroyed by the greed of the upper world
With total disregard and because the people can't see yet
The damage that's being done, they turn a blind eye
To the horrors of the deep'
'Until a hundred years ago, nay even just the past fifty
We lived in harmony, all creatures under the sea
Yes, there were dogfish eat dogfish and schools of fish
Lost their lives in one small gulp, but there was a natural order
And we all lived with what we called, mutual respect,'
'But that's all gone.
No living sea creature from the smallest to the big fish
Live in harmony anymore,
It is fear and loathing and…
well—it's just not what it used to be
species almost wiped out by oil spills
by tsunamis, that rock our world to the core'
'But because the people of the upper world
Can't see what's going on below, they just don't seem to care
While we struggle for survival, what you need to know
In no uncertain terms is that we are all connected and if you destroy
What's beneath the surface, just because you can't see what's going on
Then you will starve, and eventually suffocate—the people need to understand.

The Earth is one-third land, two-thirds ocean and as people-folk continue to destroy the Earth they destroy the oceans and as they continue to destroy the

oceans they destroy the Earth;
And we are all in serious danger,
But they just don't seem to understand
They just don't seem to care,
They are too consumed
With consumption, they have no time to think
About what's really going on which is what
The Underworld and the greedy people they control up on land
Want.
'Do you understand?'
They nod.
Manitee says:
'Message delivered loud and clear?'
They say
'Message received, loud and clear.'
'Good, now part two
Here's what I've been sent to do;
To tell you…'
'The Underworld has been expecting you
The crash landing has hailed your arrival;
When you leave, through Levi's mouth
I will guide you to where the Earth's plates
Are shifting'
'Then a gap will appear, and it will grow wide enough
For you to descend to the Underworld, be careful
Hold on to each other, for grim life!'
'Do you understand?'
'Yes.'
'When everyone is through the plates will close and for what you are about to do;
I salute you.'
They nod.
'Don't worry about me, I will take care
Of Levi and see her to a safe place, I have reinforcements
On their way, to take her away and don't worry about those ugly
Skanky sea spectres, they just exist to scare, they will soon fade away

And disappear.'
'Levi will be alright; she'll be back.'
'Will you be okay Manitee the Manitou?'
Asks the Little Odd
But he looks away and says
'I'll be fine, I have bigger fish to fry
Now let me see you all safely into the Underworld
And remember, everyone up here, is rooting for you
Our radars will point your way and where there's a will there's a way
And we will will you all, back to safety as best we can…'
'Now please follow me.'
And now they are all out of the belly of the whale
On terra firma, where no foot has ever stepped before
And the Friendly Farmer knows this is impossible—she says
To the Young Buck—'How is this so, we have human lungs
Yet we can breathe, we are alive!'
He says, 'There are more things between heaven and Earth
That we do not understand,' and she looks at him funny;
For she'd never have thought him one for Shakespeare!
They all bid farewells to Levi
And kiss her big head and wish her well
And in the moment, she summons enough
Energy to open her eyes, her big whale eyes
And give them a wink!
Then at that moment the Earth's plates on the ocean floor
Start to rumble and rub each other up the wrong way
With one almighty roar then open up, and a surge of heat
Flurries up but the Little Odds know they have no choice,
But to enter here, where all else fails, and they have no fear!
The Manitou shows the way
And beware all ye, who enter here…
But they do because they
Know no fear.

***

Chapter Three
Introduction to the Underworld

And it's not nice.

The Little Odds' first impression
Of the Underworld, is how it blows hot
Then cold.
They hold onto each other
For grim death, is standing over there;
Grim-reaper-esque, the first thing they see
When their eyes adjust.
They appear
To be floating,
This way and that
As if in a breeze, unpleasant
Flotsam and jetsam then Thank God
They are holding on to each other for they take a tumble
Down, down, down, a spiral, like a water slide, but not in a good way
'Hold tight, hold tight,' they scream as they twist and turn this way and that
As if in a theme park ride, tumble in the dark, tossed this way and that, full circle!
Then they land in a heap and the Great White Rabbit says
He is too old for that.
His wound opens, and he bleeds
But the Little Lion Man says it will be okay
And takes off his jacket, and holds it to the rabbit's head
The Great White Rabbit says
He is too weak to carry on
But they say, No, it will be okay

But the Great White Rabbit says
He will hold them back they must go on
They have work to do, but they say no!
Not without you, your wisdom to guide us through!
'Well, if you insist,' he says
'I don't want to hold you back
I don't want to be a burden,'
And he wipes, his broken glasses
One last time…
'I may be more use to you in spirit
Than alive, have you considered that?'
But they say
'Noooooo.'
And with that,
The Great White Rabbit breathes
His last.

***

They are beside themselves with grief, the Little Odds
Words cannot describe, what they feel right now
As they holler and howl, into the dark night, of the Underworld;
This is no place for one so Great as He, to die—old and infirm and so far away
From his family…
They weep and wail and console each other
The Great White Rabbit is dead, and what will become of them?

***

They have no idea how time passes
In the Underworld, but they just stay there
Holding his worn-out body and sobbing
For there is no consolation
No one knows quite what to do
And from time to time
They look at each other

And shake their heads and sob
Stuck, in this terrible place
Like nothing on Earth.
They whisper
Please Great White Rabbit,
Please Wake Up!
But they know it's too late
They are in a terrible state
Over there they see
Zombies, black shapes,
Rise from the ground
And ghost across a field
Barren and dark and deserted
and desolate, except for these dark figures
as if in a dream, a nightmare, of obscene
proportions.
They huddle close to what appears to be a hedgerow
Some thorny bush, and hide, for they cannot move,
With fear and hope, they pass by this zombie crew.
They feel paralysed with fear, and loathing
They cannot leave this place, without the Great White Rabbit
Then the Little Lion Man sees, a cave, there is a light,
Dim, as if an orange fire burns within...
He sees shadows on the walls of the cave and says
Ssshhhh, look over there...
The Little Odds watch the scene unfold
The Friendly Farmer and The Runaway
Hold the Great White Rabbit in their arms
Afraid to let go
The shadows on the orange walls
Are long and thin and lanky
They are in pain as if tortured there
They can see a bridge, a drawbridge, a drop-down lever
And two figures, twelve feet high, shadows on the orange walls
Emerge, slowly and ungainly and let the lever down and out of the cave
They can see, the shadows drop to half their size, now, they are just shadows

Crossing the bridge, two figures, walk their way
Once men, they wear loincloths and rags
Their grey skin hangs in folds, scorch-marked
And ashen, their fingers and toes, long and emaciated
And they walk their way and crouch down, beside the Little Odds
As if wanting not to be seen
The Little Odds are less frightened now
For the figures say, 'We are your friends,
And you will not find many here
We have volunteered
To put our necks on the line
To come help you for you are in great danger;
We are the lost souls, and we come from the Pits of Despair
We do not belong in the Underworld but wound up here
For one reason or another, we each have a tale to tell
Would curl your toes if you have any.'
The Little Odds stay silent
But twenty-two terrified eyes
Stare at the men who look at each one in turn
Lock eyes, sad eyes and say
'Do not be afraid, we mean you no harm.
From the cave, we saw the grim-reaper over there
Look! He hovers still! And we knew one of you was in peril.
Your elderly friend is dead, but his soul is alive and well and intact
And will not leave here, without you.'
'Let us carry him into the Pits of Despair
We have prepared a special place, where we can keep his body safe
Until you return, to claim him, his body and free us all from this dreadful place
For that is why you are here, isn't it?'
'Ummm, dunno,' says the Little Odd
And they look at each other confused.
'Well, that's what we were told,
But we understand, you have work to do.'
And they have no idea, what that is or where
Or who or how or anything… all they know,
Is their sorrow, in this moment

And the Hollow-men promise
The Great White Rabbit will be safe in their care
Until they come to reclaim him and restore their souls
To Elsewhere.

***

The Little Odds look at each other and agree
They don't have a clue what else to do and so
The Young Buck and the Little Lion Man,
Carry the body of the Great White Rabbit into
The Pits of Despair and the rest of the Little Odds
Follow the Hollow-men in a procession, silently trip-trapping
Across the drawbridge, and after the bridge rises, they are closed inside
The Pits of Despair.
And what a sight they see there
Caves and cliffs and pits of fire
Leap up and engulf and quagmire
The Hollow-men say there is no need for them to go any further
For they have seen enough for one lifetime and the Hollow-men direct them to a cave
A hole, in the wall, and gently, with dignity, they place the body of the Great White Rabbit in the tomb, and the Hollow-men place a stone, the size of a giant rock in front, to mark the spot.
There will be no mistaking that when they come to reclaim him.

***

So they each stand by and say a few words
About what the Great White Rabbit meant to them
And tears flow, and where they land, crystals form
Little dots of light, glisten in the darkness of the
Pits of Despair.

***

There are no flowers in the Underworld
For the Little, Odd asks the Hollow-men
Who says they remember flowers, in the upper world
But no, there are none here, no pretty scents, just
Thorny bushes and trees
With no leaves
For they say
The light
Cannot penetrate
Here.

***

It's strange for it's been a long time since they ate
But no one feels hungry here, how could you eat
In a place like this? When your guts are tied up in knots
And where on Earth, would you find a loo, in a godforsaken place like this!
The Little Lion Man
Solemnly, shakes the long bony fingers
Of the Hollow-men and thanks them for their help
And so the Little Odds all follow and do the same
For it's as though the Little Lion Man is all grown up now
And somehow, instinctively knows what to do.
The Hollow-men say it was their pleasure to do some good
To make recompense, for they are a glimmer of hope
In a place bereft and if there's anything more they can do
Anything at all to help, they are at their service and so
The Little Lion Man says,
Actually, there is…
Please lend us your ears.
The Hollow-men say they would happily lend them their ears, but they don't know what good it would do them for in the Underworld, nobody listens
Everyone chit-chatters
It's cacophony, it's chaos
And no one hears for they close their ears
And there are none so blind as those who will not see

But the Little Lion Man looks them in their deep sad eyes and says
'You can be, our ears and our eyes, for we need to know, the lay of this land.
We are strangers in these parts, and we are frightened.
I am a Lion and yet even I
Am easy prey!'
'We are lambs
Before wolves
We are doves
Before danger…'
(The Humming Bird nods and shakes her beak
To acknowledge this comment and Crispy Duck
Agrees)
'We know only one thing,'
Says the Lion Man
'We are here for a reason,
But we know not what or why!
Please tell us about this place,
So we can comply?'
The Hollow-men say
'Sit down, we'll explain why.'
So in awe and angst
The Little Odds sit
Cross-legged, those that can
Wide-eyed and frightened
And the Friendly Farmer and
The Runaway link arms and the
Young Bucks feels oddly protective of
This pair, and in his pocket, Vermin quivers
But the Young Buck whispers
'Be calm.'
Puzzled, Crispy, Fantabulous and the Humming Bird
Hover close, while Gurney Cat, links paws with the
Lion Man. She appears to have grown in stature, as if
She is a lioness in disguise.
The Hollow-men seem
More relaxed now and say

'Welcome to this introductory course
To the Underworld. Please listen very carefully
For everything we tell you will come in useful at some stage.'
'There is nothing about the Underworld that should come as a surprise
We have been here, oh, how long! Ha, more of your Earth years than we care
To remember… chuckle, chortle.'
(They seem to have grown in stature, to have taken on a new mantle,
to have some sense of purpose)
'So I am Dim, and this is Dumb and on Earth
We had a sense of purpose, but that's another story for another day
I did Dim things, and he did Dumb things and somehow we ended up
In the same place—haha, hoho
So welcome, to this introductory course to the Underworld
Did we say that already?'
The Little Odds nod
'Ah, then let us begin.'
'The first thing you need to know about the Underworld
Is that it is very, very, dangerous, there are dark places and…'
'Excuse me,' says the Lion Man
'Can you cut to the chase, we get the gist…'
'Ah yes,' says Dim,
'Of course,' says Dumb and
The Little Odds liked them better
Out of character, when they were the Hollow-men
More true to form.
'We just want to know the bones, the bare facts,'
Says the Lion Man, who has really found his voice now
Some confidence, no longer suffers fools, for too long
He suffered, tolerated fools
And the last thing he needs in the Underworld
Is training for beginners, 'so help me God.'
'So tell us
Who's who
What's what
Where's where
And how's how

Just stick to the facts,
Please and thank you!'
'Ah,' say the Hollow-men
In unison, and this is getting tiresome now
'We need to confer…' and so they go
Talk among themselves and the Lion Man
Is getting impatient and angry for one so calm
And patient most of the time, and he says
'I hope you are not taking the minx out of us
For we are fools for no one'
And then he roars
This big Lion Roar
That shakes the Pits of Despair
And there are cries and wails and
The Hollow-men say
'No, no, no, so sorry—so sorry'
We just instinctively slipped back into character
Ha ha as if we were back on Earth and all we were missing
Were the suits and shoes, we just got carried away, for we had this thing
Called information, and we knew that that was the very thing
That you needed, and we were going to see what we could get out of you in exchange
And now we know that was wrong, and we will never get out of the Pits of Despair
Unless we see the error of our ways, and you'd think we'd have learned by now
But we thought we could make a quick buck out of the knowledge economy
Isn't that what they say, I have information
You need information
You pay—but we sold our souls
And now we pay but did we learn
The errors of our ways
And they get confused and angry
With themselves, for all this time they've been here
You'd think they'd have learned something
Some wisdom from their mistakes
And the Little Odds looks at them funny

And wonder why
They'd want to stay
In the Pits of Despair!

***

Chapter Four
The Hollow-men

Around the Underworld

'Shame!
Shame on us!'
Shout the Hollow-men
At each other,
'Look how easy
We slipped back into character!'
'Have we learned nothing from this place!'
And they agree, to put their necks on the line
For that's what they did in their places of business
Day after day, for no pay worth mentioning in the Underworld
For they'd sold their souls years hence;
They confer
And agree they have nothing left to lose
But to show the Little Odds around the Underworld
So they can see, with their own eyes, and hear with their own ears
Just how ugly
It is.
In reality
For on Earth
The Hollow-men lived
An illusion in the Underworld
They live, in reality, and if they'd only known
It would be like this,
They were consumed
In consumerism

Until it burnt them out
And now they are consumed
In this!
Why didn't any body tell them?
(Excuse me, but they did
You chose not to listen!)

***

So the first thing the Little Odds
Need to know about the Underworld is this:
The Underlies, are the Underlies
They patrol this place, there are Underlies
Everywhere
And their specialist subject is
Lies
The Underworld is ruled
With an iron rod of Lies
Lies are the currency
They call squiggles
Same as upon Earth
It's just a turn of phrase
And for once, the Little Odd
Understands
Underlies = squiggles
And Underlies are often
Under-written by those who do something
Called underwriting which is usually just more
Underlies, for Greed and Gluttony's sake
Greed and Gluttony are the High Lords of the Underworld
No, that's a poor turn of phrase, they are the low lords of the Underworld
But they dictate everything that happens, from below and
They have been given iron rods, to rule, and have got away with it for far too long
And every time, they are challenged, they lift those iron rods, with Ferocity

Who is their great black dog with the vicious teeth, and he wields his dark power
In a way, the good cannot be comprehended;
They are given strength by the Underlies—
The Underlies, who are charged with spreading
Their lies and wanton damage, their danger
And although the Underlies are just pawns in their game
They want to please Greed and Gluttony and their friends
Lust and Pride come before a fall, so they bolster her up
And tell her she's this and that and the other for she is a shallow sort
She is needy and greedy and full of her own importance, and they laugh at her
But need her all the same for she is very influential in her own way, Pride
And she can't do her dirty work without her sibling, Lust for they walk this way
Hand in hand.

***

'Beware the Underlies,
They lurk in every corner of this place
They cannot be trusted, they dress themselves
In grace'
'See through them
Transparent, ignorant
But they try to be nice
They prey on victims of vice
But we've been told
Your hearts are pure
Which is why you were hand-picked
To grace this place, and we bow, before you.'
The Little Odds look at each other funny
They think this is all a bit weird.
Crispy Duck says
She has had enough
'Can we go now, can we go now?'
But they say, 'No, shhh, listen up.'

‘Your greatest challenge,’
Say the Hollow-men, ‘is the Queen
Of the Underlies,
She has a Lackey
Who bows to her every whim
But he can sink or swim, she is the one
You need to overcome!’

***

The Little Odds are very worried
About venturing into the Underworld alone
But the Hollow-men say, ‘We will be your guides
For we have nothing left to lose, you see above
We gave it all away, for avarice and the way
We lived each day, for we lived each day
With Greed and Lust and Pride, and shame on us!’
‘And when we came to this place, the Queen of the Underlies laughed
And said we were her’s forever and a day but when you arrived, well
We saw a glimmer of hope, there is a chance of redemption…’
‘So says the Young Buck, will you be our guides from a pure heart or from selfishness,
Your chance at redemption, are you using us for your own ends?’
The Hollow-men look at each other and say
‘Good question,’ which makes the Young Buck feel good;
‘You are right, on both counts, and well done, for your wisdom.’
The Little Odds confer for a moment and agree, they need the Hollow-men
On their side, by their side, for they have nothing left to lose
Having lost it all and if they can be reunited with their families and children
Then surely that is a good thing to be condoned?
So they say to the Hollow-men, please, be our guides;
Even though they know, your conscience should always be your guide.
The Hollow-men confer and agree
The best thing for starters, is a tour of the city
For at its core, is the castle of the Queen of the Underlies
And surely, that is where they are meant to be?

'Why?'
Says the Little Odd
For it is frightened of this
Ugly queen thing and what it might mean;
'Well now,' say the Hollow-men
For they speak in unison as if they are conjoined
The truth is this… one day, an angel, a being of light
Infiltrated the Underworld and no one knew how she did it
But she came into the Pits of Despair and said she brought us a message
Of Hope, 'that one day a group of strange creatures would arrive out of the blue
And liberate you,' and we didn't understand for it made no sense to see a figure of light
In this dark place, but she laughed and said, 'You'll know them when you see them,
For they are a complete mess!'
And then she left,
Us in Hope!
'Despite, the Pits of Despair.'
The Little Odds look at each other
And wonder, what's going on?
Then the Hollow-men say
'Today is a so-called holiday
In the Underworld, which means
The great and the good get to party
And we underlings get to serve them
Again, so it's a break only for them;
'But the good thing is, most of the Underlies
Are off duty, so we can show you around, without
As much fear as is the norm; for fear is normality here.'
'What do Underlies look like?'
Asks the Little Odd.
'Ah,' say the Hollow-men
'they look like nothing on Earth
Even though they haunt the Earth;
They take on whatever shape or guise suits
The moment of their evil deeds, but down here

They can shed their guise, they look like
Evil pixies, and gremlins and sprites;
They loiter and linger, and spread their lies.
They love to gossip and guffaw and giggle, despised.'
'Oh,' says the Little Odd
Feeling somewhat out of its depth.
'So,' says the Little Odd
'where do we go from here?'
'First,' say the Hollow-men
'We want to show you this thing they call sport;
So you can get an insight into these beings;
Then tomorrow, we will take you to the Castle of the Queen
Of the Underlies so you can infiltrate, you see you are here
To rescue the keys…'
'What keys?'
Asks the Little Odd
Innocently.
'Oh my…'
Say the Hollow-men in unison
'The three keys!
Didn't anyone tell you?'
'No,' says the Little Odd,
Innocently.
'The Three Keys are this:
to the Pits of Despair
the key to our hearts
and the key to happiness!
Didn't you know?'
'No,' says the Little Odd
And it looks at its misshapen feet things
And wonders, why nobody said.
'Why—the angel said!'
Say the Hollow-men
But the Little Odd feels lost and alone
For it is frightened, that it is not strong enough
Or bold enough to deliver, for the Queen of the Underlies

Sounds like a nasty piece of work!
And in that moment—the Little Odd realises
That they see it as the Beacon of Hope and in that moment
The Little Odd realises it is not sure it can cope,
With the weight, it feels on its shoulder right now
And instinctively the Little Odds understand and say
'Together we stand.' But the Little Odd fears, it may fall
For it feels weak and tired and ill and the Little Odd wonders
If it can go on, then falls, to the ground, and cries. Big deep guldering
Cries; and in that moment, the Little Odd feels more alone and more frightened
Than it has ever felt before, and in that moment, the Little Odd feels
In the Pits of Despair and in that moment, there are friends who stand by
And know not what to do, but say, 'o'
'Little Odd, we are with you'
But the Little Odd is consumed
With fear and loneliness and
Wants with all its heart and soul
To feel the arms of its mummy and daddy
So far away, and the Little Odd cries, aloud
'Mummy, Daddy, where are you?'
But it gets no answer.

***

The Little Odd
Has never felt so alone
And lost in all the world.
The Little Odd is afraid it might die
In this godforsaken place, the Little Odd
Aches, with all its body and soul and no one
Can reach it here.
The Little Odd fears
It has got
Stuck
In the Pits of Despair
Forever and a day

The Little Odd
Can see no way out
And is going to have to take on
The Queen of the Underlies
And she is
A nasty piece of work!

***

Chapter Five
A Nasty Day Out in the Underworld and Watching the Queen of the Underlies

AT WORK
REST
LUNCH
AND
PLAY

(So they know what they are up against)
'The first rule of business'
Say the Hollow-men
'Is keep your enemies close.'
'Why?' asks the Little Odd
'Is that a turn of phrase?'
'No,' say the Hollow-men
'It is a fact of life.'
'Oh,' says the Little Odd
'I think that's a shame!'
(for it is beginning to find its voice;
The Little Odd, at last, beginning to find
Its way in this world, this horrid Underworld)
'Yes, indeed,'
Say the Hollow-men
'It is a crying shame, but
It is a lesson we had to learn.'
'Why?'
Asks the Little Odd

But the Hollow-men say
'Let us show you, by actions
Rather than words, let us take you
Deeper into the Underworld.'

***

'Do you have a map?'
Asks the Little Odd
'Is there a Visitor Information Centre perhaps?'
The Hollow-men exchange glances
And for the first time, they smile and
For the first time, they recall, how that feels and say
'No, Little Odd, you have to find out for yourself as you go along';
And this way they speak in unison, freaks them out, the Little Odds
But they are eager to learn, for it might be a case, of life or death.
'Let us explain the lay of this land,
For it is complicated and confusing
Nothing in the Underworld
Is straightforward and nothing
Is quite as it seems, so beware!'
'Please,' says the Young Buck
'Explain, for we can see
This is a place of extreme
Pain.'
'Full marks for Observation Young man
Let us explain—the Underworld
Is divided into two
As you would expect
And within the division
Are many different sects
Sections, we mean, sections
For they like to divide everything up
Into sections, The Government of the Underworld
Is obsessed with sections and labels and everyone has to wear a label
You are either a this or a that and within the "this" and the "that"

They will label you as one thing or another; so there are scales
That do not balance, for in the Underworld, nothing adds up;
They get the sums all wrong, which is what's missing most:
The beauty of the universe, where the sums make sense
And everything adds up but it is out of balance now
For the Underworld has got a grip, and is causing chaos
For that is what it does best.'
'Pain and Panic
Chaos and confrontation
No peace or harmony
No love, or affection just
Emptiness.'
'Oh,' says the Little Odd
'That's really hard for up where I live
On Cloud Ninety-Nine-a-Hundred, there is harmony'
'There is music, and this thing called honesty
There is friendship and love and peace, hollow-man
I mean, men.'
'We are not men
Little Odd, we are forsaken
Of that name, we are the Hollow-men
You can bank on that,' and with that, they look at each other
And sigh.
'So we must be discreet
Here, look, a dandy sandy patch
By the river, hidden by thorn bushes
Let us all go, so we can sketch out the Underworld for you
It is very confusing, so try not to get lost, for at Lost and Found
They just laugh at you, believe us, we tried!'
So the Little Odds follow the Hollow-men
To a place of discretion, beneath the thorn trees
Where no one can see but the first thing the Hollow-men
Need to tell them about the Underworld, is that nothing goes unseen
There are Underlies, everywhere, there are Underlies reporting back right now
Even those not on duty, for it is their way, to cause pain and panic and chaos
Their obsession with gossip!

'Right, it's like this—
Here is the river, brown and swollen
Dirty and deserted, except for the spectres
That shadow the banks, oh yes, the banks'
'They control everything here,
Or like to think it so but the real power
Is the Queen, of the Underlies, she is obscene!
She is rarely seen, for she likes to keep her Royal Ugliness
Under wraps, except when she has to address the whole scene
And work the room, they say you should see her work the room!
Dis-grace, all glammed up to the ninety-nines, smiling, assassin!'
The Hollow-men look at each other and say
'We have said too much, we are dead meat anyway
The Underlies have heard and are on their way, to alert
Goody-two-thousand-shoes, aka, Queen of the Underlies
That you are on your way…'
'She's been expecting you.'
'What will we do?'
Asks the Friendly Farmer
'For we need to protect ourselves
And each other? Tell us what we need to know?'
The Hollow-men look at each other and say
'We'll keep you to this side of the River, for over there
Is Despair, you really, don't want to go there.
'We will take you to the race track, where they exorcise their sport;
Then to the Castle of Catastrophe, the residence of the Queen of the Underlies
For that is where you will find her there.
Be strong, be wise, be vigilant;
So let us go then, you and I
To the horror, Hallow'een,
Celebrations, annual Bank Holiday
When the bank staff, get a day off, but it's obligatory
To attend the whips and saddles.'
'Come—follow us
We will show you how
To lurk in the shadows and

Observe, for they say, this is what they deserve
These poor animals.'
They stay close, to the thorn bushes
As told, by the Hollow-men and weeds and roots
Rise up and try to trip them up
They follow, the Hollow-men
And up above, drifts the hummingbird
In silence, and the Gurney Cat has been quiet of late
For she was told to hold her tongue, just in case,
The Puzzled Penguin shivers for it has never been in a place so cold
While everyone else says, it's roasting, and they say, perhaps, it has the fever!
The Young Buck puts his hand in his pocket to check that Vermin is safe
And he wraps his little paws, around his finger, there, there you are friend!
'Shhh, hold tight, you are safe and well and undiscovered. Let's keep it that way.'
He says.
Mother and daughter huddle tight, for it is pitch black night;
Then the Hollow-men know where there is a gap
In the barbed wire where they can snuck in and watch
So they do, silence ensues.

HEREWITH THE SPORT FOR THE *BANK* HOLIDAY
IN THE UNDERWORLD

First up
The greyhounds
The poor souls, barred
From the performance up above
The Under-achievers, and shame on them
So they let them loose, from their cages
And the stadium goes into an uproar
Chase after chase after chase
Poor bunny rabbits and their thoughts
Are turned to the Great White Rabbit and his cold body
Wrapped in rags, in a cave, far far away, for that's how it seems
Though it might only be a stone's throw away for everything is not as it seems

In the Underworld.
When the poor skinny sad greyhounds
Are done and dusted and sent for
Incarceration, on account of under-performance
They are locked up in a pound, and the value of the pound is low
Which makes it even worse for the Banks, that control this place
Are out of control and it's all about control, everything is about
Control.
So they need escape goats, and they lash out
At the greyhounds, lean and sore and hungry
To kill white rabbits
Next,
The Escape Goats come, let out of their pens
And everyone is encouraged, members of the audience
To lift the whips, supplied on the way in, the workers:
The scum of this place, to exorcise their frustrations
On the Escaped Goats who run this way and that
For from the stadium, they flick their long whips
Lick-lashing tongues, tongue whipped, get a move on
I have a bet on you; stupid ugly things and up in the special box
The Queen of the Underlies, sips champagne and says
Aren't they amazing? The way they run this way and that
Please, when it's all over give them a cake, here look,
I keep some under my hat
For the Queens of the Underlies
Is obsessed with hats, she makes them
From scratch, from felt, and she makes them mad
And obscene for her greatest desire to be seen and for everyone to say
Did you see that hat?
Where did she get that hat?
So she can say, I made it from scratch
And they will say what a wonderful creature is she
Look! Look! How she works the room!
(Where did she leave her broom, giggle the Little Odds)
Look, look, step aside, give her room, to breathe
(and the Little Odds begin to see the

And think her the most disgusting creature
They have ever seen).

***

Next up
Says a voice
And oh no, how did he get here?
It is the Ringmaster! Roll up roll up
He chants and flicks his whip and says
Next up after the stupid escape goats is the
Wonky Donkey Derby—place your bets here
Bankers, call yourselves bankers, where are you?
Roll up, roll up silly siblings of the great and mighty
Show your worth, place your squiggles here
For the Ringmaster is obsessed with squiggles
But how did he get here, to torment them?
And one by one
The sad and tattered donkeys
Take their place and one by one
He whips them just for fun
And the crowd, roars,
Shame on them
Bank holiday
Is not the same
Without a whip and a
Thump for fear they forget the game

***

The Little Odds, watch in disgust and horror
And then realise, the worst is yet to come,
For the donkeys fall at the first hurdle and succumb
To the harassment of the crowd, and then
And Ringmaster takes to the stage and asks
If they are enjoying the entertainment and the stadium

Erupts
He says
The best is yet to come
Hold on to your hats and with that
The chariots line up, and this is the Pinnacle
Of the Bank Holiday entertainment and shame on them
As the horses, disturbed and distressed
Line up at the mercy of the chariots behind them
And the crowd bays and the Underlies say
Isn't this just the greatest day, ever
And so the Ringmaster flicks his whip and says
They're off!
And one by one
The chariots whip each other
Just for fun, for entertainment and
One by one, they fall, to the wayside
For entertainment and the Queen of the Underlies
Thinks this the greatest sport ever, sips champagne and says
Isn't it great, to see the Underlies have a day out and try to copy
My expertise in hats! Guffaw, guffaw!
And she takes great delight in seeing all that
Poor creatures in pain, such delight and no fright
And she scans the crowd for signs of weakness
Eagle eyes, no place for weakness in the Underworld
Anyone showing a glimmer of light will be assigned
To the Pits of Despair, East of Eden.
Shame
Shame on them
Stupid squiggle pushers
And why won't they see
The way they are being used
Blind, leading the blind.
And when all is said and done
She says, what a wonderful day
Let's go home to bed!
For tomorrow is another day

And frankly my dear, I don’t give a damn
That the Little Odds have arrived for all I care
They are here to stay.
I have them in my grip
For I am all-powerful
I am
The Queen of the
Underlies
And, with that, she rattles off
One ugly whiff of laughter,
Cackle, insane.

Chapter Six
The Little Odds Enter the Castle of Catastrophe

And Find a Lackey There

'What will we do now?' whispers the Little Odd to the Hollow-men.
'We stay hidden here until the stadium is silent, then we will follow to the Castle of Catastrophe, for tomorrow, you will find a way in.'
They all huddle silently in the hollow where they hid
Security shines a light their way, 'There's something there!'
Shouts one but the other says, 'It might be Underlies,
Getting up to mischief, just ignore them, the sooner we get home.'
'Lucky you have a home to go to,' sarks security one.
'I don't, it was just a turn of phrase,' sighs security two
And they disappear into the night and lock, the stadium doors.
The Little Odds can hear
Whimpers and cries of pain
The poor animals have been cruelly,
Without dignity, thrown into a black hole
To fester there,
Some skinny greyhounds hang dead,
By their hind legs,
The donkeys lick their wounds;
The Escape Goats, are too tired and beaten
To even try to escape and the poor horses
Just hang their heads in shame, defeated, in despair
The Little Odds are upset
They cry, they offer help
But the poor creatures say
What can you do?

The Little Odds say
They have to go to the Castle of Catastrophe
But when they've finished there, they will come back to set them free;
And the animals say, 'That would be lovely,' and sigh, for they know
That there is little hope, by tomorrow, they will be cleared away
To make room, for the next show,
When the Ringmaster shouts
Roll Up, Roll Up!

***

In the dark, dark night
The Hollow-men show the way
To the Castle of Catastrophe
And they can see its opulent grandeur
In the middle of a lake of sulphur
That bubbles, and crocks in the night
Huge amphibians, eyes above water,
Are guards of the hubble bubble
They feel the eyes of the Underlies on them
The ever-watchful screwed-up hardened little pixie eyes
Of deceit and delight in it, and by the bridge, are three witches
Stirring a cauldron, toil and trouble—the giant frogs are scared of them
For they know the witches are preparing for their brew
And that means, three frogs, will turn into stew
But the witches are busy arguing, they start to fight
The amphibians take fright and dart underwater
Then the Hollow-men say, 'Quick, fast, this is our chance
When they are all distracted, let's advance.'
And fast as a flash, before they even have time to think about it
The Little Odds dart across the bridge, and huddle and hide on the other side
Just in time to hear the roar of the troll, thunder,
'Who's that trip-trapping across my bridge?'
Roar, and roar, like thunder and that will alert, the frogs and witches,
The Hollow-men say quick, here's a drain that will take us to the sewers
And one by one, they jump in as if their Little Odd lives depended on it!
Well, it did!

It stinks down there
Of sulphur and ammonia and other nasty things.
They all want to be sick, then they realise they haven't eaten for days
How would you have a stomach for food in a place like this?
And it would only be junk anyway!
They will have to find a way out
Pronto!
Poor little Vermin peeps his head out
And says he always wanted to visit a sewer
But now he's here, it's not what they built it up to be
'Anti-climax,' he says, 'not what I expected at all.'
And with that, he reckons, it's best to keep his head down.
The Hollow-men say, 'This way, follow us.'
As if they know, turns out they don't
And the Little Odds go deeper and deeper into the sewers
Until they see a sign, that says, Dungeons.
'That might be our way in,' say the Hollow-men
As they grin.
There is a large black cast iron gate
It should be locked, but it's not
Some security man's lapse on account
Of the Bank Holiday, perhaps
Are they prepared for what they see within?
It isn't pretty; it stinks, black goo slimes down the walls
There are the bodies, of Underlies, scattered
And swept up by trolls,
It is the darkest of the dark and no one
Should ever see a place like this,
Strangely no one seems to notice them
As they slip through, and up twirled stairs
Round and round and round, like ghosts in the night
They tread, until they come to what looks like a large pantry
And there is a fat cook and a tall skinny butler, asleep, their heads
On the huge wooden table, they snore and snort, before caskets
Of green beer and other goo,
The stench of rotting flesh… and the Little Odds

Have to cover their mouths, to avoid a belch
The Little Odds, tip-toe through the pantry
And slip out the door, and before them they see
This huge marble hall, all fancy
On one side is a rail
Of fancy coats, on the other a rail
Of the most ridiculous hats
And for a moment, the Little Odds forget themselves
Forget where they are and giggle, as they dress up in gowns and hats
And parade around the hall, making fun of this charade, and giggling at how
Ridiculous each other looks, and for thesecond time, the Hollow-men smile
For they had forgotten what it was like to be a child and to play dressing-up games.
They keep a watchful eye
They know this is not wise
So they say, 'Hey, Little Odds,
Put that stuff back, we need
To be vigilant and take care.'
'Look, inside there!'
They indicate behind the two large black iron doors, locked
'There is a huge banquet going on, sssshh, listen…'
And the Little Odds, stop, look, listen
They can hear, ridiculous laughter,
They can hear, this horrendous noise
This banging and clattering make no sense
That couldn't be described as music, there is no melody,
Just insanity, no rhyme or reason, just cacophony!
'What should be done?' asks the Little Odd
'I'd love to see what they're up to
Behind closed doors.'
The Hollow-men say it would be too dicey
They might be gambling;
But the Little Odds say,
We have to do something!
The Hollow-men look at each other and shrug
Then, in unison, they say;

'Okay
We guess
If we were gambling men
Which we are for we toiled in city banks
That if we can slip up the stairs, there is bound to be a way in
For they are sure to have a balcony in the Castle of Catastrophe
For the Top Hats and the Hob Nobs love nothing more than an audience!'
'Let's slip upstairs and see what we can find,
Some nook or crannie.'
So the Little Odds,
Slip quiet as little mice
Up the stairs and the carpets
Are so thick, they sink into their knees
But at least it means no one can hear
Footsteps.
And they giggle at the portraits
Of all the ugly people, in the huge
Gold-gilded frames, and wonder why
You'd want to hang such ugly paintings
And why are they all upside down?
They find a nook and a cranny
One by one, silently, they squeeze through
The smallest through the nook, the bigger through the cranny
And then they are on the other side;
And can see, what's going on
From a great height, and there is not another soul in sight
Up here, for the Underlies have been banished for the night.
And they don't have souls anyway, in fact, the Little Odds
Are the only souls worth mentioning.
Down below,
Is one godforsaken almighty banquet…
There are pigs on spits and fires and
It seems, there is a masked ball, to cover up
Their ugliness, or maybe, that's just the way they look
And sitting on her throne
Is the Queen of the Underlies

To her left, the Lackey
A great big stupid-looking black dog
Jaws dripping, slabbering over a bone
And to her right, is the Ringmaster
Lording it over everyone, and he looks
Even uglier and even scarier than before
For she has got him in her grasp, and given him his place
At her right side which was what he wanted all along
And to her left, she lifts her leg and kicks the stupid big black dog
And makes him lame; it yelps and says, 'Thank you, Queen of the Underlies,
Just let me be your loyal Royal Lackey.'
The Little Odds watch them all from afar
Aghast, and afraid, very afraid for tomorrow
When they have to take them on
So tonight, they must prepare
For battle yet they don't have a clue,
what to do?
As the night goes on
They watch the guests
Slump into a drunken slumber
Bodies all over the tables and chairs and floor
And up on the stage, the Lackey and Ringmaster
And Queen of the Underlies slumps, as if they are no more.
The banquet is over, and tomorrow, who will clean up?
Well, the Underlies, of course, whisper the Hollow-men
'That's why they exist, to do the dirty work.'
The Little Odds huddle in a corner
And try to get some sleep, but the Runaway
Cuddles into her mother and asks,
'Mummy, you are such a lovely lady,
How did the Ringmaster get to be my dad?'
And the Friendly Farmer sighs and says
'He used to be a very nice man, a very, very nice man
He had the loveliest smile that went from ear to ear
And he had a warm heart and a nice face and was kind and dear,
And when he was like that, he became your dad, but sadly, he met the

Queen of the Underlies one day, and she twisted his mind and strangled his heart
And stole his soul, which she said, she'd come back to reclaim one day, and sadly
She did, and it breaks my heart, to see him like this for he was not a bad man;
Just a stupid and misguided one. But rest assured, when he was nice,
He was very, very nice
But when he turned bad
He grew wicked.'
And they both cry
For what seems like
Forever and a day
And in the silence of the dawn
If the Underworld has a dawn
The lesser darkness, it would be known;
It dawns on them, that the Little Odd is not what he used to be;
His vibrant rainbow colours have disappeared, and now, he is all
Shades of grey,
Fades to grey, and they worry
For the Little Odd, looks very sad
Very sad and lonely, and they try to talk to it
But the Little Odd appears to be in some far out place;
And big blobby tears run down its face
It says it would like to be in a different place;
Far, far away, on Ninety-Nine-a-Hundred
For it is afraid, it is very afraid.
The Little Odd
Wept;
While they slept.

Chapter Seven
The Little Odds Search for the Lost Keys

In the ache of the night
One by one, the Little Odds
Fall asleep for they are exhausted
And that's understandable.
They have been awake for days
And had no food, not a bite passed
Their lips,
The Little Odd sighs,
As it looks over the balcony
At the chaos down below.
'Oh Mummy and Daddy;
I just want to go home;
Please, what do I have to do
To get back to Ninety-nine-a-hundred?'
Then out of the blue
In the dark of the darkest of nights
It dawns on the Little Odd—
That strange dream, that comes to mind
Now that it thinks of it, just before it fell to Earth
It went something like this:

The Little Odd is lost and lonely
In a very dark place then there is sunlight
And a nice kind lady guides the Little Odd into a room
And shows it a desk, a very fine and fancy desk
Then she takes a key and opens a drawer and inside

Are three keys lying side by side, and she says
Pick a key
Any key.
The next thing the Little Odd remembers
It has fallen to Earth and that seems like a lifetime ago.

The Little Odd casts its tired and weary eyes
Over its friends and smiles, at how unlikely it was
It would gather together this motley crew
Of misfits and undesirables and the Little Odd
Looks at them as they sleep, exhausted, stir from time to time
Safe in the knowledge that it is watching over them, for the Little Odd
Doesn't need much sleep.
It sighs, in love and admiration at
The Runaway, her beauty, unknown and undiscovered
At the Gurney Cat and Vermin, cuddled in together, and who'd have imagined that;
Beside the Young Buck, the Humming Bird in his lap;
The Friendly Farmer cradles her daughter and besides that
The Odd Couple—Fantabulous and Crispy Duck who appears
To have taken the Puzzled Penguin under her wing, like a prodigal child;
Then the Little Lion Man, slightly aloof, apart, but one of the gang
Sleeps with one eye open and catches the eye, of the Little Odd as if to say
You are not alone, I am with you.
The Little Odd counts, on his hand-paw things
There are only eleven, someone's missing
And he gets a pang of fear and pain and despair
For the Great White Rabbit isn't there
Yet it knows, he watches from afar.

***

The Little Lion Man stirs and silently says to the Little Odd
It will not be long until they start to stir down below
And the Underlies will creep out of the woodwork
When the Top Hats and Hob Nobs start to go;

We need to get ready, for what lies ahead
For we just do not know!'
The Little Lion Man
Has never seen the Little Odd
So sombre and so grown up
All shades of grey and it says;
Bowed head and lowered eyes
'You are right, Little Lion Man,
We need to get prepared.'
And down below
The greedy and the gluttonous
The bad and the ugly start to stir
And grrrr, for they are hung over and bad-tempered
But they don't want to disturb the Queen or the Ringmaster
So one by one they leave the great big bad hall and one by one
They gather their great big coats and their ugly hats and their emptiness
And leave this godforsaken place
As the skinny butler says
'Get the hell out of here
You have overstayed your welcome!
Have you no homes to go to?'
But they are too proud to admit
That they have no homes to go to
Forsaken long ago.
And one by one they realise
In their drunken stupor, they left their winnings behind
Their precious squiggles, all the precious squiggles are tied up inside
They protest but the skinny butler says
Tough!
Too late,
No re-admittance,
Step outside.

***

They have no choice but to leave
Without their ill-gotten gains
For they would not want
To annoy the Queen of the Underlies
Swift to anger and not known to forgive;
'Finders keepers,' she cries, as she takes another
Swig.
There she is stirring, swigging, trying to jig
But she's all over the place, shame on her.
And she takes a tumble, back onto her throne
And snores, like thunder;
Falls back into deep and drunken slumber.
Then the Little Odd sees
The glint of a key;
Around her neck
On a noose of leather;
And instinctively the Little Odd knows
That is the key to the Three Keys!
'Look Little Lion Man!' whispers the Little Odd
'Do you see, that key around her neck?'
That is the reason we are here, but it is not the key
It is the key to The Three Keys, it came to me
Last night, in a memory.
'Somehow, we have to get that key
It is our way out of here!'
(Turns out it is a spare)
'I see,' says the Little Lion Man pensively
For indeed he did see, for he is all grown up now
Almost eighteen in Lion Man Years;
Then it dawns on him
The only option is to ask Vermin
Who will be accepted here, to slip up
And around her neck and try to steal the key!
Then they will have to find, the drawer and the secret
To discovery—some way out of here! (There must be some way out of here)!
So the Little Lion Man silently wakes the Young Buck

And they talk and the Young Buck nods and gently takes Vermin
From his pocket and the three explain to him, what he has to do;
Vermin nods and listens very carefully
For he will hear this only once, and
Knows, his life depends on it;
They will have to pick their moment
But they will have to act soon
Before it's too late and No!
It's too late!
There is this almighty alarm!
It wakes the cobwebs up
This great big blaring siren!
The Underlies scuttle around the Big Bad Hall
Clearing up the mess, but the Queen of the Underlies
Has risen and Oh my! She looks like a mess! Her hair stands on end
Her face is that of an old hag, the make-up drowns her cheeks
Her propped-up lips, have drooped, and how dare they see her this way!
The Ringmaster and the Lackey, are still asleep but start to stir and before they see her
She darts off to her chamber, screaming and screeching in tones, beyond the siren.
So they missed the moment and maybe that was how it was meant to be!
The Little Odds stay silent and sullen on the balcony, as the Ringmaster and Lackey
Stir and grrr at each other, the Big Black Dog bares its dripping lips,
At the Ringmaster who flicks his whip, in one almighty flip
And brings it down on the jaws of the dog.
Yelps,
Goes off
Stage left
To lick its lips
And wounds and says
'Growl, you'll regret that
Ringmaster, my day will come!
For every dog has its day,
And hey, I'll do it my way.'

'Is that a threat?'
Says the Ringmaster
Petulant, as he tosses the whip
Above his evil head, and the Lackey says
'You can bet on it!'

***

The Underlies scurry off
Sensing a fight, and they've gossip to spread
Lies and terror and fear;
Some stay behind
For the fight, but the Ringmaster
And the Lackey are too tired and too devious
To do it here, so they scuttle off, to lick their wounds
And think through their stratagem—
The dog says, I will win for I have teeth and strength
The Ringmaster says, I will win for I am devious and have
A whip
I am the chief whip
I can do whatever damage I want
I will displace the Queen of the Underlies
And her stupid pup and then I will rule
The Underworld, with a rod of iron!
And, with that, he cackles and exits
Stage right.

***

The Friendly Farmer has been watching from afar
And says, 'Looks like we have a fight on our hands;
But don't worry, I know his ways, he is not all bad;
There is a glimmer of hope.'
Then the Little Odds realise
They are all alone in this place;
It is deserted now, so they can breathe

A sign of relief.
There is no daylight here,
Just shadows.
And the Little Odd
Is still, shades of grey.
It doesn't know what to say,
So stays, with its misshapen feet things
Curled up to its body and wraps
Its hand-paw-things, around itself
To keep warm, for it shivers
It is a cold castle, for Little Odds,
And all who enter here.
There is a second loud blasting siren
That seems to last forever and it's so loud
Even those Little Odds with no obvious ears
Cover them;
Until it dies down
And in the blink of an eye
They can see, a door at the end of the balcony
Has swung open?
What lies behind it, they wonder?
And where are the Three Keys
And how do they get the key
From around the neck of the Queen of the Underlies,
So that they can get out of here?

Chapter Eight
Secure the Key to the Three Keys

(But How Do They Get Out of Here?)

So the Bank Holiday is over
And the Little Odds slip through
The door on the balcony
And down below
Is a place of work
And misery
This huge factory
That stretches for as far as the eye can see
And they are making squiggles
For the Queen of the Underlies
Is obsessed with squiggles and in this place
This sad and forsaken place, devoid of humanity
The children and the women and the men make squiggles
For the powers that be
And shame
Shame on them!
No mystery
In all this pomp and ceremony!
Just hypocrisy
And how Just
Is that!
The Little Odd says
'Let's watch awhile.'
The Little Oddis silent and tired of it all
For it has grown weary

Of those who do not want to see
Where is the joy!
None, nada, empty
So from afar
The Little Odds watch
The Underlies and their Underlings
Make Squiggles for the Powers that be
And wonder at the sense of it all
But this obsession with squiggles
Is overwhelming and all they want
Is to keep the Queen of the Underlies
Happy.
Then crawling out of the woodwork—
As the less favoured Underlies
Toil and cause no trouble—
Comes the two chief whips!
Little Miss Skinny-Wiry-Hair and
Little Mister Skinny-Wiry-Hair
And they walk up and down the aisles
Like deadwood, skinny and wiry-haired, they
Lash their whips and complain to anyone who'll listen
About a moment sucked here and a moment sucked there
Like going to the toilet to get tissues, to wipe the tears away
'Back to work, back to work
What do you think this is?
Slacking on your employer's time!'
For they have no time, just eternity
In a place, devoid of humanity.
Shame
Shame on them
But they suck the workers dry
And one masquerades as a good guy
And one can't be bothered anymore, and she says
'I am corporate, and you are union
Don't matter, let's just flick our whips for we are one and the same,
When all is said and done, exist—to spread the misery, sans mercy

Ha ha ha ha! High-five!'
And down below
The rows
Of sad and forlorn
Squiggle makers just get on
With the job at hand for they have lost faith
In the employers and the unions they paid
To protect them and that is the saddest tragedy of all.

***

The Little Odd says
It breaks its heart to see
Workers are treated this way
Such exploitation
To make squiggles for
Those who deserve them least
And with that
They see whips cracked
Over the slackers with disregard
That they may have fallen ill!
'Nah, they are just slackers,'
Say Wiry and Wiry, for they have lost all
Goodwill.
Sold out
Sold souls
To the company store;
They cackle and bore.

***

The Little Odd goes pale and weak
And falls onto its feet and says
It just had a vision,
That key around her neck
Was just a spare, there is another

'Hidden down here! It is also
The key to her chamber!'
'So where is the key
To the three keys!'
Asks the Little Lion Man.
'It must be in the safe,'
Says the Friendly Farmer!
'But where is the safe?'
Says Puzzled?
'How will we open it?'
Says Gurney
And Vermin pops his head out
Of the Young Bucks Pocket
And says he knows a way,
'I can chew my way, through anything.'
And by sheer chance
They see a sign that says:
Safe
And even though they are anything but safe
They decide they have nothing to lose.
The safe is a big steel box, the size of a tardis
So they quietly, gingerly, slip their way over there
And hide behind it, so as not to be seen
And Vermin checks it out, for weak points
And hahaha! There's one, a little blip!
So he starts to chew and chew
Chew-chew, like a train in the night
And he keeps going, long-haul,
Chew-chew; chew-chew
Chew-chew-chew-chew
Chew-chew-chew-chew
Until he has nibbled away a hole
Big enough to squeeze in and so he goes
Into the safe in search of the key to the
Three keys.
The Little Odds

Huddle behind the safe
Waiting for Vermin to re-emerge
It seems, forever and a day has passed.
And the poor squiggle makers have not had a moment's rest
They can hear, the shop floor sounds and sighs of endless squiggle making
And the cracking of whips and cackles and cries.
Eventually
Vermin comes out
With the key, in his claws
There is a tag, that says
Lady's Chamber:
Queen of the Underlies.
And Vermin is pleased with himself
As he should be and the Little Odds
Pat him and pet him and say
Well done!
'What was it like in there?'
Asks the Young Buck
'Ugly and smelly and vile.
There are squiggles as far as my little beady eyes can see
And documents, all bound up in leather and pleading to be released;
Secrets and lies, and videotapes;
Spiders the size of seals;
Gagging clauses, and choking things;
Bats and twats and torture wheels
And things, I never want to see again.'
'Oh, poor Vermin,'
They all say.
'Let's get outta here,'
Says the Little Odd
Who has changed
Changed utterly
It has grown dark and dismal
For there is no joy and colour,
There is no Shining Light.

***

So they are all so busy
Doing nothing but making squiggles
That the Little Odds can slip back from whence they came
Unnoticed,
By some sheer miracle
They slip out back onto the balcony
Of the Great Hall, which is empty now
Silent and sullen, suffering, from the strains
Of the night before.
But now,
They need to find the chamber
And seek the keys, that linger there.
It doesn't take long
For they see these huge double doors
That say, 'Queen of the Underlies:
Do not disturb! Enter here, at Peril of your life.'
And the Little Odd knows
What do not disturb means
But is confused about
Who Peril is,
'Is she a friend, of the Queen of the Underlies?'
And the Friendly Farmer says;
'You could say that Peril is not nice;
It's a good idea, to avoid Peril at all costs.'
And the Little Odd looks into her Swirly eyes
And asks, 'Is she just a turn of phrase?'
And the Friendly Farmer says
'You could say that.'
Outside, the huge double doors
To the chamber of the Queen of the Underlies
Sleep two drunken guards—the Ringmaster to the Right
The big black dog, the Lackey, to the Left and even in its sleep
It growls and grrrrrs. And the Ringmaster tuts and grinds its teeth.
'How are we going to get past them?'
Asks the Runaway;
'There must be another way in!'

'Servants quarters'
Says the Little Lion Man
'We should go back down to the pantry
And hope the Butler and Cook are still in a drunken slumber
And slip past them and find a way, some back stairs or some other way
To the chamber'
They think this a good idea
They think the Little Lion Man
Shows such signs of wisdom and leadership
And consider, how he has grown in stature,
And grown a little lion beard.
So like thieves in the dawn
They slide against the walls
Down the stairs, of the great hallway
And back below to the basement
Where they see the Butler and the Cook
Asleep at the big wooden table, they grunt and snore
And the Little Odds, slip by, silently and there
are the back stairs
Behind the pantry!
Just like they thought there would be and so they
Gingerly,
Creep up the stairs
And see the door that says
Servant's Entrance:
'Chamber—Queen of the Underlies.'

***

The Little Lion Man
Takes the key and gingerly
Turns the lock, so silently and one by one
They slip into the room and though it's dark
And barely candle-lit they can look around
Fingers to lips
They stand and stare

For the Queen of the Underlies
Is asleep, upright in a chair,
Her head nods forward, and her crown has slipped
Dangles from her fingertips, pointed claws, and
Vermin has offered to look for the three keys
For he can flit here and there, silently and get into awkward places
Easily and can chew through anything, and there is a dresser, with a mirror and over the mirror
A curtain is drawn, so even the Queen of the Underlies, so vain, so ugly, can't see her reflection
She just lets everyone tell her she's lovely
for the Underworld is full of liars and thieves and brats and twats
And they just make it up as they go along.

16.11.11

Chapter Nine
Chamber of Doom and Beyond

The Blue Moon

Here's what they find out
In the Chamber of Doom
Gloom, and more gloom
No room, to breathe
No air, just fear, and stifled
Snores
But it's not snoring as we know it
It's like a machine, droning on and on and on
A noise, absurd!
The Little Odd
Nods
Knows instinctively
Where the keys are
For it remembers, the moment
In the dream, long ago and far, far away
On Ninety-Nine-A-Hundred, when it dreamed
Of a drawer and a lock and a woman's hand opened the drawer
And it saw three keys and thought it had to choose one but now it knows
What they are, and they must take all three, or they won't be able to get out of here
And the Little Odd, can't tell them yet what the keys are for in case the weight of the task engulfs them, and they crumble,
when they have all come this far, and so the Little Odd says
'Ludwig, Little Lion Man, give me the key'
And the Little Odd, grey and dull as can be

Walks bravely to the dressing table and inserts the key
In the drawer—as was prophesied in the dream
There are three keys
Laid out the way, it saw them
Gingerly
The Little Odd lifts each one
And places one in the paw
Of Ludwig, one in the pocket of the
Young Buck and one in the hand
Of the Friendly Farmer for safekeeping
And whispers that it will be explained later
When they are safe from this place.
The Little Odd says
'I fear, we are now in great danger
I fear, for Vermin, has anyone seen him?'
They look silently around the darkened room
And can hear only the drone, drone, drone,
Of the noise that comes from deep within
The Queen of the Underlies
And there is Vermin
Crawling around her neck
As if he has discovered something
So the Little Odd whispers
'Vermin, Vermin, don't go there!
Please, come away, into the Young Buck's pocket.'
But Vermin says, 'Look at the back of her neck,
How it lies open, disconnected from her head!
Look, Little Odd, look, she will not wake
For she is nothing but a mechanical fake!'
'I can see right into her, to the pit of her emptiness
Please, let me go in there and take a closer look!'
For they can all see now
That the Queen of the Underlies
Is nothing
But a mechanical fake!
A machine, of hate and destruction

And the Little Odd says
'Please, no Vermin, there is no time
We are all in great danger'
And with that
The Queen of the Underlies
Shakes, like a mechanical fake
Coming awake and Vermin
Loses his grip and falls into the pit
Of the Queen of the Underlies
Down to the bottom he tumbles and sees
The most wicked pixie, the ugliest troll and
The sickest sprite, and they are all at the controls
And the wicked pixie shrieks,
'We've got one, now they are all history!'
But Vermin is smarter than that and leaps
Like a grasshopper
Out of the gaping mechanical fake neck
Of the Queen of the Underlies and the troll
And the sprite stays at the controls, the CCTV
Cameras, and the wicked pixie leaps out
And chases Vermin, around the walls
Determined to catch, the dastardly creature
And the spiders, the huge spiders in their giant webs
That creep around the ceiling, reach out to catch Vermin with their legs
But he is too quick for them and the Little Odds, are frozen in fear and horror
Until they find the strength, to tackle the evil pixie, who catches Vermin
As he falls, from the walls and twists his neck and with one almighty crack
Vermin is dead and tossed, aimlessly in the air, and lands, miraculously
In the pocket of the Young Buck and now
They can hear, marching noises and know
That the sprite soldiers are mobilised
And coming their way, and they must
Get out of here, so they run, back the way they came
And into the dungeons which are the same as before and back
Out through the sewers where they find, the Hollow-men still waiting there
And now, there is no time to grieve

They must leave, they have the Three Keys
That's what they came for, even though
They didn't know it at the time and so
Where do they go
From here?
The Hollow-men have an idea
There is this place on the edge of the Underworld
Called the Pyramid of Protection, but you can only enter
Once in a Blue Moon, and they say, there is no other way out of here
But it's worth a try, for they heard, there was a blue moon nearby.
So the big tall gangly Hollow-men run
And after them the Little Odds, and the
Humming Bird, flies high, to show the way
With her gentle hum, so they can be followed by sound
For it's pitch black in the Forest of the Night
'Quick quick,' says the Young Buck
But Fantabulous, who is tired and in need of water
And Crispy who is tired and in need of water
And Puzzled, who is tired and in need of water
Find it hard to keep up
So the Hollow-men stop
And lift Fantabulous and Puzzled on their tall shoulders and
The Friendly Farmer takes Crispy under her wing, for no one gets left behind
No one;
You hear,
We need to get out
Of here!
Says Ludwig
Authoritatively and even
The Little Odd has grown tired
So Ludwig the Little Lion Man
Gives it a piggyback.
And behind,
They can hear
The thud thud marching
Of the Sprite soldiers and the sounds

Of distant drums and up in the deep
Are the pixies, cackling and creeping;
In the undergrowth are the trolls and
Ugly things, that reach out to trip them up
The zombies of the night, rising like dirt
From the undergrowth of the Underworld
And it doesn't get much darker than that
And now way up ahead, is an indigo glow
Quick say the Hollow-men, there is a blue moon
Once in a blue moon, there is a way out of this place
But legend has it, first, you have to find some way in
To the Pyramid of Protection and there it is, in all its majesty.
The Pyramid of Protection glows indigo blue, and there is the door -
But who has the key?
Ludwig tries,
No
They can hear
The sprite soldiers
March near
The Friendly Farmer tries
No, she is wrong key woman
Then the Young Buck steps forward
And tries, and no, none of the three keys fit
The sprite soldiers are almost there
The wicked pixies, flit here and there
The trolls, awkward and gross, creep out of the shadows
Then the Little Odd, grey and listless and tired and sad
Steps forward and says
'Young Buck, inside your pocket
Is our dead friend, and in his little claw
You will find clasped, the key from round her evil neck, for even
In death, he refused to let it go for the key
To the Chamber of Doom, is the same key
For the Pyramid of Protection, the only difference
Is love, for Vermin so loved his friends, that he gave his life
For them, and we are forever, indebted to his grace and wisdom and kindness.'

So the Young Buck takes Vermin's broken little rat body from his pocket and there
Still clasped tight in his little claw, is the key to the Pyramid of Protection and just
As the sprites are about to strangle them until they breathe their last,
The Young Buck, takes the key and the door, to the Pyramid of Protection swings open
And they all make it in just in time, even the Hollow-men and the door swings closed
and they lock it
Tight
And breathe
They breathe
Deep and long and
They laugh, they laugh
Long and loud and then they sigh
And collapse to the ground and cry
'Vermin, Vermin, you are the saviour
Of our world.'
And with that
Vermin bounces back to life!
Hurray,
Hurray
And Vermin
Is so happy
And so are all
The Little Odds
That they neglect to see
Inside the Pyramid of Protection
For they are filled with love and admiration
For the rat, that they said, spread only germs
Then
In a moment
Of majesty, they all stop
And stare, at the creature over there
It is a stag, a magic reindeer, so indigo blue

And it steps out, majestically from the edge and walks forward
Head held high and says,
'Hullo
I've been
Expecting you!'
'There has not been
A Blue Moon for a Hundred Million Light Years
So this is indeed a great occasion, you are welcome
Little Odds, but here, we know how much, you all
Want to go home, but I hope you realise, you have done
Great works but it's not over yet, there may be trouble ahead
But while there's blue moonlight and love and romance,
Let's face the music and dance.'
The Little Odds
Have been devoid
Of music and love and dance
For so long now, that they are delighted
To hear, that they can rejoice in here,
Safe and sound, such beautiful sounds
The Stag stands by and smiles, while the Little Odds
Dance and sing, full of joy and slowly, but surely
They see the shades of indigo blue come back into the Little Odd
To replace the grey and for the first time, since they hit the Underworld
They see
The Little Odd
Smile
And dance
And jump around
Then the Runaway says
Please show me your shiniest happiest smile
And he does, and she shows him hers
Then they jump up and down;
They all do, wearing their shiniest happiest smiles;
But the reindeer of indigo blue says
'Don't believe that all is right with the world
You still have work to do, but tonight, let's party!'

So they do
Until they grow tired
And even though, they are in the Pyramid
Of Protection, they need to sleep for it's been a long time coming
And tomorrow, they hope, they are heading home, for better or worse;
For richer or poorer,
In sickness or in health.
And one by one
As the Little Odds fall asleep
Until only the Little Odd watches them,
From afar, and even though it is indigo blue
And glows and is getting its true colours back
Hopefully, the indigo reindeer says, Little Odd
Let me explain, the secrets of the keys
And the Little Odd, says
'You don't need to
I know what they are
There are three of them
And my job is to turn them
Into truth for they are not just
A turn of phrase,
They are
The three keys of truth
For I am not, as stupid as I look!'
And the Little Odd looks the stag
In the eyes, and connects for they are one and the same
And will never be the same again, on account of the journey
But the indigo stag says,
'I understand that
You understand that, but
You still have to take on
The Dark Horse, you still have work to do?'
And the Little Odd understands, for it knows
That it is on a journey, and there are still hurdles
To be jumped, and they are still twenty thousand leagues
Under the sea and somehow, they have to get back to dry land!

(How the Blue Moon got down there, it doesn't understand!)
So the indigo stag says
There is a back door
To the Pyramid of Protection
And it is the one and only way out
Of the Underworld, and when they wake
He will show them the way
To where they will find the Blue Whale
For she is well again and ready for the journey
And it is her job, her joy to see you all safely home
But beware, of those that will still try to snare you Little Odds;
'Now Little Odd
You need to get some rest
I will watch over you, but be assured
You are safe and secure, here,
In the Pyramid of Protection.'
And with that the Little Odd
Yawned and the indigo reindeer
Lay down, and the Little Odd
Slept in the cradle of its wings.

Chapter Ten
The Little Odds Journey Home

But the Fight's Not Over Yet

As the Little Odds were taking some well-earned rest
Under the watchful eye of the great stag
The Little Odd has a very vivid dream.

It is standing at the edge of the Pits of Despair
But the screaming is not there, just the heat of the moment
And over there
One by one, the Hollow-men and women
Are hauling each other, one by one
Out of the Pits of Despair
Then they sit in a huge circle,
Silently as if waiting for some signal
Some ritual
Then out of the cave
Comes the Great White Rabbit
Surrounded in Light
He glides, floats
Like an angel in the night
To the centre of the circle
And sits there silently
He takes off his glasses
And wipes them with his kerchief
And smiles, sagely and says
It is his great pleasure
To be here, to see this moment

These souls saved from the Pits of Despair
For it broke his heart to see them languish there;
He says
Once in a blue moon
There is a way out of here
And two of your kind have shown the way
Through kindness and care
To my friends and so therefore
They have rescued you, from the Pits of Despair
And so I can take you all from this place
But not the traditional route up through the ocean
So when I say the magic words we will all vanish
In a puff of air and each of you will find a moment in time
To go visit your loved ones and through thought-by-vibe,
Tell them you are fine and on your way to a better place;
We will not meet again, but I wish you well and I too
Must go see my loved ones and let them know,
I am fine and well, but my time on this Earth is done
Yet I will watch them from afar,
For where there is love there is wisdom
And where there is wisdom, there is a way out
Of the Pits of Despair.
For a moment in the dream
The Little Odd sees
The Great White Rabbit
Look directly at it
And nod his head
In admiration and so
The Little Odd looks back
And with its little paw-hand thing
Risks a wave, and through thought-by-vibe
They know they will meet again, perhaps
On Cloud Ninety-Nine-a-Hundred.
And with that
The Great white rabbit
Says to the Hollow Folk

Clap your hands three times
Close your eyes and think of home
And with that, they are all gone
In a puff of smoke and the Little Odd
Wakes up and thinks,
What was that all about?

***

So if you were to see the Pyramid of Protection from the Outside
Here's what you would see right now
It is surrounded
By sprite soldiers and
Wicked Pixies and Underlies
That skulk in the night.
The Pyramid of Protection glows
In the dark and behind it, much bigger—
Surrounding it in the night
Is the biggest blue moon you ever see
The size of a massive, blue balloon!
Inside
The Little Odds
Are safe and dry and warm
For no harm can come to them
In the Pyramid of Protection which
Is a place some might call a "den"
One by one
The Little Odds
Stretch and come alive
Refreshed after a good night's sleep
Without fear or fright of things that go
Bump in the night.
The Indigo Blue stag,
Stands by, watching over them
And says, the time is near,
Here's how you will get out of here,

For there is still danger, in the passage
From the portal to the whale.
They can only go
One by one
With the exception of
Vermin and the Young Buck
And Fantabulous and Crispy who are
Joined at the hip.
There is a nanosecond in time
When it can all go wrong and one of them
Could be sucked right in, so they have to listen
Very carefully and follow the instructions:
One by one
The portal will open
And from the Blue Moon
Emerges a big blue bubble
And they must jump
From the portal into the bubble
And when all the bubbles are safe in the blue moon
It will float away from the Underworld to the bottom of the deep blue sea
Where the whale waits silently, for her passengers, do they understand?
They all nod.
Any questions?
No, the Little Odd
Says, 'We just want to say
Thank you, for having us
And taking care of us, and we'll
Never forget you!'
The Indigo Blue stag nods his head
And says, 'It was my pleasure to rescue you
And have you as my guests in the Pyramid of Protection;
And I will never forget… you.'
The Little Odds queue up:
The Runaway—takes a flying jump and the stag confirms,
She made it safe and sound;
And the Friendly Farmer breathes again;

Next the Young Buck with Vermin in his pocket
Take a running jump and yes, they make it;
So Crispy and Fantabulous are next to take the plunge
And it's a successful leap of the imagination, then
The Humming Bird, but she's light as a feather and in the leap
Of a nanosecond, her small blue bubble looks like it might
Float away for she is light as a feather but somehow, a strange hand
Comes out of the Blue Moon and rescues her;
The Blue Stag is concerned, now that the smaller Little Odds may be too light
And suggests that the Puzzled Penguin and the Gurney Cat
Might like to share a bubble from the portal, and they are grateful for that,
And off they go.
The Friendly Farmer nods at the stag
And off she goes;
That just leaves Ludwig,
The Little Lion Man and the Little Odd
'After you,' says Ludwig
For he wants to make sure no one is left behind
Especially not the Little Odd
'No, no after you,' says the Little Odd
But the Indigo stag laughs and says
They are too polite and suggest they might want to both
Take flight, as it appears—there is only one bubble left
At the portal, and they better go now, before it's too late
So the Little Odd takes Ludwig's paw, and they look at each other and yell;
'Geronimo!' and with that, they leap into the Blue Moon which floats away
Like a big blue balloon out of the Underworld to the bottom of the deep blue sea
Where they can see, from inside the Blue Moon, the fixed and healthy body of the
Great big mummy whale who smiles with glee;
So here's how they get back into the belly of the whale
One by one, the trap door at the bottom of the Blue Moon opens
And one by one each bubble floats down to the air hole on top of the whale
And drops them in—very, very gently,
and do you know what happens to the blue bubbles from the blue moon?

Go on—guess?
You'd never guess in a million years!
Well, one by one
Each Little Odd lands safely in a seat in the whale and puts their seat belt on
And one by one each blue bubble, turns into a giant jelly fish—
a kind and helpful giant jellyfish and who'd have ever thought of that, huh?
Well, there you go,
Just goes to show,
That anything is possible.
The Little Odds all clap and cheer
And the lovely mummy whale is so pleased to see them all again
As they are so pleased to see her fit and well, and she explains
That after some rest and tender loving care, she was put back together again
And now her job is to see them safely back to the island, from whence they came
For that's what she promised the chiefs, when they placed the Little Odds in her care;
However she says
Like before, it won't be plain sailing
'So hold onto your hats!'
The Little Odd says
'We don't have any hats'
And the mummy whale smiles and says
It's just a turn of phrase and the Little Odd's cheeks go pink
And everyone cheers, for it has got another colour back again
The Little Odd is all pinky-blue.
And now, another thing they didn't expect
The Blue Moon can speak, and she says to the mummy whale
'Are we all present and correct and ready to go?'
The lovely mummy whale revs up her engine and says
'Aye, aye cap'n ready for take off,' and the Blue Moon says
'Then follow me, i will guide you from this place, and the
Giant jelly fish will protect you from attacks
By giant sea monsters—who are afraid of nothing
Except giant jelly fish, and up, up and away they go
Where it is pitch black and only the ancient sea monsters of the deep

Linger there, until bit by bit they start to see sea creatures they know;
They see Manitou the Manatee who waves and smiles,
And Fantabulous sees his friend Cedric the skate and his skate family
And they wave,
They don't stop this time in the city of Atlantis, for there is not time
They still have work to do, but they are going home
And everyone is happy
So they sing that song again
About living in a Yellow Submarine
For they change the words to fit the tune:
For we all live in the belly of a whale,
The belly of a whale,
The belly of a whale.
And this makes the lovely mummy whale
So happy, she starts to blubber, and shudder
And apologises in her captain's voice,
'for we are experiencing a little turbulence'
And all the Little Odds laugh out loud.
Then the lovely mummy whale
Says she has a special announcement to make;
She will be stopping for a short break
When she reaches the surface for she
Will need to re-fuel.
They will be free to leave the belly of the whale
For a short time only as long as they promise
Not to go far away, some light snacks may be available.
Every one claps
For they are starting to feel a bit cooked up
And some fresh air will do them the world of good
And now as they can see the light stream down into the ocean
They realise, that it is time for the big blue moon balloon and the
Giant jelly fish to disappear, their work is done
So through the windows
The Little Odds wave and shout
'Thank you blue moon balloon,
Thank you Giant Jelly fish!'

Who wave back with their floaty
Tenticles, and off they go,
Somewhere beneath the sea.
For a while
The whale sails
Half in half out of the ocean blue
And now they can see all around them
Daylight for the first time in what seems like centuries!
The lovely mummy whale advises that they are just pulling into the fuelling station
And the Little Odd asks, what is the name of this place?
The lovely mummy whale says
It's called the Antarctic and the Puzzled Penguin
Thinks for a moment and says
That sounds oddly familiar.
It scratches its head,
And one by one
As the whale docks
Beside a large flat ice block
The Little Odds disembark and go
Brrrr, for it's very cold but very refreshing
And Crispy and Fantabulous can't help themselves
They see a gap between the ice and dive right in and
Fantabulous does great big leaps of glee and Crispy flaps around
Somewhere, beneath the sea and then comes up for air, and they are so
Happy.
Everyone is out now
The Humming Bird, brrs
And flies around,
The Puzzled Penguin
Comes out and looks around
And it's all so beautiful…
The Puzzled Penguin says to the Little Odds
'I feel as if, I've been here before, it feels like home.'
The whale gets on with re-fuelling and there
On the edge of the ice

Is a sad and lonely penguin
Looking way out to sea
To see what it can see, see, see
And all that it can see, see, see
Is sea, sea, and sea but not the one thing
It wants to see.
It is not aware of the Little Odds
Who wander over to it for they know it is a penguin
Just like Puzzled, perhaps a little bigger and the Little Odd
Says, 'Hullo'
For the Penguin is in a world of its own
'Oh, hullo,' says the Penguin, 'I didn't see you there,
We don't get many visitors here.'
'Are you a penguin?'
Asks the Little Odd
'Why, yes,' says the Penguin.
'One of my best friends is a penguin,'
Says the Little Odd,
'Why are you standing there looking forlornly out to sea,
And what is that thing between your paws?'
'Oh,' sighs the Penguin,
'I am looking for my one true love,
She got confused one day and floated away,
When the big tanker came aground and then they got it on its way
And she wanted to know if she could follow out and see what was out there in the world
For she was convinced there was a whole big world
that she just needed to see
and it seems
She forgot all about me and our baby egg
and so I promised to keep our egg in safe custardy
until she found her way home and remembered who and what she was,
'She was just a puzzled penguin who forgot she was about to be a mummy,
But she is the most beautiful penguin in the world to me, even if she is a bit dippy,

I know she will be a really good mum, and I know that some day she will come back to me,
For if you love someone, let them go and if they love you too, someday,
They'll come back and let you know.'
'Oh, I see,'
Said the Little Odd
'Why do you think she'd go?'
'Oh well, one day, she slipped on the ice
And bumped her head, and she was a bit confused after that.'
'Oh, I see,'
Said the Little Odd
'That explains *a lot'*
And all this time
The Penguin with the egg
Didn't take his eyes off the horizon
Then the Little Odds parted and the Puzzled Penguin
Stepped forward and said,
'Um, hullo Percy.'
'Puzzled—Puzzled, is it really you?'
And she waddled to him and said
So I am a mummy penguin and Percy said
Nothing
but just wrapped her in his flippers
And gave her the hug of his life and in that moment
The egg cracked open and out came a very puzzled looking
Little Penguin who looked at Percy and said
'Hullo, are you my mummy?'
And all the Little Odds
Jumped up and down
And wore their shiniest happiest smiles
And hugged Puzzled and Percy
For now, it was time to go.
They all jumped in the belly of the whale
And set sail for the last time, and Puzzled and Percy and the baby
Stood on the edge of the Antarctic and waved,
Until they could see the whale no more, amidst the waves.

Chapter Eleven
The Little Odds Retrace Their Steps

And Some Things Start to Make Sense

The Little Odds will never forget Puzzled
And who'd have thought that would happen!
But the lovely mummy whale is on the last leg
Of the journey for she has to bring them back safely
To Paradise Island, like she said to the chief and now
She sails on the surface, and up ahead they can see the
Golden shores, like before, of the paradise they left behind
What seems like a lifetime ago, for they have been to hell and back,
These Little Odds
And like specks of dust
On the shore, they can see
The dots that are people gathered there
For they've been expecting them and now
As they get nearer and nearer they can make out
The shapes of these beautiful people, so simple and so kind
Lined, along the waterside, to welcome them home, to dry land.
And as the lovely mummy whale washes up onto shore,
They applaud and the drums start, slowly then some more
And one by one the Little Odds jump out of the air hole and land
Safely on dry land and everybody cheers!
The chief comes forward and in his native tongue
Makes a little speech about how they chanted and prayed
For the safe return of the Little Odds, to the island and for the
Whale to get well again for they are close to nature and knew
She was unwell, and they give thanks, for their safe return and

Celebrate, until the dawn and when they wake, as the big orange sun
Rises on the horizon, the whale, says farewell, and they wave her off
Into the waves and watch, as she sinks, somewhere beneath the sea
But they know, they will always be connected, through the sacred bond
Of nature.
The chief gathers the Little Odds around
In the cool light of day and says he understands
They must be on their way, back from whence they came
And he is willing to provide the guides for the journey and the canoe
That brought them here and the Little Odds are happy to hear this;
Then the chief says a strange thing—
'There is one among you, who wants to stay here.'
The Little Odds look at each other confused
For they all want to go home, wherever that is;
Then out of the pocket of the Young Buck
Pops Vermin who jumps down to the ground and bows
Before the chief and says
'Um, yes, excuse me,
But um, you were all very kind to me
And made me feel at home, you didn't judge me
Or make me feel like dirt, and if it is okay with you
I'd really like to stay and settle here.'
With that, Vermin bowed at the chief
Who picks him up in his hand and says
In his native tongue,
'You are very welcome, little one,
We will take you for who and what you are
The children can play with you and know no fear
For we can see, that your heart is pure.'
And with that, they nod at each other,
On cue and Vermin wants to know
Can he learn to play the drums and
The chief says, 'we will make you a little one.'
Sagely, slowly
The chief walks
To the edge of the river

Where the canoe is waiting for them
With the same crew of two men
And the two gentle tribe girls
Like spirits, their eyes averted, to the water
Neither of this planet or the next but waiting gently
And kindly to take the Little Odds, back from whence
They came.
Vermin sits
On the shoulder of the chief
As the Little Odds board the canoe
And drift up river, waving and sending their love
Through thought-by-vibe, and they'll never forget him
Especially if and when, they are down in the dumps.
They wave until the chief grows small and Vermin is just a dot
On his shoulder and it's the Young Buck in particular who feels so sad
Until big blobby tears roll down his cheeks and the Runaway and the Little Odd
Take his hands, and say
Nothing.
Just let the ebb and flow
Lap the sides of the boat
As it flows, back from whence
They came and with the gentle
Sounds of the river, all the Little Odds
Slip into silent reverie.
Eventually, they can see
That they are floating back through
Cheerie Valley and there walking along the river banks
Is the kind and patient gentleman, who nods and waves
Then smiles, as if he knows, in his understated wisdom
Where they have been and why and is so pleased, to see
Their safe return.
The gentleman pauses
And watches as they sail on by
Then he nods, at the Little Odd
Who nods back and in that moment

Another colour returns, this time
It’s green.

***

The tribesmen and the tribes girls
Do not speak, for they are gentle spirit souls,
And the thing is, Cheerie Valley looks the same
But different, as if there has been some sea change
Of mystery—this time, the children come and stand and wave
Their mothers stand behind them, and this time, they look alive and not
In some lost and lonely haze, it’s like they have woken from some catatonic state
And realised, they are alive, and there is hope, after all.

***

The next phase of the journey
Draws near, there on the jetty
Is the innkeeper and his wife,
As if they haven’t moved, since they left
But that can’t be true, suspended in time.
And there is much joy
So the Little Odds jump up and down
And wear their shiniest happiest smiles and
Once again the innkeeper and his wife have prepared a great feast
And have kept their places by the fireside warm, and they must not fear
The pirates and crew for they have seen the error of their ways and are now
Friends, who go to sea in a beautiful old pirate boat and rescue those, lost at sea!
And so all night long,
They party and wouldn’t you agree
That the Little Odds have had some great parties
Amidst all their ups and downs!

***

During the party
The Humming Bird
Feels a little bit lost and lonely
And goes outside, to get some air
And sing her melodies and the innkeeper's wife
Comes out and says, all the time she was away
Every day, dawn and dusk, this condor would swoop down
Amidst the trees that hang over the river and sing his song of longing
So the hummingbird asks
Where is he tonight?
The innkeeper's wife says
The night is young, perhaps
If you set your hum aside
And sing, instead, he might
Hear your song.
The innkeeper's wife
Goes back inside, she says
'It's chilly'; and the Humming Bird
Hums, then hums some more and from somewhere
Deep inside her, she finds the song, and sings, as if she'd never sung before
Then out of the blue, the span of the condor's wings, cast a shadow on the river
As he swoops, more near, and she feels his presence, like the breeze, and she hears
His song and like a wisp in the night air, he lands at her feet and says
He's missed her, his hummingbird and would she leave everything behind
Her friends, her life, her past and come live with him on a mountaintop and
She doesn't have to give it a second thought, and she knows,
the Little Odds will understand
So she leaves each one a feather of remembrance for there is only this moment, this now
For this is her time, to soar—she's felt it in her bones,
in her feathers all her life, that she would one day
Have to leave everything behind and follow her heart
but she knew that those who loved her and understood,
would know the reasons why and so
The Condor and the Songbird,

for she is a humdinger no more
Soared in to the mountains tops
Where they both belonged.

***

And now, there were nine.

***

Inside the parlour of the inn
There is a feast and much joy and dancing
And here's the most amazing thing—the pirates
Are their friends, for they have seen the error of their ways
They now know that it is mean to terrorise innocent people and steal their things
For they understand now, that greed is bad and brings no happiness or joy
But being kind and a friend, is much nicer and the innkeeper and his wife say
They are happy to have the pirates as allies for instead of bringing fear and terror
They bring tourists who love this place and are very happy to stay a while and everybody benefits.
So just for old time's sake
The Little Odd and the Runaway
And the Friendly Farmer go up into the attic
And look around and think how far they've come
But isn't it a pity, that they could do nothing about the Ringmaster?
They ask the Innkeeper
Whatever became of the Ringmaster?
And he says, as far as people know he got his comeuppance?
The Little Odd wants to know what that means, is it a turn of phrase?
But the Innkeeper says, no—this is, he got what was coming to him;
'What was that?'
Asks the Little Odd
Simply, and the Innkeeper says
'He told so many lies and was mean to so many people

That one day, it all caught up with him, so he chased his tail
For he was always chasing his tail like a mad dog and no one
has seen or heard from him since!'
The Little Odd looked sad and said
'That's a shame, for every one deserves
A second chance, and even a third to prove themselves
They even deserve ninety-nine-a-hundred chances,
But it will only work, if they learn, how to forgive themselves
And to say sorry, and really mean it, not just pretend, **really** mean it
Not just an "I'm sorry now get me out of here". But an "I'm sorry, and I really
want
To make amends".'
The reason
This made the Little Odd sad
Was at the end of the day, if the Ringmaster
Was the dad of the Runaway—then he can't be all bad
For she is so lovely.
The Little Odd
Bowed its head and
In that moment another colour
Returned, this time, it was all
Yellow.
Then the Little Odd fell asleep
And in the morning it awoke
With a new sense of splendour
And said, to the remaining Little Odds
'We must return, to the Land of Wonder!'
The kitchen parlour is in chaos
And the Little Odds are all a bit of a blur
They want to know why! Can't they stay
And have a holiday and the Little Odd says
'No! Not until our work is done and then there will be time
For rest and play.'
They don't question the Little Odd
For they are used to its ways, and
Where it goes, they will follow.

‘We have to go back
To the Land of Wonder;
I had a vision last night
That it had fallen into disarray!’
And in slumber all around the pantry and the inn
Inside and out where the pirates, and the Little Odd
Rounded them up and said, ‘Can we count on you?
How many of your are there?’
But the pirates made a motley crew and said
‘We have no idea, but we are with you all the way,
Little Odd, for we heard, too, that there is trouble, ahead.’
So outside the Inn
They counted nine Little Odds
And around ninety-nine-a-hundred
Motley crew and the Little Odd
Looked at the ground and wondered
What words of wisdom he could say
To the Little Odds and the Motley Crew
That might see them on their way,
Like Warriors of Light but all he could think to say was,
‘Um, let us go then, you and I…’
And they waved
Bye-bye to the innkeeper and his wife
As they marched this way and that
To and fro, fro and to down the hill
All a-wobbly, in the morning light.

***

And bizarrely on the way
A twist of fate they met the nice doctor
Who filled them in on the state of the Land of Wonder
She couldn’t stop long, she was busy for there was so much illness
And every one wanted, a pill for every ill instead of looking deep inside themselves
For the answers.

She looked sad and tired and worn, this nice doctor and said
'Remember to tell them, that hospitals are places to heal
Not steal.'
And her eyes were sunken and tired
As she carried on her lonesome way
And the Little Odd thought
The lovely doctor, didn't look well
Didn't look well at all, as if, she had the world
On her shoulders.
So he stood and looked after her
And as if she could feel the eyes of the Little Odd on her back
She turned around and came back and whispered in his ear;
'The Dark Horse is back,
There will be trouble in the Land of Wander
Beyond the chaos that exists there, now, but
The chaos is nothing compared to what the
Dark Horse will do if it has its way and already
It is gaining force, in the skies and the Earth;
The Top Hats and the Fluff Dragons are poised for battle,
And you need to go there, and put an end to all that,
For it will be the destruction of us all.'
And with that the nice doctor
Fixed her meaningful dark eyes
on the eyes of the Little Odd,
then she turned, and walked on
her weary way.
The Little Odd has no idea
What this all meant, so it shrugged
And carried on its way, with friends
Back to the Land of Wonder
And whatever lay ahead.

***

17-18.11.11

Chapter Twelve
Finale! The Fluff Dragons

TAKE ON THE
TOP HATS
AND
ALL IS RIGHT WITH
THE WORLD
AGAIN
THANKS
TO THE
LITTLE ODDS!

The Land of Wonder
Has turned cold and grey
No children play, the streets
Are deserted; the shops are locked
And hollow-eyed lonely folk, look out
From doorways
The Little Odds are shocked
What has happened to this beautiful place!
Then there is this almighty roar of thunder
And up above the dark clouds gather, and as if by magic
They turn into Top Hats, dark marshmallows, that roll and thunder
And spit on them, then to the right, they can see, glimmers of blue sky
And the Fluff Dragons, try hard, to push their way through, but there are way too many
Big Black Top Hats, and they are so angry, for they are losing their grasp, on the world economy

The Head of the Top Hats, looms large and loud, down onto Main Street and says.
'Get out of our way, Little Odds and you Motley Crew, the Land of Wonder is ours!
Look—here comes the Dark Horse who has taken charge, of the dark brigade and The Warriors of the Dark Horse are all over this place, and they are strong and mighty
And have billions and zillions of squiggles behind them while you—Little Odds and Motley Crew
Have nothing behind you but that miserly band of Fluff Dragons, too weak to be more than an evening hue!'
And with that the Head of the Top Hats lets out an almighty roar of evil laughter that tolls
Like a roll of rattling thunder!
The Little Odd steps forward and
Puffs out its chest and says
'Shame on You!
Nothing but a big bully!
You and those horrible Top Hats
All sickly sweet on the surface but dark
Like glue with greed and gluttony and shame!
Shame on you!'
The Top Hats
Throw back their heads
And laugh out loud at the Little Odd
Until it tolls like Earth-rip-roaring thunder
All across this land!
No wonder!
Then down Main Street
Strides the Dark Horse, as if
It owns the place, and when it sees
The Little Odds, it neighs up into the air
And throws its front legs, forward then snorts;
As if sending some sign into the ether and with that
The clouds burst, the Top Hats, flick their whips to high heavens
The Little Odds

Just stand and stare
Shutters go down
Children, that came out to stare
Are whisked in by their parents
So there is not another soul in sight
In this Land of Wonder, just fright
And fear and loathing—then Ludwig
The Little Lion Man says, 'What are we waiting for,
Let's fight!'
But the Little Odds look at each other and say
'We are love and peace man, we don't fight'
Then Ludwig says
'This is the good fight
And the Fluff Dragons are on our side.'
'So are you gonna stand there
And let the Dark Horse and the Top Hats
Take over this place—and the world,
For they have no love of nature or music
Or literature or culture, just money and greed and
Gluttony!'
'Look around you Little Odds
If you let them take over, they will take the music
And the words and the laughter and the love!
Given half a chance, they will take your humanities away;
Then where is the love? We will all be slaves, to squiggles
For they only care about the squiggles, and the Underlies;
The sprites, the pixies and trolls, and those who do their
Dirty work!'
'You are right, Ludwig'
Says the Little Odd
'But what should we do?'
'Something we haven't done in a long time
Little Odd, something we have forgotten about
When we got stuck in the Underworld.'
'What's that?' ask the Little Odds.
'We forgot about the music, Little Odds

We forgot to sing and play our instruments!
Let's fight them, with beautiful things, for that will
Be torture to their ears and to their evil eyes!'
'We must fight them with song, with dance, with our love
And respect for the beautiful things, for flowers and trees
And birds and bees and all the things, they want to destroy.'
This made the Dark Horse
Very, very angry, for it knew
If the people, had their souls
Opened one more time, just a glimmer
Of hope, then they had lost the battle
But not the war!
The Dark Horse
Stamped its feet in the ground
And the dust rose like dynamite
That made booms, as if the core of the Earth
Had opened up one last time, and in that moment
The heavens were taken over, by the Top Hats that roared
And lightning struck to the core of the Earth which opened up and
Out came the Underlies to take over the Earth, and the pixies and the trolls
There, down on Main Street
Strode the Queen of the Underlies
To her right the Ringmaster, cracked the whip
To her left, the Lackey, the Big Black Dog with saliva
Dripping from its lips;
And on sight
The Dark Horse
Rode up with devious delight
And lifted its legs into what was now night
For there was no light anymore, on the horizon
The Fluff Dragons seemed to disappear in fright.
The Dark Horse
And the Queen of the Underlies
Did high-five and said, 'We are the champions
For we hold the squiggles in our power, and you
Stupid vile Little Odds, are nothing but thorns in our sides

Be gone!'
Then they let out this cackle
That made the heavens open
And the Earth was tore open to the core.
Molten lava
Seeped through the streets
Until it petrified then Ludwig said
'Little Odds, what are we waiting for!'
'Let's FIGHT!'
The Little Odds
And the Motley Crew
Looked at each other in fright,
For they didn't have a clue
What to do!'
Then Ludwig
Took his flute
From his pocket
And played it, as if by
Magic,
The Gurney Cat
Played mock guitar
And the Young Buck
Sang a new song,
Afraid at first…
La-la, la-lala
Lalalalalalalalallalalalalla
Then
Slowly
Gently
The Runaway
Joined in
La-la
La-la-la…
Llalalallalalalalalalalalla
Then her mother, eye balled
The Ringmaster, and her eyes

Swirled this way and that
La-la
La-la-la
La-la-la-la
Lalalalallalalallalala
The lava flow
And the thunder
Seemed to subside
Crispy and Fantabulous
Looked at each other and wandered
What they could do, so they began to dance
La-la
La-la-la
La-la-la-la
Lalalalalalalallla
Then the Motley Crew
Who were standing by
Ready for the fight started to dance
And sing, la-la
La-la-la
La-lala-la
Lalalalallalalala
La-la
And all the la-las
La-la-las
Rose up into the air
Like energy swirls
Like bubbles of air
And somehow
They were stronger
Than the Top Hats
and the Thunder clouds
The swirls of sweet sounds
The twirls of energy, dispelled them
As if by some beautiful magic
La-la

La-la-la
La-la-la-la
La-la-la-la-la
And soon
The la-las
Took on a tune
That everyone seemed to get
And the louder it got, the more powerful it became
La-la
La-la-la
La-la-la-la
Lalalalalalallalalala
The Top Hats
Could not bear this beauty
As the energy swirls pushed higher and higher
Into the sky and soon, the Top Hats began to disintegrate
And float away into nothingness and the Queen of the Underlies
And the Dark Horse screamed, 'Where are you going, come back! Come back
You have work to do, have you forgotten, about the squiggles we promised you!'
But the sound of music
Was way more powerful
And drowned them out and
All you could hear, all over the Land of Wonder
Was this:
'La-la
La-la-la
La-la-la-la
La-la-la-la-la…'
And soon
The shutters came down
And the doors and windows
Began to open and slowly but surely
The people began to look out their doors…
Then the Queen of the Underlies
Yelled at the Dark Horse

'Do something!' but the Dark Horse
Was lame now and said, 'You do something
For you are nothing but a bully!'
And she said
'So in my moment of need
You turn on me!' and with that
The Gurney Cat, with a sound like a
Guitar solo, out of control leapt to her neck
And ripped it open and exposed her as a
Mechanical fake, and she shuddered and imploded
And all her cheap finery fell away to show, the evil pixie
At the controls, and it was so in chaos and insanity it didn't even know
That everyone was laughing, and when it lifted its ugly head to show
It's true colours—the darkness, then imploded, into a sizzling mound
Of green glug
Sizzling on the Main Street
Before a lame horse, the Dark Horse
Redundant now.
There is no place
For a Dark Horse
In the Land of Wonder
Somehow
The Ringmaster
And the big black dog,
The Lackey, looked lost and
Empty as the la-la
La-la-las
Filled the air
And all the Black Clouds
The Top hats of despair
Had dispersed, into the emptiness.
In a miracle, the sky turned blue
And the Fluff Dragons, filled the hue
For they didn't have to do much, but
Blow, the darkness from this place
With their gentleness and still the air was filled

With the la-la-las
La-la-las
The children
Came forth from the houses
And danced and their parents
Emerged, blinking in the new light
The Little Odds
Had forgotten how beautiful
It was to sing and dance and so
The whole of the Land of Wonder
Was filled once again, with the sound
Of music
And dance
La-la
La-la-la
And up in the heavens
The Fluff Dragons danced
The Little Odds forgot
Themselves until they saw
Two old friends float down
Onto Main Street
The Elegant Elephant
And the Unicorn.
The Unicorn says
'Come this way,
To the park, where
There is a stage,
And you must say
What you have to say
For the people need to know
About the three keys!'
And with that
The Little Odds
Look at each other
And remember the keys
Entrusted to them, stolen

Long, long go.

***

It seems like a lifetime
Since the Little Odds
Did that concert in the Land of Wonder
But the people didn't forget, and want an action replay
For they have lived in the dark too long, since the Little Odds
Left to go to the Underworld and the Land of Wander, descended
Into darkness
The park is full
Of the people still singing
La-la-la
La-la-la
La-la-la-la
Lalalalalalala
So the Little Odds realise
They have to please the Like Minds
Once again and put on a show
But they don't have a clue, what they are doing
Until Ludwig, picks up his flute, and plays, and the notes float
Into what is now the cool evening air and up above, the Fluff Dragons
Provide cover and protection, for the Top Hats and the Thunder have gone away
And one by one
The Little Odds remember
On cue their party pieces
Gurney plays gee-tar
The Young Buck sings
And if that doesn't disperse those black clouds
Nothing will, then Fantabulous and Crispy do their dancing thing;
And mother and daughter
Sing a new song.
But as they are in mid-flow
The Ringmaster appears and cracks his whip

And wants to know, where his squiggles are
The one's they stole from him and the crowd go
Booooo
Until the Lackey
The big black dog comes out
And bullies them too…
Then the Friendly Farmer
Wrestles the whip from him
And she cracks it, in his face
And says, 'shame!
Shame on you!'
'For you
Are the King
Of the Underlies!
You told so many lies
And destroyed so many lives
With your insensitivity!'
She dangles the key before him.
'Do you recognise this key?'
And he crumbles to her feet and says
No!
'I didn't think so
This key, is to truth
It was entrusted to me
By the Little Odd, and this
Is the Truth, we all hold
The Truth within our hearts,
Until it is unlocked'
And with that
She threw the key
To Truth into the audience
And it split, into a hundred thousand keys
So everyone who was there, caught a fragment of
The one true key to keep close to their hearts—
To hold it as a legacy.

***

And as the Friendly Farmer
Held the gaze of the Ringmaster
He fell to the ground and gasped for
Forgiveness
But she said
It is not mine to give
First, you have to tell the truth
Then, you have to ask, for forgiveness
For without honesty and integrity, you are
Nothing.

***

Next
The Young Buck
Steps forward and sings a song
About how the Runaway holds the key to his heart
Even though, the key is in his safekeeping, in his pocket
But her heart, won't open, until, he has opened his own
And the song is so beautiful
The people with closed hearts
Start to open theirs and the Young Buck
Takes the key and shows it to the audience
Then hands it to the Runaway who looks at the floor
Then the audience scream for more, as she takes the key
From his hand and examines it, then she looks deep into his eyes
And says, 'you have opened my eyes and my heart and my soul and if
I can pass that on, let it be so'
She goes to her dad and says
'Can I open your heart?'
And with that he melts
Then cries and gives her a big hug
(for he's not all bad).
So with a flourish and smile and a laugh
She takes the key and flings it into the audience
And it splits into a hundred million keys to open the eyes

And the hearts of the audience, so they can love with purity
Then the Young Buck and the Runaway kiss
And the skies are filled
With fireworks.

***

The park…
The entire Land of Wonder
Has come to life, and all you can hear
As far as the eye can see is this new song
So simple
La-la
La-la-la
La-la-la-la
Lalalallalalallalalala

***

Then the Little Odd
Comes to the front of the stage
And it has a new colour
Orange;
Then he says
There is one more key
But only those who recognise it
Will see;
And so
The Little Odd
Bows its head and
The crowd goes silent;
The Little Odd
Does not know
What to say
For it does not hold
The key to their hearts

Or their souls, just their
Imaginations
The Little Odd
Holds the key to
The sun and the moon
And the stars
But doesn't know
What to say so it looks
At its little misshapen feet things and says
'Hullo'
The crowd
Goes wild and the
Little Odd, gets even more shy
And says,
'It is time for me to go now, soon;
But I do not know what to say
Except this
My friends
I have made so many…
Beautiful friends, and we have had
Such amazing adventures, and we are
Friends forever, but I have one last key,
Entrusted to me, and I hope, I can share it with you,'
'It is the key to happiness,
The key to a hundred million suns
so when I fling it into the audience
It will disintegrate, into a hundred million sums
Of one part, for I cannot do the big sums will you promise me,
That you will hold it close to your hearts, your minds, your souls?'
And when the Little Odd looks up
All it can see is the people, willing it to be so
Then he takes the key, the last of three and flings it
Into the air and it disintegrates into, a hundred million keys
To be shared among their hearts and minds and souls
But what they do with it, from this day forward is up to them
And future generations…

No one knows
Where the fireworks came from
But suddenly the air is filled
With fireworks and Catherine wheels
And whoops and good wishes.

***

Then the people dance
Until dawn, for the children
Have been cooked up too long and
Suddenly there is the sound of silence
As the distant sounds of fireworks, fade into the night.

***

All things have been put to right
In the Land of Wonder, and tomorrow
Is another day, when we will see the Little Odds
Go their separate ways
But there is one more thing to say
In this story, and that's called
An epilogue.

***

Mañana, little ones (that means tomorrow☺)

Epilogue

IT'S JUST THE END OF THE STORY
BUT THE LITTLE ODDS LIVE ON
FOREVER
AND
EVER
HURRAY!

Well, what a night the Little Odds had
As they helped, put the Land of Wonder
To rights.
The people, partied all night
But now it is the dawn, with
A beautiful pinkly blue hue
Across the heavens.
The Little Odds,
Sit in a circle and wander
What happens next?
The Little Odd smiles
And all his true colours
Are back, and it shines
Luminous.
The Little Odd says,
'We have a few things left to do;
Some odds and ends that need tied up
So we can go back from whence we came,
Forever changed.'
'Look, there's the Elegant Elephant and the unicorn
Back to see it through!'

‘Before the people rise
We should just slip through
The gates to the Land of Wonder
And somehow, I have no fear
That we will find no danger, anymore.’
‘Come,’ says the Little Odd,
As it rose to its little misshapen feet things,
‘Let us go then, you and I…’
They all rose
And held hands and paws
And walked to the gates of
The Land of Wonder
With Elegant and the Unicorn
On either side, then for one last time
They stopped and looked around, and saw
How beautiful it looked, under a pinky-blue sky
Where Fluff Dragons winked, and the birds could sing,
Once more.
‘You must be tired, but happy, Little Odds’
Said Elegant,
‘Here, hop aboard.’
The Friendly Farmer
The Young Buck and Runaway
And the Little Odd, hopped on to Elegant
The Gurney Cat
Fantabulous and Crispy
With Ludwig the Little Lion Man
Leapt onto the Unicorn,
Who rose up into the sky
To fly.
‘Where are we going?’ laughed Ludwig,
‘You’ll see,’ says the unicorn.
Then they landed, not long after
Beside the Old Oak Tree!
Ludwig ran and hugged his friend,
Climbed up into the leaves, and laughed

Out loud and one last time, played his magic flute
And let the notes float high and beyond, while the Little Odds
Danced to see such glee, and the Oak Tree, was very happy,
To see them all again.
'Ludwig,' says the Oak Tree, 'You are my beloved Little Lion Man
In whom I am well pleased, but look! How brave you've been and
Look! How grown-up you are, now—one last thing, before you leaf me
Forever, and I know you'll never forget me for I am always here, your tower of strength;
The time has come, for you to go home, you are needed there, they miss you so and are sorry
They just didn't understand where you were coming from when you tried to make them see,
All those years ago, that you were just a little odd, go forward, and take your rightful place,
As the Head of the Pride.'
Ludwig looked confused and said,
'Are you for real, Grand Old Oak Tree?'
Who laughed and shook his leaves and said
'Of course, look it is late autumn now,
It is time for me to sleep until spring,
When I will wake, and sing, a new song
Your music, lives within me!'
They climbed aboard
One more time, and Elegant
And the Unicorn took Ludwig home
To the Land of the Lions, where they welcomed him
With open paws, and he wrestled with his siblings, all grown now
Who were delighted to see him home and said,
'Look, how you've grown, you are a Lion Man now!
You have just turned, eighteen!'
And the whole pride
Sang Happy Birthday out loud
And gave Ludwig, a little golden crown
Which made him very proud.

***

So Elegant and the Unicorn
Looked at each other and said
'Just a few more stops then?'
'Where next?'
Asked the Little Odds
Who were loving this jump-on, jump-off experience
'Why, back to the Dump of course!'
They hugged and waved good bye to Ludwig
And the whole Pride waved them off;
Then they landed,
Down in the Dumps.
There wasn't one Little Odd
Who wanted to stay there
But they had to go see old friends
And settle old scores.
The Dump Dwellers
The rabble-rousers
Had never seen the likes of this
As the Elegant Elephant and the Unicorn
Descended down amongst them.
'What is this strange and beautiful thing?'
They said, 'On this fine new morning?'
For the Dump was such a dull and dreary place
Day after day after day, that it was nice to see something
Different happening, then the Dump dwellers and the rabble-rousers
Recognised the Runaway and Gurney and pointed their fingers and said
'Where is that Vermin?'
But the Runaway said
'Vermin is alive and well and living happily
With people who love him for what he is—so shame on you!'
They hung their heads, then the nastiest of the rabble-rousers said
'There is that mutant—look—the odd looking one, grab him, nab him;
Beat him up and stab him!'
But the people, bowed their heads in shame and said
'We are not listening to you, for look, can't you see,
That these are beautiful things, and it is not the beauty

That has betrayed us but you!'
The rabble-rouser gathered a few yahoos around
But no one was listening to their views, anymore,
For they knew it was all a load of rubbish, designed
To just keep them down in the dumps.
The Runaway said
'Don't worry, we are not staying long,
We just wanted to come say good bye
To our good friends Faith and Joy—
Do you know where they are?'
And in that moment,
Out of the crowd
Walked the two old ladies
Hand in hand… when the Runaway saw them
And the Little Odd, they ran and hugged and held
Them tight, for they will never forget how kind
Faith and Joy were to them a long time ago;
The Runaway said
'Dear Faith and Joy
These are our friends,
Why don't you join us
For we are going home?'
But they smiled and said
'Although we'd love to,
Our place is here, in the Dump,
We have work to do, but will never,
Ever forget you, dear Runaway and Little Odd'
The Runaway said
'I understand but let me introduce you
To my mummy!'
Faith and Joy jumped up and down
And hugged the Friendly Farmer for they had heard
So many good things about her and the Friendly Farmer
Could say
'Thank you so much
For looking after my daughter

When she was lost, but now she's found
And is coming home, with me!'
'Mum, Mum,' shrieked the Runaway
'There's one more person I want you to meet,
A kind man, his name is Bert and there he is over there
Feeding cardboard boxes to the Big Blue Machine!'
'Bert, Bert—come meet my mum!'
Big beautiful Bert, had been immune to all that was going on,
So busy feeding cardboard boxes to the Big Blue Machine, too afraid to stop
For fear of its angry hunger…
Bert stood up tall, ten feet tall
And rubbed his eyes and wandered
Where all this noise was coming from
Then he turned around and his eyes went
Wide and swirly as he saw, for the first time
The Elegant Elephant and the Unicorn and the Little Odd
And his dear Little Runaway, and he ran
And scooped her in his arms for he never thought
He'd see that strange little girl again!
'Bert, Bert! I have so much to tell you!
I've been on a wonderful adventure, but Bert!
Bert! I'd like you to meet my mum!'
Ten foot tall Bert's eyes
Met nine foot tall Friendly Farmer's eyes
And his swirled blue and her's swirled red
Then turned into a pinky-blue hue!
And for a moment, the world stood still
And disappeared.
The Runaway stepped forward
Then held Bert's hand and said
'Dear Bert, you were always very kind to me,
We are all going home to my mummy's farm
And she could really do with some help from a big strong man;
Why don't you leave this dump and the Big Blue Machine and come
Make vegetables and things with my mum?'
'Errr, ummmm,' says Bert;

And the Friendly Farmer said
'I'd like that very much, and what have you got to lose;
I can make you strong coffee, for we get up at dawn;
And work hard as the day is long, then in the evenings
We can disappear to the lake and listen, to nature's songs.'
'Errr, ummm,' says Bert,
'I think I'll come, if that's okay'
For Bert, had never fitted in anywhere
Before, not even in the Dump where no one understood
His kindly soul, except, this strange Little Runaway.

***

'Well then,' says the Runaway
'Our work here is done, good bye,
Faith and Joy, we love you so,
Don't we Little Odd?'
So they all jumped up and down
And wore, their shiniest happiest smiles.
The Little Odd, mind you, was confused now
It was just going with the flow, it knew somehow
That everything would work out fine, but the Little Odd
Sighed, for it would very much like to go home,
Then watch them from afar…
Still on the last leg of the journey
The Little Odds got on the Unicorn and Elegant
And rose out of the Dump waving farewell to Faith and Joy
Who seemed happy, to be left behind, and from a distance
The Dump, took on this pleasing glowing hue
Of red and yellow and pink and blue
Purple and orange and green…
By Elegant and Unicorn
It was just a short haul flight
To the Friendly Farmer's farm
Where they found, every thing
Just as they left it.

'Home, Sweet Home'
Said the Friendly Farmer
Jumping off the Elegant Elephant
And throwing her arms out wide.
'Coffee, anyone?'
As she ran inside to say hullo
To the Singing kettle.
Bert said
He wouldn't say no to a coffee,
For he hasn't had one in as long as he can remember,
This gives him a warm glow,
Gurney asks politely
'Would you like a farm cat? I will be kind and gentle
To the mice and rats?'
The Friendly Farmer said she'd like that;
Fantabulous and Crispy,
Dive right into their pond
And splash about as if they'd never left.
Then the Runaway and the Young Buck
Look at each other then look at their toes
'Would you like to stay with me and Mum,
You could work as a farm hand?' she says
And he says, he'd like that very much
To feel he belonged;
Then she takes his hand
And leads him to the water's edge;
Where they hold hands, and play
Teenage Kicks, inside their heads.

***

From the Friendly Farmer's kitchen
Comes the sound of the Singing kettle;
Warm coffee all around,
Glows and smiles and everyone is happy—
Aren't they?

The Little Odd looks at the ground;
And big gloopy tears fall from his eyes
And glisten in the light of the sun,
Which turns its tears,
into all the colours of the rainbow.
'What's wrong, Little Odd?'
Asks the Friendly Farmer
Then the Little Odd sighs and says
'I am so very sad and so very happy
All at the same time...'
'I love you all,
So very much
You make me so
Very happy, but the
Truth is this;
I want to go home,
See my mummy and daddy.'
More big rainbow tears bounce out of its eyes
Until, over the lake, and the setting sun,
There drifts down a big blue moon,
Like a big blue balloon,
Slowly, silently
It drifts down,
As the sun disappears behind
The horizon
And they all stand and stare
At this beautiful vision
Of a blue moon
Which is a big blue balloon
that lands, at the edge of the lake
And would you Adam and Eve it?
Who steps out of the basket,
But the Great White Rabbit,
All a-glow!
He takes off his glasses and wipes them
With his handkerchief and says

'Hullo.'
The Little Odd
Runs and hugs his friend
As do the others, all a-glow
For the Great White Rabbit is back!
He laughs and says
'I've been sent on a mission,
To take the Little Odd back
To cloud Ninety-Nine-a-Hundred.'
But we don't have much time
His mummy and daddy said,
I have to bring him back before dark;
'Oh, and they said, to give the Little Odd this,
They said, it would be missing, this…'
And the Great White Rabbit
Handed the Little Odd,
The Little Xylophone,
Harp-thing that looked
And sounded like an
Egg-slicer, like nothing
On Earth.
The Little Odd
Jumped up and down
And took the little egg-slicer
Xylophone thing and began to ping
Until the notes twirled, like coloured
Energy swirls into the sky.
They all lined up
To say good bye
The air was filled
With emotion
As the Gruney Cat
Fantabulous and Crispy
Stepped forward first for hugs;
Then the Young Buck and the Runaway
Next the Friendly Farmer and Bert

And there were happy tears and sad tears
Which ripped at their hearts, but the Little Odd
Was glad to go and sad to go and held on to their hugs
For just a moment too long;
'I will never, ever forget you;
And I will watch you from afar
With my cirrusoscope on cloud
Ninety-nine-a-hundred,
You just have to look up and will
Easily recognise it';
Then the Great White Rabbit said
'Have I got news for you, Little Odd
I am right next to you, on Cloud 101!'
So they all jumped up and down,
And wore their shiniest happiest smiles;
But it was now time to go.
The remaining Little Odds
Gathered round, the basket
Of the big blue balloon
Which was also, the blue moon;
Fantabulous and Crispy danced
And Gurney played gee-tar
Bert reached out, and took the warm hand
Of the Friendly Farmer;
The Young Buck and the Runaway held hands
Then she ran, one last time, to hug the Little Odd tight
Then they jumped up and down,
and they wore their shiniest happiest smiles
For each other, one last time;
Then the Little Odd
With the Great White Rabbit by his side
Soared, up into the heavens at the end of the day;
They climbed out
Of the Blue balloon
And waved down below
At the Friendly Farm, all a-glow

The Little Odd landed safely
Back on its cloud
Ninety-nine-a-hundred
And the Great White Rabbit
Leapt like a young thing, across
To cloud 101 and down below
The Little Odds sang, the La-la-la song
And they all joined in, until the Little Odd
Did one last ping, then said
It's time for bed
Sleepy heads
But just one last thing
As it winked one eye
'I love you all'
La-la-la.

The End